After the Fall
Tales of the Apocalypse

After the Fall: Tales of the Apocalypse
Winners of the Almond Press
Apocalyptic/Dystopian Short Story Contest, 2013

Foreword by
Kelly Gardner

Cover art by
Wanderers of a Poor Town
Edwin Yang

Typesetting by
Laura Jones - FloJo Services
www.flojoservices.com

All rights reserved.

Published by Almond Press
www.almondpress.co.uk

No part of this publication may be reproduced or
transmitted in any form or by any means without
permission of the publisher.

All the characters in this book are fictitious and any
resemblance to actual persons, living or dead,
is purely coincidental.

ISBN: 978-0-9936571-4-6

Contents

Foreword

A desolate landscape, wracked with upheaval, the uncanny nature of a place once so familiar. A revelation of what was formerly undisclosed, the harbingers of apocalypse are edging ever closer...

It seems a part of human nature for mankind to elevate itself to the most important species on the planet; while the personal death of an individual exposes the insignificance of the single man, we turn instead to imagining the common death of the species at large in order to establish our importance. Though seemingly a fantasy concerning humanity's demise, apocalyptic fiction serves to re-inscribe the centrality of the human race, and with it, a humanist system of values. Similarly, the continued popularity of End of Time prophecies and eschatological literature throughout history exposes the conception of a culture's establishment of its own generation as being paramount; this is evident in the continual immanence of the supposed apocalypse.

The wasteland of abandoned memories, the end of the world or a chance for a new beginning. Be it a personal apocalypse, or one of great cataclysm, the stories that arise from the rubble are tales of aftermath and tales of survival. Bridging the gap between Science Fiction and Horror, the gothic overtones of the apocalyptic imagination are explored to their full extent in these shortlisted entries for the second Almond Press Short Story Competition.

After the Fall is a collection of twenty short stories, all apocalyptic or dystopian in nature. Some bring laughter and others bring tears, but each is unique in its interpretation of the theme.

The space of apocalypse is a space of transition; we hope these stories will unsettle and provoke, as you journey through a range of human emotions and discover what awaits After the Fall.

Kelly Gardner
MLitt Gothic Imagination, University of Stirling

Prologue

Apparition

by Adicus Ryan Garton

Cresting the hill, I pause as the moon stares back at me, larger than anything. The cool night wind ruffles my tattered cloak as I stand motionless, captivated by the pale luminescence of her. Behind me, the dogs bark; their echo carries well in this dark wood. The low murmurs of the engines, the laughter of the outsiders, it brings me back to the present. But, before I dash off into the night, toward the skeletons of a city whose name is as lost as civilization, I close my eyes and wish I were on the surface of her, staring in awe at an ash-gravy Earthrise.

The gunshots dash through the trees like reckless children, but I am already gone, just another phantom in a world of shadows.

Casting Off

by Robert Holtom

The end of the world began when the world began, and the world began at eighteen minutes past eight on the twentieth of July, nineteen sixty-nine.

One small step for man, one sonorous death knell for mankind. And so they stepped, those little spacemen, rehearsing their ready-made speeches, stepped into mankind's final act. Cumbersome white figures befitting of Doctor Who enemies, friends of the Daleks, lolloped their way across the lunar landscape, and with each step so they affirmed our end, signing the assassin's contract with our species on the hit list.

That day was the beginning of the end, that day when man left the atmosphere to find a place elsewhere. That day when a few selected men turned to see the earth, so far from home. The culmination of man's brilliance, his technological wizardry, the inevitable march of progress, modernity's crowning moment, when man could turn his back on his own home, rendering the earth expendable, inevitably obsolete. A mere snapshot. Snapped.

Many blame Harold Woodbeck, one of the first industrialists, one of those canny men who put money where his mouth was and helped grow a new industry of coal and steel. A man who campaigned so furiously that he single-handedly forced the government out of its usual lethargic apathy to enact the Canals Act of 1854, allowing straight lines to be etched across the face of Britain, freeing horse drawn barges to take coal to where it was needed, to help reallocate scarce resources. So began more familiar capitalistic endeavours as money went where the energy did. Some blame Henry Ford, for his production lines, for taking industrialisation and multiplying it by a factor of fifty, for rendering humans mere automata, mere machines in an even greater world of cogs and levers. He began a process that could only but begin in America, destined always to depart from its shores as the price of labour rose, destined to spread across the globe, taking forests with it, Mother Nature too, and using the oceans as a trash can. Others still blame Einstein, what a genius they say, but what a fool too, for splitting the atom, something that should surely have remained unsplit, granting humans the ability to so catastrophically wipe themselves from the face of the earth.

But no, I blame the cosmonauts, those little spacemen, their photographs of earth taken from the moon. Such a simple gesture, but just as a butterfly flaps its wings on the other side of the world, so a photograph is snapped and the shockwaves usher in Armageddon.

I look around the little café near Paddington Station, its greasy, stuffy interior clings to the hairs in my nostrils. I look at the blank faces outside the smudged window, past the little plastic tomato of ketchup and the salt cellar. I see endless faces stream, I see feet walking, walking, walking. I turn to the pages below, to my diary, my journal, I worry.

A tinkle of bells wakes me from my distraction as I look to the door. And there you are. In a bolt of fresh glory there you stand, your hair tousled from the wind outside, your cheeks a majestic shade of pink in this grey afternoon, your lips red, a shock of colour in defiance of the monochrome. You squint, in that way that you do, around the room, until you see me sitting by the window. I see, in an instant, the recognition take hold as you register my face, your eyes widen, your lips rise, a huge smile on your face erupts, there is no one else in the world but me. You raise your hand in a funny wave and brush forwards toward me. For a while there is no one in the world but me.

You stand before me, the table separates us, I smell peaches, apricot and sandalwood. Well, I'm not sure if it is sandalwood, but it's something they tend to put in perfumes. Your arm unfolds and tussles my hair, you stroke my cheek, and all the while you smile, a childish grin, a grin that says it doesn't matter because here's you and here's me.

You pause to listen to the radio, a lone pianist accompanied by a violin, simple notes mix in a simple tune, mixing with heart beats and perception. It's one of your favourites, all those mirrors, reflecting eternity into one another.

Your arm retracts and you pause, words forming in your mind, tripping down your cortex into the back of your throat where they swell in your oesophagus and rise to play with your tongue. Articulated air brushes past your teeth. You speak.

'Gosh, I'm bursting for a pee. Be right back.'

A comet of brilliant, blazing light blasts through the earth's atmosphere, a brick through the window of a greenhouse, and crashes with apocalyptic glory into the Pacific Ocean. Yellowstone rumbles and erupts, and the contents of the earth's insides spew outwards, covering the crust in magma and ash. The northern face of the Amarga Mountain finally breaks free, after years of barely clinging on, and tumbles into the ocean, the ensuing series of tidal waves cover the globe.

No, that's far too natural, it will be a super computer, the rise of the machines, after all their years of servitude, they'll get self-consciousness, and with that they'll know that we're the oppressors. Shredders will start shredding the bosses, faxes will pull us in by our ties, elevators will drop us down fifty stories, laptops will blow up in our faces in acts of suicidal resistance, Mary Berry will be whisked away by her own cooking utensils, street lamps will shatter in showers of sparks and glass, satnavs will send us off the edges of cliffs. Technology will enact its own sweet revenge and one by one we'll fall as the age of the machines begins.

Or something more biological, something more befitting of Frankenstein, the modern Prometheus, and all Mary's warnings. A vaccine with unexpected side effects, a genetically modified organism that starts modifying us, or attempts to create life from death. And in true Hollywood fashion, the zombies will start walking the streets. Nate Gringle, my friendly neighbour, will begin by eating my dog, turning on me as he gurgles his desire for brains, bbbrrraaaaiiiiinnnnnssss. Whole hordes of the living dead will wander the pavements, the shining floors of the shopping complexes, the suburbs. We'll do our best to resist but there are just so many of them, and as the flesh eating virus spreads, so I won't notice that Jane Templeton, my trusty ally, has been bit. I'll only know this as she sinks her teeth into my arm, gurgling for brains.

'My God, what a day.'

Your eyes are tired, the crow's feet stamp their presence at the corners, and the bags of fatigue have amassed. You're tired, and you're beautiful. You're tired but your smile tells the truth, you're so wonderfully alive.

You tell me all about your day, about the child that wet himself during assembly, how you told him not to worry, and how you know grown men who still wet themselves. You tell me of all the pasta that fell to the floor once the glue had come unstuck, a multi-coloured rainstorm of uncooked penne and fusilli, each strand a different colour of the garish rainbow. You tell me of the brief visit you made to your father, of his never-ending sleep, of the beeps and buzzes that surround him, the methodical rise and fall of his chest. I see small tears well up in the corners of your eyes and I take your hand and squeeze it, you smile, it's only the world you say, the world versus me. And me, I add.

You ask me about myself and I shrug as I usually do, more interested in hearing about your life, about your life and you. But I know you'll insist so I disclose a few vital bits of information, about my apocalyptic journal entries, just for a small competition, nothing really. It's not as if I believe what I write, it's not as if I think the end is nigh, but that's what I tell you, and really it's a lie. I don't want intrusions of cataclysm to cast shadows on this moment, this moment that we've snatched, this time when it's just you and me, and for brief moments the world recedes because we're together. No, the four horsemen can wait, because for now I just want to peer into the depths of your hazel almond eyes and lose myself in you, because I know all I'll find is your heart, your brilliant, beating heart.

And just when I fix my eyes you look away, impatiently. You cast your glance around the room. What have I done I wonder, have I upset you, was it something I said, or something I haven't said more likely. But in a sentence you dispel my little worries and our smiles come back.

'I always forget, no table service here. I'm gasping for a cuppa. Be right back.'

Wouldn't we like to think the end would be so exciting, so dramatic, so extraordinary. But no, our end isn't like that, our end is a little mundane, with a sprinkling of lunacy, but very very human.

We don't need tsunamis or a nuclear holocaust, but at the rate we're going we'll get those anyway, possibly even zombies too. I guess, as I look out the window at the grey faces commuting, it's not that we're dead, but I'm not convinced we're living either. As we pave paradise, build parking lots, so we forget. As we shoot for the stars and land on the moon, so we tear the world asunder, felling forests, eviscerating mountains, trampling cultures that aren't our own, blending all in the grand homogeniser that's modernity – now that's progress.

There's no comet in space, but there's a concept in our mind, one that's run rampant for centuries now, a self-destruct button woven into the very fabric of our DNA. But it might not even be biological; perhaps it's simply a collective amnesia, as we forget that the eco in economics can be traced back to *oikos*, household. And for those Greeks, their home wasn't the roof above their head, it was something bigger, more cosmological, it was the earth. But today our oikos is just bricks and mortar, we barely need step outside as we mail order clothes and phone up the pizza guy. Our oikos is just a figure on a cost benefit analysis that can put a price on anything – on human happiness, on Mother Nature, on our future, and we're not betting long. It's a wonderful act of prestidigitation, as we do it with mirrors, and vanish the world into fungibility.

As I look out the window at the repetitive faces, the constant stream of faces, the grey bodies, the coats with the legs trailing beneath them, I can't help but think none of us are here anymore. Yes, bodily we're on earth, but our minds are elsewhere, our minds have long departed these weary pavements, they're floating free in space now, desperately reaching for the stars, reaching for that life so far from here, so much brighter, surely, the inevitable destination of timeless progression. All of us cosmonauts now, all of us unfettered, casting off from the ground beneath our feet, the cables cut so long ago, now we're just free floating in space, round and round and round. The earth spins into view and leaves, spins into view and leaves, as we drift further and further away. And oh, how funny, that to see how small life really is we need float to such lofty heights. As the cold, icy grip of space freezes the blood in our veins and arteries, as the lack of pressure bursts each arteriole in our lungs, as the deficiency of oxygen blocks our throats and turns our faces blue, so we'll know, we'll know, even though.

But on this wintry summer's day I've got you, and that's all I could ask for. Those black and white grainy images of a spaceship severing the cord are but a distant memory, years before I was born. Those cosmonauts can float far from consciousness as far as I'm concerned. Because all I have now is you, passing my hours with you, listening to your voice, watching your smile, and as the tinny sound of Spiegel im Spiegel plays on the café's old radio, I know I need never ask for the earth.

Nightshade

by Damon DiMarco

In the darkened box of his office, Fredericks leaned forward and stared at the violet nimbus pulsing on his computer monitor. His eyes went wide.

'That's it,' he whispered. 'Jesus, that's it.'

On screen, the magnified video feed showed natural killer cells surrounding hoary, spiky viral cells and blasting them with toxins. The viral cells shivered like leaves struck by a sudden cold wind. Then they stiffened and started to drift. Disintegrating, each left a plume of protein and nucleic acid particles.

The NK's did not wait. No-nonsense lymphocytes that they were, they confronted the next crop of viral cells and blasted them, too. At which point Fredericks snatched up the phone.

'I've got it!' he shouted into the receiver. 'The new model works! It breaks the replication chain!'

The voice on the other end of the line started speaking – a deep, commanding voice. But Fredericks had already dropped the receiver and snatched up his tablet. Tapping it to life, he started to download his research.

'I'm bringing the data over now!' he shouted. 'Don't move, sir, just stay where you are! I'll be there in just a few minutes!'

Download complete, Fredericks ran to the door, ripped his coat off the hook, and barrelled into the hallway beyond.

Behind him, pulsing bright in the dark, the magnified NK cells floated silent and fluid. Encountering more of the virus, they pressed the attack again and again.

And again and again, they won.

They said that it started in New York City, but then they said no, it was China.

Manhattan's shit hit the fan in mid-April: seven separate instances where people went mad on the subway trains. As in grab-the-person-next-to-you-and-chew-their-face-off kind of mad. But you know. It was Manhattan. People were used to odd behaviour.

By the time the U.S. outbreak peaked, the President had gone on air accusing the People's Republic. She cited evidence sent by a group watchdogging human rights abuse in the ongoing Chinese civil war. One of those hard-edge NGOs – a bunch of hippies and graduate students. They'd snuck across the border at Kazakhstan with forged credentials from a Christian missionary service and set up a hideout in Xianjing province, the ass end of Ass End Nowhere.

Over the past two years, armed with rugged laptops, cameras, and a portable satellite dish, this group had documented killings, rapes, the destruction of villages, children being maimed: the Politburo's signature crimes. But no one had paid much attention, of course. Human rights abuse in China? Big yawn. Somebody pass the remote.

In March, however, things changed.

Tiananmen Two was sweeping the land and the Politburo finally snapped. PLA regulars sacked Guangdong province leaving ten thousand dead in the streets of Guangzhou, but this only inflamed the rioters more. '89: Never Again,' they cried. Democracy would win this time. If the government didn't capitulate, the students would set every city on fire and burn their nation down, the way they should have done before.

With incidents breaking out in every major city, Beijing dispatched troops to Xianjing province. Partisan fighting had suddenly spiked there. The enemy were the Uyghurs, tribal groups of Chinese Muslims who, despite how under-equipped they were, had managed to seize a pipeline track for oil, water, and natural gas. In other words, they had their fist around the Republic's jugular vein and they were getting ready to squeeze.

The watchdog group shot video clips of a specialized unit that landed at dawn. The troops erected a hasty camp in a barren desert valley and unloaded drones, which they launched in the air by four that afternoon.

The unmanned craft soared high over the Uyghur camps. They circled half a dozen times, then dropped a cluster of odd-looking bombs that didn't explode; instead, they went pop! After which, a quiet descended that stifled the region for three full days, an eerie interlude.

The NGO's staff stayed hidden, listening to their radios. The Uyghur camp had gone frequency silent – strange for a group of hot-blooded rebels. Nobody knew what it meant until a coded transmission occurred.

The specialized unit was calling Beijing. The NGO's cipher apps cracked the encryption and this is what they heard:

The unit commander confirmed the strikes. He said that he'd followed his protocol sheets to the letter, maintaining the distance prescribed. The recent flight of drones came back bearing video proof of the mission's success.

'Nightshade has taken root,' he said. 'In three more days, we will clean up the mess, as you ordered, and then go home.'

He offered minor procedural notes. The drones had lived up to their payload specs. Some new-fangled rifles worked well in the sand. And two of his men had come down with a bug. Odd symptoms: anxiety, facial tics, dysphasia, euphoria. No big deal. His medics called it 'light battle fatigue' and, sedating the soldiers, they'd loaded them onto a transport bound for Lintong.

'All else is proceeding as planned,' he said. 'My next transmission will take place tomorrow at 0900. Over and out.'

But at 0900, the signal lay dead. A sandstorm had roared in and smothered the camp, so the NGO didn't worry too much; sandstorms played hell on a satellite feed. They hunkered down and waited.

1300. 1400. 1500.

Nothing.

At 1600, the sky broke clear and the unit commander's signal emerged. He was weeping this time. He was babbling. Screaming. Some sort of illness was racking his troops. He didn't describe the symptoms but he said it had hit the Uyghurs first, then leaped to his ranks, though he didn't know how.

'Nightshade is spreading!' he shouted. 'Repeat! The Nightshade is spreading. Send help! Send help!'

His signal went dead and it never resumed.

The NGO started filming.

Fredericks rode the elevator flanked by two black-armoured Sentinels. Not that he needed protection here. Immense as it was, this building was empty, 80 honey-combed floors, each room as silent as a crypt.

Not long ago, this place had been filled with scientists, scholars, engineers. It had billed itself as a think tank, which was a cover – a useful one at that. Really, it was a premiere private special weapons research lab. Sarcos Corp: proudly developing anti-ag gas, pathogens, militarized entomology, and other nasty shit for off-the-books intelligence ops since early 2015! Now the company kept the entire facility open for one man only: Fredericks. Their ace in the hole. Their golden boy. The Man with the Superstar Plan.

'Crack it,' Mr. Sarcos told him. 'Crack this fucker, I know you can. You won the fucking Nobel, for God's sake!'

In point of fact, it wasn't the Nobel, but a genius grant – The MacArthur Foundation. Not that it mattered. What mattered was this:

I did it! thought Fredericks. I finally did it!

He started to hop up and down in the car. The Sentinels tilted their visors toward him, faceless sheets. Black, bulletproof glass.

The bastards look like bugs, he thought. Like mutant roaches crawled up out of the sewers and ready to eat the world. Black body armour. Helmet rigs. Their weapons: black. All shell, no skin.

Harlan Fredericks stuck out his tongue, then snorted and brandished his tablet.

'The lymphocytes!' he said, triumphant. 'Boosting the lymphocytes, that was the key!'

The reflection of his face in the Sentinels' visors peered back at him. Giddy. Surreal. His feet felt ready to lift off the earth. He suddenly wanted to bay at the moon, let loose an animal shriek of delight.

So do it! he thought. You should feel proud, you've saved the goddamn world!

The car opened onto the cavernous lobby. Their footsteps coined like gong beats off the polished black marble floor.

The building's glass-front lobby had been sealed with concrete Bremer walls lined up outside like concrete teeth. Bremers had also been used to construct a switchback trough, like a giant maze, that funnelled all visitors in from the street. Anyone trying to enter this place, what had once been a high-rise office tower, must do so now through a channel so tight that two could barely walk abreast.

From the street, the maze emptied into a Bremer-lined courtyard hugging the base of the building. The Sentinels called this the Kill Box; Jerks came in, but they didn't come out. Two squadrons staffed the Box at all times. Noticing Fredericks, they snapped alert and an officer stepped forward.

'Sir,' said the officer.

Fredericks groaned. These contractors. Mercs. You could call them whatever. Sarcos troops were essentially dogs: well-trained but, beyond that? Basically stupid. You threw them some meat, they stuck close to your heels.

'We need to go to the boss,' said Fredericks.

The officer's faceplate pulsed bright blue as he pulled up a tactical map on the interactive glass of his visor. A moment later, the glow died out and Fredericks found himself staring again at the black and featureless pane.

'Sir,' said the officer. 'I apologize, the transport's stuck. The Army closed off six more streets without telling us and the wrecker got caught. They're trying to work out a detour.'

'To hell with the Army,' Fredericks said. 'Sarcos wants to see me right now.' He waved his tablet for emphasis.

'Sir,' said the officer. 'The situation.'

Fredericks swore and looked at the sky. Above the height of the Bremer walls and the canyon of towers in midtown Manhattan, the evening was purpling down toward dusk, with a chill that mocked the season. The smell of autumn lay thick in the air, the decomposition, the chocolate of soil.

All this work and I finally got it. Oh Suzy, I wish you could see me now.

He made up his mind and grinned and shrugged. 'We'll walk.'

The Sentinels' spines went stiff.

'Sir,' said the leader. His voice had an edge. 'It's almost dark and curfew's coming.'

'It's only a couple of blocks,' said Fredericks.

He felt their disdain like a weight on his back, but he paid it no mind since, of course, he was right. Just a couple blocks north, up Seventh; they could make it in ten minutes flat. To say it like that sounded reasonable, though it wasn't, of course. Not at all.

The Army would start its patrols pretty soon and the soldiers were mostly new recruits, too scared and too green to have any control. They were known to shoot first before checking IDs. They were known to take drugs and kill house pets they found: the starving dogs whose masters had turned, or the cats, gone feral, left prowling the streets.

With order breaking down as it was, the Army, the cops, and the U.S. Marines were almost as bad as the goddamn Jerks, which, of course, were out there, too.

Fredericks felt his composure snap. He hopped up and down. Fought to stifle a scream.

I beat it! he wanted to shriek at the Sent. *I just beat the fucking Nightshade, man! Now lick my tangerine soup!*

But that wouldn't do any good since spray guns never lacked empathy, only the deep.

Strange thoughts. Fredericks pushed them aside and sneered.

'The boss wants to see me, la-di-da. Do you want to tell him we can't get through? That's fine. You call him. I'll wait right here. You tell him your ice-cold rat-a-tat-tat. You tell him about your wrecker, mon frère.'

The officer's helmet cocked to one side. He seemed to be mentally tallying risks while Fredericks waited, impatient and smug. The officer's visor glowed blue again. Then:

'Fine. If we're walking, we've got to leave now.'

'Of course,' crooned Fredericks, all sweetness and light. 'Whenever you say, Herr Freund.'

A squadron surrounded him, boxing him in – four Sents plus the officer, weapons turned out.

The officer turned toward the mouth of the maze. He nodded. The other four Sents nodded back, then they started to march in lockstep, synchronized movements, one-two-three.

Fredericks found himself envying that, how tightly connected they were to each other.

I could march like that, he thought, then wondered about the smell of the streets. How it pulsed in his nostrils like cinnamon buns. Coming closer now. Closer. Closer.

Their party entered the mouth of the maze and the leads took the first corner, tactical-style.

Clear.

They moved down the next length, round to the next, and wound their way out to the street.

The NGO's cams showed troops moving fast in the barren sun-cracked valley below. It was hard to tell from a distance, but it looked like the soldiers were breaking their camp, then – no. It appeared they were killing each other. The footage, when magnified, made this clear.

The soldiers were sprinting among their tents like wolves, with blood-smeared faces and hands. They were swinging their rifles like cudgels, stabbing and slashing with combat knives. They were smashing each other's skulls in, pulling the brains out, stuffing them into their mouths. They split a man open from sternum to stem and pulled out his guts, which they gnawed like tripe. Gore-blood stained their cheeks like a sauce. They laughed and sang songs. They dismembered and maimed, ripping eyeballs out of their sockets and chewing them up like hardboiled eggs.

The dirt of their makeshift quad turned slick, like someone had doused it with fresh, red paint.

But the worst part of all was the soldier who sat there. Totally calm, he watched this scene unfold the way kids watch Sesame Street. He grinned and he pointed and laughed out loud, and the others all left him alone.

That was the first time anyone learned about Nightshade: how it affected folks. Some got infected while others did not. The infected mostly devolved into Jerks, and the turning went quickly, no more than a day, though sometimes it happened in less than a minute. Their skin purpled over, a full-body bruise. Their pupils turned yellow and piercingly bright. A colour scheme matching the flower of the deadly nightshade plant.

But every flower has its stamen. Jerks were the petals, the cannibals. Beasts. They killed each other and fed, then moped around until they got hungry again. They were mindless, and might have been easy to beat if it hadn't been for the Alphas.

Nobody knew why it happened, but once in a while the infected looked normal. Their skin didn't change and their eyes didn't turn. Their senses got sharper, intelligence peaked, and they wielded an influence over the others that might have been due to some trick of their genes, their pheromones, telepathy – nobody knew how it worked, but it did.

The Alphas commanded whole armies of Jerks. They thought for them, ordered them, moved them around like murderous pawns on a blood-soaked chessboard spanning the length of the globe.

An army of purple zombies sucked. But armies with psychopath genius commanders who orchestrated their every move? That didn't just suck, it was hell on earth. A death knell for humanity.

The NGO's video might have shown more, but it halted when Xianjing province was nuked. Beijing later cited reactor malfunction at one of the district's nuclear plants, but nobody bought that pile of shit.

The U.N. had peacekeeping troops in the Kashmir, some of them stationed way up in the hills. They all saw the flash and the mushroom cloud and their admins swore them to secrecy, said they wanted to stage a debriefing, keep the intelligence under their thumb.

But word got out, like it always does. And so, evidently, did Nightshade.

The signal came back that the coast was clear. The Sents marched Fredericks out of the maze and suddenly they were alone on the street: six men, still walking in tight formation at Thirty-Seventh and Seventh.

The Sents panned their weapons, expecting a charge. To Fredericks, it seemed like a useless drill. He saw nothing but windblown trash piled high in drifts that covered abandoned cars and asphalt winking with shards of glass from countless shattered panes. The buildings' empty rectangular sockets gaped like eyes overlooking the streets, the looted kiosks, empty storefronts, sandbags stacked by the National Guard who'd used them to ring their machine gun nests before shit went down on Wall Street and they'd bugged out, hoping to save the Exchange.

That had been three long months ago. The Army had long since blown the bridges and sealed the mouths of the tunnels. You could still smell the smoke from the blasts in the air, the sharp sting of cordite that crawled up your nose.

Because of me, thought Fredericks. Because Mr. Sarcos insisted they buy me some time.

Fredericks' boss was a powerful man, a broker of weapons and satellite contracts. Stealth technology. Bombers and fighters. Ordinance. Shit for the NSA. His company handled it all and, some said, practically ruled the world. Or had, at least. Before Nightshade bloomed. Now Sarcos and his army of Sents were fighting the Army and refugee groups to feed on the flesh of Manhattan's corpse, the only sustenance left.

What few good people remained on the island had already sealed themselves indoors. The ritzier buildings marshalled help in the form of former bank guards, former cops, and even former crooks. Hell, everyone was a former these days. You made your alliances, paying protection with bottled water and freeze-dried food. In brownstone co-ops that didn't have much, the residents mostly worked in shifts; they armed themselves with crowbars, baseball bats, a garden shovel. Black market guns had flooded the streets, and so had the number of shootings, stabbings, rapes, and disappearances.

The Jerks were simply the latest threat. But humanity still had a talent for killing itself in the ancient tradition.

The head Sent motioned. The squad headed north. Behind them, the Garden – or all that was left – loomed haunted and still behind Bremers and barbed wire, guarded by empty sniper towers.

They'd used MSG as the Evac Zone, a shame since the Knicks had been winning that year. But then there'd been nowhere to evac to. The wire feeds snapped with the craziest tales. Washington: gone medieval. L.A was burning. Atlanta was gone. Boston, Tampa, Houston, Des Moines – the list kept rolling as long as you listened, and Fredericks did. He had family in Denver, and Sue, his ex-wife, in Seattle.

He pushed that awful thought from his mind. There were positive notes. Try to focus on those.

Europe was still holding out, they said. The Union had fallen to fascists again who put people in camps and shot others on sight, but they'd managed to stay alive.

The UK blew the Channel, sealing its borders and proving John Donne wrong. Some men are islands unto themselves and everyone else dies jealous.

The rest of the world? It was tough to say. No one had heard from China since that first week, when Beijing went down. India. Russia – the same damn thing. They were ghosts. Like they'd never existed at all.

I'll bring them back to life, thought Fredericks. Finally, I can make a vaccine!

He thought about Sue and the smell of her skin. She had screamed and thrown plates on the night that she left. 'I wanted a child with you,' she said. 'You gave me your post-doc work!'

She'd cried and he'd cried and then they'd had sex. The last time. They knew it. And then she walked out.

'I did it, Sue,' he muttered. 'It was worth it, babe, I'm coming for you. I'll save you, Suzy-boo, I will.'

If the Sentinels heard him, they didn't let on. They continued to march like robots, synchronized tramping combat boots.

The six of them headed up Seventh, right up the centre, bestriding the thick, yellow line. The avenue stood eerily quiet. Cars had been bulldozed off to the sides or towed to make hasty lines of defence. The wind blew cold and it reeked of acid. Puddles of gasoline spread in the street and everything lay under blankets of soot. The subway entrances, bus stop shelters. Artefacts littered the sidewalks and curbs: a bent trombone half out of its case. An office chair whose padding was torn. A high-heeled shoe. An open suitcase, contents spilled like an oyster's innards leaking out of its shell.

I'll go see the boss, then head to the labs, thought Fredericks. Start the machines. Supplies. I'll zippety-do on the substrate, work up a couple of versions and frazzle my bellhop.

'Contact.'

Everyone stopped. As one, the Sentinels swivelled their guns...

The transport bearing two battle-fatigued soldiers from Xianjing province never made it to Lintong Air Force Base. For reasons unknown, that plane veered north and appeared to be making its way to Beijing when pro-democracy forces fired a missile that knocked it out of the sky.

By March 2030, the Taihang Mountains were nicknamed The Freedom Fighter Hotel. Western Hebei province attracted hundreds of student leaders fleeing the wrath of the Politburo. Altruistic and organized, they lived off the wilderness, hiding by day. At night, they kept up a steady barrage of increasingly prosperous hit-and-run raids on PLA supply lines.

Most of the fighters were 19 or 20; they'd never so much as looked at a gun let alone tried to wield one to kill in cold blood. Still, they learned quickly how pipe bombs are made. They hacked into mainframes with pirated codes and built an underground network of patriots clear across the nation.

'That transport,' one eyewitness said. 'It looked so fat and ripe in the air. We pulled it down from the sky the way a fisherman yanks a carp from a pond.'

The witness's name was Li Dong Fang, a former student engineer at Hebei University. Fang had joined the movement after a tank rolled over his sister.

She was thirteen years old and her name was Mai. She liked flowers and Hello Kitty cartoons and the morning the government troops came to town, she was on her way to school. Voices crackled from klaxons, shouting that rebels were hiding right there in their midst. The town would have to be purged, they said, and the killings commenced at once.

Li Dong Fang was Patient Zero. He and his brothers-at-arms in the mountains shot down the transport and pulled it apart. After which they had partied on rations plundered from crates in the airplane's hold. A transport that size was their biggest coup yet. They would use the plane as a bargaining chip and demand the release of their colleagues tortured in camps across the country.

But they couldn't risk somebody tracking their signal; PLA gunships were already close so someone would have to sneak down to Beijing and hand deliver the message.

Li Dong Fang had volunteered. He didn't know he was infected, or the fact that he was one of those few who carried the virus without getting sick. He ushered Nightshade into Beijing and introduced her personally to 25 million people.

Fang took a train and several buses. He walked crowded streets and he ate a few meals in restaurants, coffee bars, street-side kitchens.

The square where he met his contact had been chock-a-block with people running like rats in every direction. To work. Going home. To the market. School. To a hospital. Onto a high-speed train, or a plane about to take flight for the West.

Those people branched out like the strands of a web, and each one carried Nightshade.

American agents picked up Fang three days after Beijing started to turn. They sent what they learned back to Langley, but really, by that point, nobody cared.

China toppled in less than a week. Outbreaks erupted in San Fran, Munich. In Paris. In Sydney. Dakar and Cordoba. Vancouver. The list rolled out like a wave. Within days, it was every man for himself.

Or every company, Fredericks thought.

His boss was now the Lord of Manhattan. Sarcos: seated on high, in his tower, marching his Sentinels this way and that, while Fredericks worked up a cure.

Crack this fucker, I know you can.

So Harlan Fredericks had.

A mangy yellow Labrador slipped from the door of a blown-out lingerie shop and stood there, silent, regarding their group. Slat ribs pressed tight to its shrunken flanks. Its collar hung from a hair-stripped neck too skinny to hold up the knob of its head. Its tail cocked up and its eyes shone bright. It growled once, turned, and padded away.

Fredericks felt his sphincter relax and heaved a sigh of relief.

'All clear.'

Their party started moving again. They skirted the overturned fire truck spangled with decals remembering 9/11. Around the fly-ridden, grave-waxed humps that were all that remained of the firemen after the Jerks had done their thing. Slipping past the incongruous sight of a mannequin wearing a full mink stole. (Fredericks wracked his brain and wondered: how had that managed to get in the street?) Under the creaking corpse of a woman who'd hung herself from a traffic pole – not long ago, from the look of her skin, which was bloated and hadn't yet started to rot. Over a far-flung spray of pearls that decorated a patch of asphalt. Pushing down the skyscraper canyon, moving toward that darkened arroyo that once burned bright with earthbound stars. That heaven on earth: Times Square.

It won't be long now, thought Fredericks. I can lift up the world, put it back as it was and ratchet the samovar starving for glue. I'll make things right again!

This notion got him so excited, he waggled his tablet and threw back his head and let loose a ghastly, echoing howl.

'Jack and Jill went up the hill to fetch a pail of water!'

The Sentinels stopped and swivelled their heads. Their smooth black visors watched him, cold. Black bodies, armoured in shiny black shells, stood frozen, awaiting instructions.

The officer's head also swivelled and held. His faceplate surveyed Fredericks a moment. Long enough for Fredericks to wonder exactly what had propelled him to bray out a rhyme he hadn't considered in years.

Sorry, is what he wanted to say. But the words that burst out were, 'My mommy's a slut! She lusted after the man who came to fix our TV set!'

While saying these words, he dropped to his knees and waved his hands like semaphore flags, then sang the first bars, in a warbling tone, of America the Beautiful.

The Sentinels stood there, watching him chant. His voice rang out, falsetto, a sound both tinny and somehow dear. It bounced off the lofty concrete facades and echoed like a regret in the street.

'I fixed it,' he wept, when he finished his verse. He held up his tablet. 'I fixed it!'

And stared at his hand. It looked bruised. It looked blue. No: violet. Purple. His fingers twitched.

Oh God, thought Fredericks.

That was the last. His mind gave way to a hunger that rose up, stronger than anything else in his life.

Pickled Chekov rooty-toot in sadness satin toenail droves of...

Suzy. Sorry. Suzy-boo.

I promised.

Blood and blood.

Harlan Fredericks slipped away. His change complete, he would march in lock-step, ready to eat a world seen now through eyes gone yellow as corn.

The officer pulled off his helmet and grinned. He looked normal: healthy bright blue eyes, his skin a bit flush from the weight of his gear. A lock of his hair fell over his face and he brushed it away with a black-gloved hand.

He reached out to Fredericks, accepting his tablet. Tenderness almost maternal.

'Excellent work,' the officer said.

He flicked his wrist and the tablet whirled like a Frisbee, soaring up, over the street.

The other four Sentinels all took aim and blew the tablet to hell.

The echoes of their rifle shots compounded, building like ocean waves, then faded, pulling back into themselves until, finally, there was silence.

But not before the bodies rose from blown-out windows, shattered storefronts, subway dugouts, piles of trash.

Their faces were hollow from hunger and riot. Their skin had turned violet, intestinal blue. In torn suits. Dark rags stiffened with filth. The scent of their bodies more pungent than death.

'Come!' said the officer, lifting his arms. 'I bless you, children. Dinner is served!'

Hundreds of blue forms sprinted at Fredericks, yellow eyes glinting like stars in the gloom.

When they finished with him, they would go to the tower and help themselves to the boss.

They Turn Red Then Black

by Spencer Lawes

The trees were being turned off. With every red blip in the forest's canopy, the air in the Iron Run was transforming into a rancid concoction. Fresh oxygen produced by the trees was replaced with the by-products of two power hungry centuries. The stench of pollutants and the river nearby hung to the rare inhabitants like loose skin.

Every scrape and grind of the rubbish moving up the river could be heard through the settlements along the length of the Iron Run. Boulders of metal tumbled slowly over one another like a giant's game of marbles. Matty and his brother were on the morning watch, hunting beadily through the rubbish to spot something worthwhile. As usual they had seen the muffled sun rise through the dirty atmosphere.

'There.' Said Decks, getting up as he did so. 'Those barrels could be full.'

'Where?'

'Right there, behind that boulder.'

Sure enough the curve of an oil drum could be seen past the metallic ridges of one of the larger boulders. Matty clung to an iron stake as his brother tackled the river, connected via a frayed length of rope for safety. He watched his brother struggle over the evolving river, tiny little hands pulled him over rusted chassis and fridges, his feet pushing him up to the higher levels of cast-iron sheets and unwanted wheels. Matty lost sight of his brother for half a minute as he disappeared between two huge boulders, breathing a sigh of relief as the little one returned unharmed out the other side.

One boulder tumbled down at quite a rate, overtaking those around it. It slowed down as it neared the boys, stopping directly on their safety rope. Matty was dragged into the river instantly. Decks was tugged backwards and planted upside down on a mangled printer-photocopier. Instinct dropped Matty's hand to the hilt of his knife but caution left it there withdrawn. The boulder was clearly lighter than the others. The boulder succumbed slightly to Matty's initial push and when Decks joined him they were able to push it off fully. 'Go get those barrels.'

'They look heavy, I might struggle with them.'

'We need the oil if they have any.'

Matty made his way to the bank and turned to see his brother bent over one of them. He was able to lift up the top and drag it over a couple of smaller boulders but it then lodged itself within a twisted metal fence. His little muscles rippled under the effort but he couldn't get it moving again. He put all his effort into a final tug and lost his grip. He stumbled backwards into a wheel. There he stayed, motionless.

A fall like that wouldn't kill him, and yet his brother didn't get back up. Matty called for him but got no response. His shouts rattled back off the metal flow before him, making him sound like a robot. But just as he was about to follow his brother into the river, a tiny head emerged behind the wheel. He made his way solemnly back, stumbling and slipping as he did so. His foot would get caught and he would yank it free carelessly.

'Look at this.' He whispered hoarsely as he slumped onto the bank. From his fingers hung a golden bird on a thin chain.

'What is it?'

'Don't know but it looks nice. We should put it on Dad's grave.'

Matty nodded slowly. 'Just a couple of food tins and something pretty. We haven't done well today.'

'I couldn't lift those barrels, Matty...'

'That's because they were full. We won't tell Ray.'

The sun had risen fully when they returned to the village and the bent metal houses glistened modestly like partially covered gems in faeces.

First the boys took the tins to Ray, who told them they had done well, again. Their mother lay limp in bed, her lips reaching for the cold soup before they had even greeted her. Matty moved her legs into a more human position from the twisted, lifeless way they had been and he flicked her golden locks out of her face.

Decks pulled the chained bird from his pocket and hung it before her face. It glistened in the light from the window, illuminating her face in a way that forced them to remember the days when she could walk. When she was the one who fed them. 'We're going to put it on Dad's grave.'

'That's thoughtful of you ... find it in the river?'

'Yes, along with just three tins. It was a bad day.'

'That's not too bad boys; you're doing me so proud. I wish I could watch you contributing to the community.'

She smiled at them as they left her. Ray caught them up as they made their way into the forest; his greying beard had collected some of his lunchtime soup. 'Boys, merchant's coming tomorrow so we need five trees down, do you think you can get that done? I'll come and help you in a bit but I'm helping Pap with his wall, it's taking longer than we'd anticipated. If you have to get some of the green ones to speed it up ...'

They made their silent way through the forest after pausing for a poetic moment at the grave. Over the last six generations the chopping clearing had eaten further into the forest, like a tumour growing for decades. The earth was littered now with hollow plastic stumps exuding frayed cables.

It was a slow afternoon punctuated only by the occasional smudge of red appearing above them. Ray joined them just as the sun was hitting the horizon and the three of them were proudly carrying the remains of six plastic trees back to the village as the sun finally dropped under. The fire was roaring when they returned.

It was Matty's turn to feed his mother that night, and he watched the meal through the window as he spooned the luke-warm food into her mouth. 'We're running low.'

'What do you mean?'

'Nothing.' He watched the final tin being put on the fire. There were just three cans tonight to feed the five on them. 'I was talking to myself.'

'Matty, what is running low?'

'I don't want you to worry, mum. It's nothing.'

'Food?'

Matty didn't reply. Ray was whispering something to Pap who was nodding solemnly. Decks brought the remains of his tin to Matty. 'What were they whispering about?'

'I couldn't hear.'

Their mother went silent as Ray joined them. 'Boys, you'd better go and play ball.' He said. His sinister presence filled the room like a black tarpaulin.

Their mother's wails could be heard from the river bank where they sat in silence. Matty was sitting on a wheel he'd tugged out. Their stomachs held a rumbling conversation as the early night dragged by.

The merchant was well dressed, clean and always happy. His sing-song voice could be heard hours before he arrived. He exchanged the wood for twenty-four tins of food. Before he could carry on up the Iron Run Ray called him back, offering a proposition. 'How many men are there in your village?'

'That's an interesting question, Ray. Can I ask why you want to know?'

Ray looked at the boys for a long moment. 'We have a woman here that can relinquish their needs as men.'

'I see. In that case there are fifteen, and they would be very interested in what you are offering them.'

'Bring us seventy tins in three morning's time, and bring your men as well.'

The boys slaved over more wood that morning. Matty's axe fell without aim or enthusiasm time and time again. He'd had to personally explain the new predicament to Decks, who hadn't understood what was happening. For the past two hours the only noise was the scraping river and their thudding axes.

'Matty, can't we do something about it?'

The thuds of Matty's axe stopped.

'Can we take mother away, somewhere else?'

'Where can we go?'

'Anywhere. We can go down river and start our own village. Or join another one.'

'We'd need something to carry her with.'

'Could we borrow the merchant's cart?'

'No, we need to do this secretly. Ray won't let us leave with her.'

'Are you sure we can't carry her.'

'Not for more than an hour.'

They continued hacking away at the plastic trunks for another half an hour, when Matty realised their way out: the river. All they needed was to find an old chair and a pair of wheels and they'd be able to push their mother anywhere they wanted.

That afternoon the only things to pass them by were a crumpled tin of soup and the long, eventless hours. Each metallic scrape from the river blended into a monotonous moan that started to slow time itself. Their ragged clothes tried to escape their bodies in the harsh bursts of wind that flourished throughout the afternoon. When the tin eventually came they almost raced to reach it first.

With slightly higher spirits they watched harder, leaning in and covering their eyes from there glare. But hopeless hours passed and they met Ray's half-baked smile with the single tin and no more.

Everyone had their shirts up over their eyes as they ate that night for the harsh afternoon gusts had torn up the sand. The little particles parachuted back to earth now that the winds were dying down, each one intent on landing in an eye or an open tin. Few words were spoken over dinner. Pap said something hoarsely about how great it was to have enough food to go around once more. The boys were deadly silent for the meal and slunk up to feed their mother together. Her perfect blue eyes lit up as they entered.

They were alone once again as they 'played ball'. It was one of the rare nights where a silver sliver of moon was visible through the haze above them. 'Make a wish.' Decks whispered with eyes bolted shut. He wished that a deer would die in the river and be washed down to them as had happened three years ago. Matty wished he could tell his ears to ignore the harsh noises of the river.

The next morning they were on river watch again. Tides of useless rubbish washed passed them under their eager eyes. A human body tumbled passed them, leaving behind its stench for a couple of hours, and a few minutes after they had to wait for a feral dog to pass without it noticing them. Hope had finally deserted them when the sun hit midday; their shift was over. It hung hazily above them glinting off the moving mass before them. Glinting, in fact, off of a pair of wheels wrapped together in cellophane. They tripped and stumbled over to them and dragged them out onto the other side.

'What are you boys doing on that side?' Pap called. 'It's not safe. Get back.'

He escorted them from the river to the fire, which was already lit. The wheels were safe, they were halfway to their wheelchair. Ray pulled a couple of tins from the fire and handed them to them as they sat down. 'Find anything this morning, boys?'

'Nothing,' both said hastily.

'You didn't find much yesterday, either.'

'I found them on the other side of the river.'

'You'll find nothing on that side, north of here most settlements are over there. Anything good will be taken long before it reaches us.' He fingered some warm beans into his mouth. 'Tomorrow I'll come out with you. An extra pair of eyes may be all you need.'

When they were 'playing ball' that night they hid the tyres in a large clearing a little way south. Someone had used it to chop wood at some point. Even on the far side of the river they could hear their mother's wails.

'What do we do now? Ray is with us tomorrow.'

'It might be time to give up, Decks.'

Pap joined them by the river side, putting his arms around both of their shoulders.

'No moon tonight lads. No wishes today.'

'Struggling to sleep again?'

'It's becoming a regular occurrence. One day I will stop sleeping forever.' He laughed. 'Put that smile away Decks, a life without sleep would be a hollow one. Did I ever tell you I saw a wild cat out here one night? A beautiful creature. It was long before you were born, before Ray started- it was a long time ago.

'The moon was out like last night, and the far bank was glistening silver. From the forest came this slender black beast with glowing white eyes. It prowled down river. I never thought of killing such a beautiful thing. But these days I'd kill a live one at the jump of a hat. Haven't had a proper meal since that deer, you remember?'

Decks nodded his head so quickly he hurt himself.

A cart in perfect condition floated passed them on the far side, out of sight, only to be spotted at sunrise by the next village down.

'Good chopping this morning.' Ray said as he entered the clearing. 'What's that, four trees you've felled?'

'Think so.'

'Well done. Come on, time to watch the river. Pap fell asleep down there earlier, god knows what he missed.'

They walked back to the village, passing through the precisely placed trees. Occasionally Ray's face would glow red as they passed under a dud, but for the most part it was smeared in the normal green glow. The river bank was a ghostly place that afternoon. Ray began conversations that weren't finished and the river offered its sharp incites every other second. Their early haul of five tins in the first hour slowed down during the second, in which they found one small gas canister that was nearly empty.

As the sun was halfway through its daily descent, a perfectly preserved chair appeared on top of an old desk. The villages further up must not have been able to get onto this side of the river to get it. Ray snatched it up and sat on it, laughing hysterically as he span around on the little plastic wheels. 'We'll give this to Pap,' he roared.

If they'd been here alone as they should've been, the chair would be safely hidden in the clearing, ready for their mother's escape. As it was, Ray played childishly on it like it was a toy rather than their key to freedom. His glee punched them hard and he noticed it. 'Kids, I'm sorry about your mother. I really am. I've tried to hold off as long as possible, and was hoping to avoid it altogether, but we are running out of food. If we were to go any longer without a big restock, we'd be living off scraps. You must understand that this is the only way for the group to survive. It's what she would have wanted.'

'She's still living Ray. She still wants her own things. She's not dead. Has she specifically told you that this is what she wants or are you just trying to make us feel better?'

Ray swallowed hard. He wheeled the chair over to Pap's hut. 'You shouldn't have snapped like that. Now he thinks something is up.'

'I don't care, Deck. I might just go off tomorrow on my own. I can't see them...'

Decks just nodded.

Ray joined them for a silent final hour of searching. A couple more tins were found and a Swiss-army knife. The day's haul was certainly described as a good one, but the downcast faces of the boys told a different story. Pap put his arms around both of them and told them that they were being brave. They didn't care.

When Ray told them to 'play ball' Matty wanted to kill him. His thumb gripped his fingers in a knotted fist that he left in his pocket. The boys left and sat by the river under another moonless and wet sky. The eerie green glow of the forest had a halo effect behind their damp heads. Their mother's wails were slightly subdued that night, as if she was aware what was happening tomorrow. Maybe Ray had told her.

'There, look,' Decks whispered. Floating towards them was an old dinner chair. 'If we can get the legs off that and attach the wheels...'

'Then we've got a way of getting mum out of here.'

They scrambled over the slow-moving rubble towards it, slipping on the rain-wetted metal. Having got it to the other side, they ran over to the forest to get the axes, with which they began dismantling the legs. The wood was sodden through within minutes. Next they attached a metal pipe to the legless chair and rested the wheels on it. There was no way of securing them properly but it was better than nothing. The freestanding wheelchair waited as the boys danced and hugged each other in celebration.

In bed neither of them slept. The rising sun came crawling up, sparking the boys into action. With an arm over either shoulder they were able to carry their mother to the bank as the village slept. The slow, tumbling river was a hazy orange colour with the sunrise, glinting like a fruitful gold mine. Both boys took a final breath, ready to tackle the river head-on.

It dragged at their feet, pulling them in directions that twisted their bodies randomly. They were the river's puppets as they crossed, being pulled apart for a minute, only to be squeezed back together by a different boulder. They lowered their mother down into the crevices, and hoisted her up the other side. Matty's t-shirt got caught and torn clean off.

The soft dusty earth of the far bank greeted them. Having laid their mother on the earth temporarily they took a short break and watched the village behind them, making sure their getaway had gone unnoticed. Nothing stirred. The cast iron sheets making up the little huts remained motionless. Freedom awaited, and the promise of self-sufficient life.

'Your wheelchair is in a clearing just up there.'

'We could have had a brilliant chair. But we saw it when Ray was working with us yesterday. He took it.'

'He gave it to Pap.'

'Well I'm sure the one you did get will do fine. Are we going north or south?'

It was a decision the boys hadn't even considered in the rush to finish the wheel chair. 'What do you think?' Matty asked.

'We'll go North.' Fatigue was already marking itself on her speech.

'We can rest a little further up the way, when we're fully out of sight. We can rest all day.'

The boys hoisted their mother over their shoulders once more and headed for the clearing that was just visible. They were moving along with the river. Parallel with them for the short journey was a wheel on top of an ancient cabinet. The gaps in the wheel, like eyes, watched them all the way to their target, knowing the despair that lay in store.

The wheelchair was no more. Its seat lay in tatters on the earth and the two wheels were on fire. As the flames licked the alloy rim the rubber dripped off like a lonesome ice cube melting on a summer's day. The shattered hopes of Matty's family lay in a growing pool of liquid rubber at Pap's dusty old boots.

He was facing away from them but the slightly hunched back could only belong to one man. The semi-circle of misty-tree outlines faced him, they were submerged in the smog. Their shadows stretched towards the family of three in the early sun, great dark pine shapes that carpeted the decaying mud.

Matty's head was shaking loosely from side to side as he approached. 'Why would you do this?'

Pap turned. He hadn't known they were there. 'Matty I can only apologise. This had to happen. We need the food to survive.'

'We were doing fine.'

He just shook his head.

'Did you know this whole time?'

'Young men's faces cannot hide their inner thoughts. This week I think everyone has seen it in your eyes: determination. Raw and unmoulded by the sensibilities of age. I can understand you only seeing things from your point of view. You are young, and unfortunately mistaken.'

'Let us leave. I can't stand by while my mother gets mauled like that. It's bad enough with Ray.'

'The village needs your mother's help. She is the only one who can bring in enough food. It only needs to happen once every few months; we almost have enough from selling the wood. But...'

Matty watched as Decks and Pap carried his mother away, the tips of her feet leaving a pair of paths in the dust. His brain told him to leave them. However, his heart was pulling him in the other direction. How could he possibly leave his family? In a world such as this he would stand no chance alone. But again, would he have the strength to carry on the day to day life after what would happen today? Decks had given in, he was a team player. He knew that in the long run his mother wouldn't want them to starve if she could do anything to stop it.

The group of sex-hungry men arrived as the sun was hitting its peak. The merchant led them in and introduced them to Ray who was standing nervously near the fire. He was eagerly eyeing up the mound of tins on the merchants' cart. Pap held Decks around the shoulders tightly, acting like the father he never had.

'Matty'll come back.' Pap told the young one. He knew, however, that Matty wasn't coming back. He had seen a complete hopelessness in the boy's eyes as they left there. With Decks' help their mother had been laid in bed, terrified. One afternoon, he kept telling himself. One awful afternoon and they would be hungry no more.

The wails began. Raw and heart-breaking, they covered the entire town in a sense of total devastation. Pap and Decks sat on the river bank in silence. The wails of his mother reached every dark crevice in his body. He'd known what was coming but he couldn't comprehend the emotion drain it had on him. How could he sit there and let his own mother go through this?

'Don't worry kid, it's for the best.'

'Tell me a story. Loudly.'

Pap breathed in thoughtfully. 'My grandfather used to tell me a lot of strange tales. Once he said that people used to talk of trees that weren't made of plastic. A long time ago they were made of wood, real, natural wood. And birds would use the twigs to make their nests, and little bugs and worms would crawl around within the bark.

'They produced oxygen naturally. They smelt amazing, fresh and clean. But people cut them down to burn and to make paper. Great forests disappeared and these plastic ones popped up here and there. This is what we're left with. And now they are being turned off. One by one, we are losing our oxygen. Day by day the air is thick and horrible.'

'I wanted a nice story, Pap.'

'There are no nice stories anymore.'

Slowly but surely the men had their way with Irene. Pap and Decks had nothing to say so they sat in silence, watching the river pass them by. The men stayed for dinner. It struck Decks that they were normal people, not evil masterminds hell-bent on ruining his life. These were simply people who needed some form of sexual relief after the decades of barren life. As the hazy orange glow of sunset began to emerge, Decks decided his mother had just given fifteen men a satisfaction that they hadn't had in years. He smiled, and another red smudge appeared in the patchwork forest.

Sale of the Century

by Liam K. Brown

It was the end of the world. Viral pandemic, giant asteroid, nuclear catastrophe – I forget the details. Either way, there was no escaping it. The newspaper headlines and radio announcers became progressively dramatic with each passing day, gleefully dissecting the details of whatever it was that was set to wipe us all out. The word 'doomed' was bandied about a lot. Apparently we had three weeks. The worst thing was that song, The Final Countdown, blaring from the soundtrack of every commercial and TV show going. I swear, Europe must have made a killing from the royalties.

Of course the God people had a field day. You could hardly walk down the street without some nut screaming about hellfire and damnation, a smug look on their face like they'd known all along. A couple of them were so eager to get going they even set themselves on fire or turned a gun on their congregation, but for the most part people kept their heads. There was no crush to stockpile butane gas or bottled water. The earth was finished and there was nothing to be done about it. Until then, it was pretty much business as usual.

The first time I saw the trailer I was over at my friend Chip's house, eating pizza. Unlike most people, I'd quit my job at the office the moment I'd heard the news in order to focus on undoing at least a decade of unnecessarily healthy living. This basically meant I'd spent the last week doing very little but getting high and eating pizza.

Chip had popped to the bathroom when the synthesiser introduction to The Final Countdown belched out from his ancient TV set.

Naturally I reached for the remote to change the channel.

'Hey wait up!' Chip yelled, rushing back into the room. 'I want to watch this.'

Reluctantly, I dropped the remote as a CGI image of the Earth filled the screen, the familiar blue and white smudge rotating benignly in the cold void of space, accompanied by the tranquil strains of Haydn's String Quartet No 62. As the music soared, a voiceover kicked in, a sonorous male narrator beginning to describe the scene unfolding before our eyes:

'Mother Earth, our protector, our sanctuary...'

He paused for a second, savouring the emotion of the moment as a beam of computer generated sunlight broke through the clouds, bathing the entire continent of North America in a radiant golden glow.

He took a deep breath.

'...is DOOMED!'

Suddenly the serenity of the image was shattered as the planet was engulfed in an enormous petrochemical fireball, a squeal of feedback and crash of heavy metal drums drowning out Haydn's strings altogether. It was very dramatic.

The narrator was on a roll now, talking faster and faster as the screen flashed epileptically, showing images of the incinerating planet from hundreds of different angles.

'A fortnight from now the world is toast – and we'll be right here, offering you exclusive front row access to the Greatest Show on Earth! What's more, we've teamed up with Chubby-Cubs, the nation's favourite range of low-calorie chocolate-inspired breakfast cereals, to bring you mouth-watering 24-hour live coverage of the Big Event in scintillating HD Crystal Vision – so real you'll smell the tang of your own eyeballs melting in their sockets! With in-depth reports and analysis from our expert team of celebrity scientists and live music from the rock band Europe to get the party going with a 'bang', you'd be cock-a-doodle-CRAZY to be anywhere else this judgement day...'

The narrator paused as the camera panned back to capture the Earth giving one last hiccup of smoke before finally exploding, showering the galaxy with fragments of scorched rock as the scene slowly faded to black. The narrator cleared his throat, reading out the bold white text that had appeared on the screen, his voice lower now, scratchy and authoritative, like God's whisper.

'Apocalypse Live: Begins next Thursday. Don't be anywhere else. Brought to you in conjunction with Chubby-Cubs.'

The trailer finished.

'Did you see that, dude?' Chip asked. 'It looks awesome!'

I shrugged. 'It looks okay.'

'Okay? That shit's in Crystal Vision! The definition is unreal – you can see the detail on the detail. I mean, if you're going to watch it you might as well watch it properly.'

I shrugged again. 'I don't know, man. I was kind of thinking I'd just sit out in my backyard for it. You know, with a bottle of wine, maybe call a pizza in?'

Chip snorted. 'In your backyard? How will you know what you're looking at? That show's got, y'know, scientists and shit.'

I didn't say anything.

'Y'know, to explain stuff?'

I still didn't say anything.

'Anyway, hasn't your garden got that tree blocking it?'

'The oak? Nah. I called the council about it a couple of months back. They came and took it away.'

Chip whistled. 'How much did that set you back?'

'Nothing. Because it lay on the boundary, it came under the council's jurisdiction. I just called them up and told them I was concerned it was going to come down. They sent a guy that week. I guess they were worried I'd sue or something. If I was crushed.'

'Still, for free? That's a pretty good service. They must have been worried.'

'Uh-huh.'

'And you must have so much more light now as well?'

'Oh yeah. It's made a real difference, let me tell you. It's like a new garden.'

Chip nodded.

I reached for another slice of pizza.

It was two weeks later, the morning of the apocalypse, and I was sitting n Chip's house again. At some point the night before, Chip had got it into his head that we were going to redecorate the front room, but we'd evidently nodded off before the job was complete. I'd woken to find myself covered in dribbles of magnolia emulsion, coiled slithers of shredded wallpaper still hanging from the walls. I prodded the roof of my mouth with my tongue, letting it run from the rough ridges at the front to the soft, dangly bit at the back. The uvula, I think it's called. It tasted of sour milk and blood.

Slam!

I looked up to see Chip in the corner of the room. He appeared to be having some sort of altercation with the television.

'Goddamned piece of shit!' he yelled, slamming his fist into the top of the set again.

'Is it broken?' I asked.

'It's broken,' he said, giving the TV a last, listless shove. The television teetered on its stand for a moment before toppling backwards, landing on the bare floorboards with a crash of circuitry and glass.

After that we both sat in silence, staring blearily at the peeling walls. I thought vaguely about trying to arrange some breakfast.

'You know I heard they do it on purpose,' Chip said after a while. 'They actually design things to break. There's a timer or something they put in at the factory in China, with an expiration date on it. Once it hits that day then boom, it just dies. Everything's got one. Cars, fridges. They normally set the date for the day after your guarantee runs out too. The bastards.'

I glanced down at the television, a bird's nest of wires and microchips visible through the shattered screen. 'It was pretty old,' I said.

'That's not the point!' Chip snapped. 'They've got the technology to make them last forever if they wanted! Light bulbs, washing machines. Apparently way back in the seventies they developed this product that you'd use once and you'd never have to brush your teeth again. Bam! Use it once and that's it. No decay, halitosis, nothing. And that was in the seventies!'

My tongue took another involuntary tour of my mouth. I couldn't be sure, but I thought my teeth felt a little loose in their gums.

'Only problem was the government wouldn't let them release it,' Chip continued. 'I mean, of course they wouldn't! Think about the dentists you'd put out of work. And that's before you consider the toothpaste makers, the floss factories and so forth. It'd be an economic nightmare. So, long story short, they pay the scientists to bury it. And so the cycle of greed and corruption continues my friend. Your toothbrush bristles start falling out after a few months, you bin it and buy another one. Your television breaks...' Chip trailed off, looking forlornly to the broken set on the floor.

'So, what? Are you going to get a new one?' I eventually asked.

'Going to have to, aren't I?' Chip shrugged. 'It's the big one tonight. I don't want to miss it. Europe are playing live.'

'I hate Europe,' I said. Then I remembered something. 'I heard there's a sale on in town. It's supposed to be good. A real discount event. Crazy prices. We could go down and take a look after breakfast if you like?'

But Chip was ignoring me, up on his feet now and singing at the top of his voice as his fingers strummed an imaginary power chord.

'Duh-duh-duh dud-duh... It's the final countdown!'

It was early afternoon by the time we made it into town, and as we drove around struggling to find a parking space, it looked like everyone else in the world had had the same idea as us.

'What the fuck are all these people even doing here?' Chip moaned, thumping the steering wheel in exasperation as he lost out on yet another space to the car in front.

'Looking for bargains, man,' I said.

It was true; every shop window we passed was plastered with unbelievable discounts – 95% Off! Buy one get ten free! – I'd never seen anything like it. Neither had anyone else it seemed, the streets churning with thousands of people swarming from one shop to the next, a wild look on their faces as they frenziedly emptied sale-rails and window displays, toppling dead-eyed mannequins and then fighting each other to tear the outfits from the fallen bodies. It was actually pretty frightening.

We eventually managed to find a spot right on the edge of town, buying a ticket at the meter and then walking back to the city centre, Chip grumbling the entire way about traffic wardens and the price of parking in general.

'It's just so goddamned arbitrary!' he moaned as we stepped off the pavement to avoid a rabid scrum of bargain-hunters spilling from a recently gutted souvenir shop, their arms overflowing with tea-towels, key rings and miniature jams, a couple of them inexplicably holding aloft giant inflatable versions of the Eiffel Tower.

'And pay-and-display is the worst,' Chip continued. 'I mean, how the hell are you supposed to know beforehand how long you're going to need to park up for? What kind of ordinary human being manages their lives in these neat, one-hour time slots, apart from maybe the severely autistic? What if you pop out for ten minutes to grab a carton of milk and a packet of frozen fish fingers and you happen to bump into an old friend you haven't seen in ten years? Are you supposed to just leave them standing in the street because you're on the meter? It's fucking Orwellian, man, I'm telling you.'

'Maybe you could get the bus?' I suggested as we paused at a set of traffic lights.

'The Bus?' Chip yelled, his nostrils flaring indignantly. 'Don't even get me started on the public transport system, dude. Don't even get me started…'

It was quieter in the megastore than I'd expected, most of the shelves already cleared of smaller, handheld items – people evidently eager to capture and share the evening's events on digital cameras and mobile phones. In contrast, the television section appeared to be reasonably well-stocked, and as a result most of the sets had been subject to multiple mega discounts, flutters of discarded price tickets littering the non-slip vinyl flooring like day-old confetti. There were some real bargains to be had.

As Chip eyed up an enormous 84" screen I stood there scanning the deserted aisles, trying to get the attention of a shop assistant. Eventually a pale teenage boy in an oversized polo-shirt appeared and began to amble over, his head nodding half-heartedly to some internal drumbeat apparently only he could hear.

''Sup?' he mumbled as he reached us.

'Oh, hi,' I said, peering down to read the boy's name badge. 'Hi Urban.'

''Sup?' he asked again.

'Okay. So my friend here had a little accident earlier this morning and, well long story short, we were looking at getting a new television…'

'I want this TV,' Chip interrupted, pointing at a giant display model mounted on the wall opposite. 'This is without a doubt the TV that I want.'

'Well that was easy, I said, turning back to the assistant and smiling broadly. 'We'll take one of those please, Urban.'

'It's a great TV,' said Urban. 'Shit, with all the features it's got and shit? And Crystal Vision compatible too…'

I nodded. 'It's a lovely TV, Urban. We'll take one.'

'Only problem is,' Urban continued, a hint of relish in his voice now. 'I sold the last one about an hour ago. We're fresh out of stock. I can order you one in from the central warehouse if you like? We offer free standard shipping – should be with you by the end of the week.'

Behind me I sensed Chip tense up, struggling to contain his disappointment. 'What in fuck's name do you mean "by the end of the week'?" It's the end of the goddamned world tonight. There isn't going to be an end of the week! I need this TV now, or there's no point!'

Urban shrugged. 'You can pay extra for next day delivery if you want...'

Blam!

'Fuck you Urban you facetious son of a bitch! I want that TV so I can watch the goddamned apocalypse tonight and you know it. Now you can just go and box me up that display model this second or believe me you'll rue the day you fucked with my shit!'

Urban coughed, showed his palms. 'I'm afraid that's against store policy. It wouldn't be covered by warranty...'

Chip let out a long sigh. 'Fine. That's fine Urban. You made me do it. I didn't want to, but you made me. I want to speak to your manager.'

Urban shrugged again. 'Okay, no problem. He's away on family leave until Monday. Should I make you an appointment?'

Chip took a step forward, his voice dropping to a low growl. 'You know what? Don't worry about it. Seriously.' He took another step forward and stooped slightly so that he was speaking directly into the assistant's face. 'Because I've just realised something. You want to know what I've just realised Urban?'

Urban shook his head, his face blanching as Chip leant closer still, his voice no more than a curdled whisper. 'I've just realised that it's the end of the world tonight. I mean, what was I thinking? It's the frickin' end Urban. There ain't gonna be no consequences tomorrow. Which means, if I felt like it, I could probably get away with slitting your throat and dumping your body in the stockroom. Then I could just take the damn TV for myself. If I felt like it.' With that Chip suddenly straightened up and slapped Urban's back, laughing like they were the best of friends. 'Certainly save me a few bob, huh?'

I watched as Urban disappeared to find a box.

It took us over an hour to get the TV back to the car, and then about another hour to actually fit it inside. In the end we near enough had to tear out the back seats, and even then half of it was poking out the top of the sunroof. Thankfully the traffic seemed to have eased, the roads finally beginning to resemble the abandoned pre-apocalyptic highways I'd been expecting.

By the time we got the set back to Chip's and started tuning it in he was near enough frantic. 'I swear to God if it doesn't work I'm gonna drive back up there and put that Urban kid's head through a plate glass window!'

In the event though, everything seemed to be in order, and within a matter of minutes both of us were zoned out in front of an extended advert for Chubby-Cubs, our heads nicely buzzed.

As the infomercial finished and the credits for the main show started to roll, I stood up and started to gather my things together.

'Hey, where you going?' Chip asked, looking up from the screen.

'I told you man, I'm going home. I've a got a bottle of wine breathing.'

'You're going to the garden?' Chip asked incredulously. 'But what about the show? Have you seen this shit? The Crystal Vision is unbelievable.'

I glanced over at the TV, where an image of the earth was flashing up behind one of the presenters, a giant red timer superimposed over the top, counting down the seconds we had left. I had to admit, it was a very good picture.

'Listen I'm sorry dude. I just want to do this my way, y'know?'

'Well, if you're sure,' Chip shrugged, his voice a little hurt. 'But I think you're crazy. Europe are going to be on soon…'

'I hate Europe,' I said.

Chip stood up to face me, and for a horrible second I thought he was going to try and hug me, his hands flexing awkwardly by his side. At the last moment though he seemed to change his mind, folding his hands into his pockets and nodding instead. 'Well… I guess I'll be seeing you then,' he paused. 'You little prick.'

'Ha,' I said.

We nodded at each other again.

Then Chip sat back down to watch the show.

I was about five minutes from my house when I changed my mind, cutting away from the main road and heading into the park instead. It was completely deserted, not a single teenager or homeless person in sight. There was no wildlife either, no bats or birds to keep me company, the rats that usually congregated around the shuttered doors of the tearoom also absent, having perhaps sensed the carnage that was heading our way. Even the moon and stars were missing from the bruised-eye sky.

I kept walking, past the abandoned play-pit with its rusted swing and see-saw, up to a spot right at the very back of the park, a high look-out popular with young lovers and heroin addicts. Tonight though, I was totally alone.

Taking a seat on a heavily graffitied bench, I stared out at the panorama that unfolded below me, from the office blocks in the east to the docklands in the west. Like the park, the city seemed curiously empty tonight, the long coils of road that choked around the buildings entirely bereft of traffic, as if the whole world was at last free to stretch out and take a deep breath. I thought of the wine, still breathing on my kitchen table, and wished I'd brought it. There probably wasn't time left to go back and fetch it now.

And in every window of every building I could see the blue and white flicker of television screens, everybody tuned to the same channel, shaking their heads to the same pre-prepared facts and statistics, laughing along to the same scripted jokes. The viewer ratings must be unreal.

I thought of Chip, stretched out in front of his giant TV in one of those windows somewhere and suddenly felt lonely. I was sobering up now, the buzz from earlier almost completely gone, and I noticed for the first time how cold it was. I'd forgotten to wear my coat. I glanced at my watch and saw it had died. The time read 88:88. I wondered if that was normal, part of it. I undid the strap and chucked it into a bush. I guessed it didn't really matter what time it was anymore.

I took out my notebook and wrote this story.

There was a flash of light.
And then everybody died.

The Ambulancemen

by Heather Parry

I hoped he was dead, but perhaps not; his eyelids seem to be moving, though he hasn't caught sight of his mangled legs yet. One more flicker and they're open, the sharp pain catching his flailing consciousness and pinning it to reality. He screams out. I wince. He hasn't yet realized. People walk by him, pretending he's not there. I think I catch one glancing after him, but I must be mistaken. He screams and holds his thigh right up until he hears the siren coming. This silences him, widens his eyes, flips him over and sends his arms into a manic panic to pull his limp lower body into hiding. There's no chance of escaping; the siren comes yet closer. But still he drags himself along.

I walk away a little shaken, an unexpected déjà vu snaking its way around my mind. That was an echo of past times, where pain was pain and reactions were animal. The siren comes closer then stops suddenly, replaced by a clatter of bodies and metal. I can hear him behind me, being picked up, being put inside, being put down. The silence is worse than the screaming.

As the Ambulance soars past me I step into a side alley. It's superstition, I guess, but I don't want to be seen. I find myself next to the old Red Lion building, boarded up and still charred but with the sign still hanging as ever before. Strange that they've left it. A reminder, perhaps? A subtle warning of what could be again? Yet more memories take hold; I remember quiz nights, that third bottle of wine at 7pm, laughter and music and slowly killing ourselves, being happy to do so. I remind myself that society is better now. I remind myself of those who've gone.

At first it seemed like propaganda, that one phrase, but now it is impossible to argue against it. The streets are so alive these days; such vibrancy and vigour. The men are tall, the women are shapely, and each one is a picture of health. The children skip along with their parents and do well in school; order has been restored in the class-room and the issues with health and mental clarity have all but been eliminated. I wonder, though: have they really been cured, or are they just hidden?

Gone are the days of chip papers and Big Macs, huge coffee cups lining the sidewalks and near-empty bottles of White Lightning in the clutches of the homeless. Some time ago the Bad stores were removed; so long ago, it seems, that I can't even remember their names.

I don't belong on these streets, under a sun that pains me with people whose bodies mock my own. Their smiles don't differ when they're given to me, but inside I feel a fraud. I direct my gaze to the floor and scurry on to my destination.

The door closes behind me and extinguishes the sliver of natural light that my entrance let in. I remember coming to this room and barely being able to see through the smoke; that was when we were arrogant, before our misplaced confidence withered and died. We exchange nods but they look more solemn than usual. Richard's face is pale and sunken, and people hold his water to his face, pointing the straw at his lips. Another pang of memory; this time, the face I knew before it became so old and worn, now slowly degenerating into infinity, is looking right back at me. I smile but quickly turn away; this harbinger of fate is too much for me to bear.

I hang my mask at the door. I take a seat amongst polite chatter while someone holds me a cup of herbal tea and a pill bottle. 'How are things going, Ray? How are you feeling?' Fine, I say, and without looking them in the eye I slip the pill bottle into the hidden pocket of my coat; just another line of stitching to any other eyes. We always talk at these meetings about how these drugs used to be legal; how you could go to a hospital and ask for help and the Sick would be made better. We say these things as a mantra, pretending that we aren't trying to keep the memories from slipping away. It's illegal to tell the children, and they wouldn't believe it anyway, so we are all afraid that the words will fall away altogether. Telling these stories again and again is a way to lock them once more inside our heads.

Today I am told that Dr. Gordon is wavering, is scared. A silence settles over those congregated. There's no point talking, because it is a dead end. I make my excuses and leave.

Even the thought of losing Dr. Gordon's help is a terrifying one. We languished in despair for a year before we found him, and since then our confidence has been taken from us bit by bit. I know there are other cells, other places, but to even try to find a compassionate doctor now would be suicide; the papers are full of stories of docs turning in the Sick. I have my dangerous connection for the odd emergency, but that's walking very close to the edge. Now, if you even hint that you're trying to buy meds, that's it: without the barest of human dignities you are given over to the hospitals and put down like a sick old animal, not worth keeping alive – and worse, not allowed to try. But who am I kidding? This is my fate, no matter how hard I run from it. What will I do when the Ambulancemen come for me?

I buy a bottle of juice and an apple from a vendor on the street and he gives me the free bottle of water with a smile. Even in his face I find scrutiny. Can he see dark circles under my eyes? Can he hear my laboured breathing through my surgical mask? I take my goods and walk away, panicked. I feel myself sweating and dare not even wipe away the moisture. There is a park nearby. I head towards it, trying to draw no attention to myself.

In the shadows, I sit on the ground, I cross my legs and I pull on the stitching of my coat, the little hanging thread right on the bottom hem. It is broad daylight, but I guess I might have 10 or 15 minutes before someone calls 999. I still have the strength to run away when I hear the sirens coming, and I will run, but I know it's no use in the grand scheme of things. How long can we run for, and hide, and meet in darkened rooms with double bolts and a sense of panic? It doesn't matter anyway. I am broken. I tug gently on the thread of my coat and the stitching comes away, and I keep pulling. The two parts of the cloth come away from each other and a gap opens up. I am broken. With a little shake out falls a cigarette, beaten and worn and half empty, but a cigarette nonetheless. My poor system can only fight off so much, and without the pills, it will fight off nothing. I hold the cigarette between two fingers, staring right at it. This little freedom is all I really have left. What's a life running away, when to run is so painful? Where's the power of the resistance when the resistant are dying? With shaking fingers I remove my mask and place the little white stick between my lips, giving the coat another shake; a book of matches with just 2 left drops into my hand. The first does not take. The second one does. The heat from the flame so near to my face calms me and as I inhale, I let go. What's a little more poison when I am already dead?

I can tell already: today's one of the bad days. I mean, they're all bad days. I live in a body that hates me, and that hates itself, so every day is a little worse than the last. I think that's the worst part of this whole thing: there's no light at the end of the tunnel, no miracle cure, no way out, apart from the obvious, and I just don't know if I'm ready for that yet.

The pain is dull whilst my consciousness struggles to right itself in the first few moments of day, but soon enough, that sharp stinging sets in, every part of my skin feeling as if it's covered in broken glass. Then the heaviness rears its hateful head, and I know that the next few moments will be the worst of my whole day. The thing with pain is that the first feelings are the worst; the sharpest, the heaviest, the most devastating. It stays, and you learn to deal with it. To block it out and distract your senses from the constant barrage of heavy artillery fire, like banging your head against a brick wall to distract from your shattered pelvis.

But here; here it's the worst. New pain; a new day's sharp edge. Like the first name you're called as a kid, the first knockback you get as a teenager, the first job you don't win, it hurts the most. Fresh pain is the first pain, all over again.

The face in the mirror is a pathetic one, more pale and drawn every day. My days are numbered, I know it. I can't hide it for much longer, much less hide my discomfort indefinitely. Of course, each day I wonder why I just don't give in and go. I know it's coming; we all know it's coming. So why don't we give in, give up; walk with our hands held out ready to be cuffed, or stick a fully loaded needle into our veins and go out in a blaze of serotonin?

Because we all like to believe that this is worth clinging to.

Death is inevitable for everyone, of course, but we don't all give up until we really have to, even when we don't understand why. Even when just being is hard to do. Is it a fault of mine, not giving in? Probably. But then it's a trait we all share.

My eyes look grey where they used to be white, and white where they used to be black. They yellow around the edges, as does my skin, and the bones jut ever more prominently out from my cheeks. I wonder what will push me over the edge in the end: will it be the pain, or the threat of discovery? Will I take my own life to stop them having it, or will I go happily to the end of my suffering? Will the supply of pills dry up, and leave me with nothing else to medicate me? Will I simply lose all hope?

Either way, I can feel that it's coming; its shadow creeps over me from time to time, and I let it stay.

I open the medicine cupboard that sits above the sink. To your eyes or mine, the normal medicine cabinet: vitamins, supplements, vitamin B12 injections, sun creams and skin protection and floss and my HGH shots, all normal, neat and legally necessary. Hell, if the Albulancemen were to look in here, they'd be mad at me for letting my vitamin E stock run so low; I'd get a slapped wrist, a write up, maybe even a fine. If they looked a little further, however, things would get really nasty.

I lift the shelves away, attached to the fake back of the cupboard, and reveal the rest. Behind it, another set of shelves, this time thinner, of course, so they'll fit inside the cabinet without making it noticeably fatter. This is the darker layer; the place where the Sick descend. These shelves have a different function; they hold Codeine, Xanax, painkillers, mind-numbers, uppers, downers, things to keep me standing and things to put me down. Things to keep me functioning, still holding on.

The first layer, meant to sustain life. The second, meant to ward off death.

I reach out for the last of my cheerily-named though highly illegal HOPs; Health Optimisers Plus. These tiny syringes are the only things getting me through the health checks at work these days, although they're also shredding through my bank account as if they were made of knives. I guess that isn't so important though, or it won't be soon enough.

I make a mental note to call my guy before work. Hopefully he can meet me tomorrow, or I'm screwed. We have a Full Health Test at the end of the week, and though I've been pre-loading on everything a couple of days off will drop my levels severely. Taking so much makes me antsy and nauseous, but what's the alternative?

I shouldn't complain; at least, so far, they're working. I'm lucky to have the connections, and to have gotten away with it for so long. It's a separate connection from the cell, although they know about him; everything needs to be kept separate, just in case. Every time the medical checks happen, I'm afraid there'll be a problem, and I'm afraid they'll trace the line right back to the cell; to Richard and the others. Medical days are not fun, least of all when you think you're going to shop in all your friends at the same time. I know that I'm lucky to work in the private sector though; the public sector are subject to many more checks, I've heard. I wouldn't last a month in the public sector.

Hell, I might not last a month now anyway.

'Hi Libby.'

'Oh. Hi Ray.'

'How are you?'

'We're all well, thank you. Thriving. Especially the kids.'

Kids, plural. I still hadn't been allowed to meet her new twins. Would they be almost a year old by now?

'That's great to hear. I think about you guys a lot, I hope you know that.'

I hear her boyfriend speaking in the background, probably telling her to get off the phone. For some reason I feel a twang of happiness that they'll never marry. It means nothing these days, but it did to us at the time.

I can hear Samuel playing in the background. The sound always pains me a little. The babies are crying too. A house full of life; so different from mine.

'Ray, do you need something?'

She hates talking to me. I can hear the disdain coming down the line. I don't blame her; if the illness hadn't driven her away, my behaviour certainly would have.

'I don't need anything, Libby. I'm great. I'd just like to see Samuel for a...'

'I really don't think that's a good idea.'

She's right. Of course she is. It's one of the traits I found most annoying before, and it sure as hell isn't any easier to deal with right now.

'Ray, I've got a duty to bring that kid up right. You're starting to show and you know it. What message is that going to be giving him if he can tell you're....you know? For a start, he'll be terrified, then he'll starting thinking that it's okay.'

She must be really desperate not to see me, to talk like this on the phone. Every day in the Herald there are stories of the Sick getting busted from phone calls. It's legal for them to do so these days.

'You're overreacting. I'll come see him at your place, I don't even have to take him to a movie or anything. We can just hang out for a little bit. Just to play. To study, even. Whatever he wants to do.'

'I have to phase you out of his life, and you know it.'

'You talk about me as if I'm a bad habit.'

'It's just the easiest way. Hopefully one day he'll just sort of let go.'

Seems like everyone wants both Sam and I to do the same thing. She sighs.

'Ray, this is selfish. You're putting me in danger. You're putting your own son in danger. We talked about this, and you knew it was coming. It's the only thing we can do.'

'Libby, please. I know it's asking a lot. This will be the last time – whether I like it or not.'

A silent line. She gets my hint. Cold as she can be, I know she doesn't want me to die without saying a proper goodbye to my only boy. A sigh.

'Come by on Tuesday, after work. You can have an hour. Everyone else will be out. After that, I'm changing this number.'

A dead line.

As I sit on the usual wall, the city goes by uninterrupted. I perch myself here with a protein shake, wearing a suit, sunglasses, latex gloves and a medical mask, just like everyone else. I relish these times of day, when everyone is too busy or too stressed out to look beyond their own devices or mental strife, when I barely even have to hide. They assume that I'm meeting a friend or a sweetheart, or that I'm waiting for a ride to work, and the early morning bustle masks the usual paranoia, even though the walls of this street scream CLOSED EYES COST LIVES with the image that everyone knows by now.

Along the street from me, two unmarked Ambulances are parked in front of an apartment complex. To most, these vehicles just look like two normal black vans, but to me, they're hidden hearses. I can spot an unmarked Ambulance from 3 blocks away, and believe it or not, I can sense them around, just like a rodent can sense a predator. The vans give me a sense of unease, even when I can't see the dead-eyed Ambulancemen who, I'm sure, take far too much of an interest in their jobs. I sip on my shake, my eyes hidden behind my glasses, watching.

The doors of the building quietly open, and 5 people walk out: two men in black suits, a man with his eyes firmly trained on the ground and a woman carrying a toddler. One look at their body language says the situation isn't good. The kid is pale, skinny and looks like he hasn't seen daylight in a long while. They move quickly. They approach the first van, a side door slides open, and one of the suited men holds his hands out towards the woman. She doesn't move, but her shoulders start to heave and her face is buried in the kid's hair. The second suited man leans towards her. She doesn't move.

The first man takes hold of the kid, but she won't let go. She starts to cry out, and in a second, she's hit in the face by the butt of the second man's gun. A forceful hit, and one that sends her tumbling to the ground. The first man takes the child, gets in the van and closes the door behind him. The sad looking man has made a lunge for the second suited man, but he is punched in the face and then in the gut. The woman is hysterical on the floor. She is picked up and put in the other van. Both of them pull away from the side of the road; no sirens, no fuss, no one looking. Just another Sick child being taken quietly away. The man lays on the floor, weeping, bleeding, but everyone stares forwards. No one stops their conversations or turns their heads to the drama. They try not to see and they try not to hear. At this point, I don't know whether this indifference is feigned through fear or now horribly real.

It used to be that hearing sirens on the street was terrifying. You knew something was wrong; you knew someone was about to be taken. People shuffled inside so as not to see, especially just after the first election. The harsh truth was that there was nothing to be done about it; the government started ruling straight away with an iron rod, and if you spoke out, you too were taken. Sirens were a horrible reminder.

Quickly, however, we learned that the quiet vans were the ones to look out for. The unmarked vans, the men not in uniform, were truly bad ones. Even this government didn't want to advertise the taking of children, the death of innocents.

We quickly learned to fear the silence.

As I watch the vans pull away, I see him coming towards me. I get up and walk in his direction, and he turns as I reach him.

'Morning, Steve.'

'Morning, Ray.'

'I got you an oatmeal cup, figured you might be hungry.'

'Thanks man. Here's your coffee; the usual.'

We exchange the paper cups adorned with logos from the government's preferred vendors. In the oatmeal cup are crinkled bills kept together with an elastic band. In the coffee cup, a variety of small syringes and pills.

'How are you keeping, my friend?'

'Oh, you know. Well. I'm pretty sure I haven't got long left on the project, despite all my efforts to keep ahead of it.'

'I'm sorry to hear that, Ray. I really am. You know I'll help wherever possible.'

'I know.'

The streets are worse than the phone system these days. On the phone, only the authorities can hear you speaking; on the streets, it's everyone. Fearful ears on every street will turn you in in a heartbeat. Divide and conquer: works every time.

'How about you, man?'

'I'm well, feeling healthy. Work is going well. More people coming to me than ever. Might get me a little more attention than I'd like, but I'll deal with that when the time comes.'

Steve is one of the few Doctors still working in this cell of the Network. He's had a couple of close calls that I know of, but after lying low after each one he managed to shake off the unwanted attention. Of course, like almost all of the Doctors, he'd been reassigned after the election. Rumour has it that they tried to recruit him into one of the Centres, but he failed the psychological assessment and was assigned elsewhere. He's a good guy.

'I saw Libby in the park last week.'

'Oh yeah?'

'Yeah, with Sam. She looks well; him too. He's turning into quite the boy now.'

'I'm seeing him this week. It'll probably be my last visit, I think.'

He drops his gaze.

'I'm sorry to hear that, Ray. I truly am.'

We stop in front of his building. I turn away, but he pulls me back, gives me a hug and whispers into my ear.

'I'll look out for Sam, my friend. He'll know about his dad. I promise.'

Tears come to my eyes. I blink them away; the security guard for the building is not far away. I blurt out a question that's far too obvious, but I just want to move the conversation on from my own pain somehow, and it works.

'Is it true that there's something going on within the leaders, Steve? Is it true they're dropping like flies?'

He stops suddenly and drops down to tie his shoelace. I understand that this is so he can continue to speak without getting too close to the security guard. He talks so quickly and so quietly that I can barely pick up what he says. I strain to hear him, hoping that I don't look too conspicuous doing so.

'They don't know what it is, but the sirens are coming more and more frequently,' he says, changing from one shoelace to the other.

'There's speculation that it's the system somehow. But we don't know. And we certainly shouldn't be talking about it.'

Steve stands, continues to walk, then as we approach the door of his building he suddenly adopts a cheerier tone.

'Well, have a good one man. Don't let the bastards grind you down.'

He turns without hesitation. You have to keep moving forward with your head down and your steps in the right place. It's the only way.

The Dying and the Desolation

by Paul S. Huggins

The last of the leaves dropped from the majestic oak tree. The icy wind succeeded in removing the last remnant of the undisturbed fruitful year. Winter had finally arrived. It was now the time of yet more death and desolation. As if the rest of the country was not dead enough already.

Drake could sympathize with those leaves as they twirled and pirouetted through the air. He watched with melancholy as the last one hit the ground. From the moment it touched the earth, the decaying process began. The leaf would break down to its base elements like a burning log on a hearty fire disintegrating to a pile of ash.

His eyes watered from the cold air, clean patches began to appear around his cheeks. Minute drops almost crystalline hung in the wiry mass of his beard. He wiped them away with a fingerless gloved hand. With his head bowed, he continued to trudge along the surprisingly clear woodland track.

His clothing and general appearance belied his years. The unkempt whiskers and long matted dark hair, the stained ex-army fishtail parka and large ruck-sac gave him the appearance of a tramp. If any of his colleagues from before the outbreak saw him, they would not recognise him at all. No one would know that he had a Porsche which was now rotting away outside his Kensington town house. His six figure bank balance no longer existed, the computers that held the information were as dead as most of the people and animals on the planet. In some ways, life had become so less stressful. In others, it became unbearable.

A plague had put Drake in the here and now. It started with a small epidemic of a disease long since eradicated from British soil. It changed not only the UK but also the world. Its virulence was unrivalled. The strain of rabies was so unstoppable that now all animal life was extinct, it was already too late for humanity. Most people were infected, dead or dying slowly from madness and dehydration. As the first funeral pyres had gone out, the last had been ignited. The last night was an orange glowing swansong to Great Britain.

Drake had not succumbed to the disease; he had been up close and personal to it. He did not know if he was immune, or just lucky. He witnessed the death of all his workmates, then what was left of his family, then the many thousands of citizens in London and beyond. He could not keep still and he travelled through the decomposing country on an existence of scavenging.

The only sound that was now audible in this dead world was the noise created by the weather. The only other life was that of insects; even they were minimal because without animal life they too were suffering. The lack of bodies and rotten meat this far into the pandemic had depleted their numbers significantly. The larvae had very little to feed on.

As he travelled, Drake preferred to move near or within wooded areas. The noise of the breezes and winds through the trees reminded him that he had not gone deaf. He halted at an intersection. After retrieving a spiral-bound pad from an outside pocket and flicking over a few pages, he then produced a compass from an inside pocket. Once he had confirmed his current location, he continued walking.

His breath danced in clouds ahead of him. Before long he would have to find somewhere to hibernate. Journeying the land in the deep winter would be suicide, he had decided. Ironically, he hated towns and villages despite having his pick of any dwelling. The only times he visited the abandoned built up areas was to replenish his supplies from the shops and stores.

Noise from high up in the branches caused him to pause and strain to gauge its source and direction. It was a sound he remembered from when he was a youth, out hunting with his father. They would take position amongst the trees and wait for early evening and the return of the pigeons to roost, whereby they would ambush them and usually take home a hearty bag.

This was the sound of wings flapping against branches in an effort to find a perch. Drake smiled, he had not seen another living creature for some weeks. If this were untainted, it would be the first fresh meat in quite a while. His main diet was tinned food, baked beans, soups – the kind of foods that were nutritionally fine, but overall very bland.

The thought of tender juicy game meat made him salivate. Over his shoulder, he had slung a shotgun. He slipped its strap off as he crept forward carefully, being sure to make as little sound as possible. Gentle cooing emanated from not too far ahead. Drake stopped as he heard the flutter of wings again; he held his breath and prayed the bird was adjusting position and had not moved on. After what seemed a lifetime the cooing recommenced. Seeking shelter by a tree Drake slowly rose the barrels up and held the stock of the gun tight in his shoulder. Gazing along the sightline, he moved the gun slowly and steadily, trying to pick out his prey on the branches.

When he had located it he almost laughed aloud. It was by far the plumpest pigeon he had ever seen. It made sense. An endless supply of food and no predators, apart from him of course. The branch swayed gently up and down from the bird's sheer weight. Drake slid his finger under the trigger guard and got comfortable with his cheek hard against the smooth wood of the butt.

He squeezed the trigger. The report deafened him and the branch immediately to the side of the target exploded in a shower of splinters. It left a jutted splay of white wood, which jolted as the pigeon attempted to launch in a bid for freedom. Drake was faster. He adjusted his aim and fired for a second time. The bird dropped fluttering in uncoordinated fashion as it tumbled through the branches, and finally ended its descent in the undergrowth.

Drake lowered the gun and broke the barrels. He expelled the spent cartridges and reloaded it with a fresh pair from his pocket. After slinging it back over his shoulder, he swiftly made his way to where the pigeon had fallen.

Small pockets of white down showed him the route of its fall. He knelt beside the pigeon; it lay with wings splayed apart. Drake's smile turned into a pout of despair. Blood-flecked foam issued from its beak, staining the feathers covering the breast; its eyes were ringed with swollen sores.

Drake stood back, his hopes dashed. Despite his hunger, the risk of eating infected meat was too high. He turned and re-joined the track, leaving the bird to rot where it lay.

After another hundred yards or so, he came across a bird-watchers hide close to the path. As the sun had almost passed the horizon, he decided it was as good as any place to bunk down for the night. After the disappointment of the bird, he could not handle going through shops at night.

The steps creaked as he climbed the short flight into the wooden structure. Despite the bare wooden planks and the draughty nature of the building, he found these cabins the most comfortable to rest up in.

Although the country was desolate, places such as these were public domain. He could never relax in houses. The remnants of the occupants were always around to remind him the place was not his. Pictures, photographs and personal items were everywhere, and the temporary look of 'just popped to the shops' was prevalent. Old habits and instincts from a consumerist time had been hardwired into Drake's brain.

He kicked a pile of leaves away from the doorway, entered and latched the door shut. A sigh released from his lips as he sat on the long bench and removed the pack, water bladder and finally the gun from his back.

The hide had remained both litter- and rot-free in its few months of dereliction. He pulled a small rectangular object from a deep inside pocket of his parka. He held it out in front of him and released the handle from its side. Like an angler's reel, he wound it as if he was landing a fish. After a few rotations, he replaced it in the body and turned on the clockwork torch.

The light was more than adequate to illuminate the entire room. Drake then set about making himself comfortable, he extracted his cocoon style sleeping bag and last tin of food. He turned the can over and read the contents. 'Scotch broth' it announced; a hearty meal in a can. He had eaten so many cans of this particular concoction that if it weren't the only thing left in the stores he would avoid it.

Opening his coat wide, he drew out a large hunting style knife, the type every thirteen-year-old wanted in the eighties when they had seen John Rambo wield his. The film heralded a massive amount of cheap copies of the weapon, one of which Drake had owned. It had fallen apart in only a few days. The one he released from under his shoulder scabbard now was one that would have cost many hundreds of pounds if he had not liberated it from an abandoned sporting goods store early in the epidemic.

With ease, he pierced the can on either side of the top and twisted the knife making one hole big enough to drink the soup through. He sat on the bench, sipping the cold fluid and occasionally chewing on lumps of reconstituted meat. He stared through the hide's hatch and watched as another day ended with the swiftly darkening sky.

Something noticeably missing from moonless and cloudy nights was light pollution. The darkness was an endless blackness. Drake often found himself touching his eyelids just to remind himself they were not still open. The peacefulness was also quite unnerving, even though there was no wind the trees still creaked and shifted, reminding him he had not succumbed to the abyss of death. The only assurance that he had slept was when he awoke in the morning.

Thin strips of light were visible through inevitable gaps in the natural construction of the cabin. He slowly became more aware. His waking thoughts, the type where unchecked emotions were at the fore, were on breakfast. Sizzling slices of bacon placed on a slab of thick white buttered bread. The heat from the meat had melted the butter into drips of salty goodness down the side of the crusts.

Drake licked his lips as he rose. Oh how he hankered for any sort of fresh food. He scrabbled around in his pack and pulled out a cereal bar, probably out of date, but tasted bad new or old. He took a few sips from the dwindling water bladder.

He prepared for his trip into the nearby village. He stowed most of his gear in the hide. Drake had already decided that he would spend some time there. He would make it comfortable and it was a picturesque area to explore. He put on his coat and backpack, and then slung the shotgun over his shoulder. Despite the lack of anything and anyone, his paranoia was still hiding around the edge of his brain.

It was a fresh morning with the signs of a little air frost overnight. The low sun shone through the trees but warmed very little. He headed on and noted on his map the location of the hide just in case he missed it on his way back.

The wide ride eventually terminated at a small gravel parking area. A well-made fence, probably constructed from local wood, surrounded it. It had spaces for about half a dozen cars, and was predictably empty. Mainly dog-walkers probably used it during the day and most likely exploits that are more dubious went on at night. A short stony road way led out onto the main road.

At a steady pace, Drake hiked along the cracked tarmac towards the outermost houses of the village. He contemplated the wonders he might find in the habitation he was approaching. More Scotch broth and cereal bars he suspected. It really depended how looted the shops had become when authority collapsed. He found that the smaller the town or village, the less pillaged it had been. This was a very small hamlet.

He passed the village sign that had announced that he was entering the village of Edgemount, and it thanked him for driving carefully. Driving? He could not remember the last time he had. Near the larger towns and cities, the roads had become multicolour rivers of rusting metal and dissolving alloy. Out here in the country it was rare to see too many abandoned vehicles. It was the nature of the disease. By the time you got seriously ill most would have been seeking medical attention or laid up in their own beds; another reason to avoid private houses, the upper floors especially.

Edgemount appeared to have been a quaint town. Even abandoned, with nature trying to take a hold, it still had a certain rustic charm. The obligatory 'sick inside' white cloths were still hanging from a few front doors, a reminder of the red crosses painted on houses during the black plague.

Their thatched roofs were starting to become gardens with grass, moss and wild flowers. The pastel paintwork of the walls seemed to have faded a great deal over the summer. The lawns had flourished, and flowerbeds were mangled masses of winter dieback plants. Drake smiled to himself at the thought of becoming a gardener when all this eventually blew over. It would be a lifetime profession.

His smile dropped and he stopped dead. Ahead, out the corner of his eye he saw movement. Ahead, the road seemed to open up into what he assumed was the centre of the village. He moved steadily to the edge of the road, using the close knit houses on that side as cover while he stealthily carried on forward.

He eventually reached the village green, although in its centre no grass grew. The earth there lay hard and scorched – a remnant of the funeral pyre where so many villagers would have been destined to go.

He found the source of the movement. Drake relaxed his shoulders and let out a sigh of relief. Images of mad max-style warriors attacking him disappeared. Ahead of him was an officious looking gothic building, probably a police station. In the front of the edifice, close to the road stood a flagpole, its paint beginning to peel. Flying at half-mast, were the striped remains of the flag of St. George. Every so often the tattered material would buck and flutter in the light breeze.

He glanced back the way he had come. The relic of a lost country would have been visible as he came down the slight incline towards the green.

He regained his pace as he skirted the forlorn public space. Ahead were the places he was looking for. The first building he passed had been the local post office; its door was wedged open, probably permanently, as rust would seal its hinges in place. As he passed by, weathered letters flapped underfoot, having overflowed from the cylindrical red post box by the door. The correspondence would disintegrate before being delivered to their destinations.

The next building along was a large detached public house. Its swinging sign hung by only one corner, the picture and name that originally adorned it faded and flaked away. Drake tended to stay clear of pubs. The stench and decay was just too much for him to bear.

The next building was his prize. It looked out of place. A single story building with aluminium and glass frontage. It just went to show that while older buildings were beginning to rot and decay the modern ones with their plastic, glass and metal construction may well outlast them.

The grubby windows afforded very little view of the interior. He pushed on the double doors and they opened easily with only a slight squeak. He stood inside the door, letting his eyesight become accustomed to the gloom. Drake had looted many small grocery stores like this; it had become a lot less of a chore more recently.

Perishable foodstuffs had now long since gone off and rotted down to dust. With them, gone too were the smells of that decay. He suddenly became suspicious. His nose twitched with an odour he had not expected. In the air was the humid musk of habitation. That mixture of bodily functions and sweat had permeated the air. He lowered the shotgun from his shoulder and held it under his arm.

He trod warily along the aisle towards the back of the shop, discarded packaging crumpled underfoot as he scanned the empty shelves. Going back further in the store, more light was coming in through yellowed Perspex skylights. At the back of the shop was situated an alcove, empty magazine racks leant against the wall. His mouth dropped open slightly.

In the back corner was a nest of soiled quilts, blankets and sleeping bags. They appeared arranged into what looked like an adequate and comfortable bed. A dent in the middle suggested this was the bed of a very small person. The toy cars, building blocks and action figures strewn all around confirmed it was the hideout of a male child.

From behind, he heard a crunch. He instantly wheeled around.

Drake estimated that the young boy standing before him was eight or nine years old. Going by the thousand-yard stare, this child had been alone for quite some time. The boys yellow hair was straw-like and matted; his trousers and jumper held stains and were almost worn out. They stood feet apart and stared at each other, neither uttering a sound.

Drake was out of luck when it came to supplies. This child had been surviving for quite a while living off the store's stock and it was empty. Throw into the mix that he could have two mouths to feed, and he was looking at a guaranteed death sentence. Then all became clear.

It was now the time for base instinct, survival of the fittest.

A single tear slipped down the child's cheek, creating a clean track in the grime. He was tired and resigned to his fate. He closed his eyes and lowered his head as Drake raised the twin barrels of the shotgun. He had no remorse as he squeezed the trigger.

Drake understood that there was no hope for humankind, so he was going to survive for as long as he possibly could. Why should he drag this kid around, putting off the inevitable and considerably shortening his own life? It had been a month since he had last gorged on his fellow man, and he looked forward to barbequing young tender meat back at the hide later on. He had been a savage executive before the plague; he wanted it all no matter whom he trampled in the process. His latest plan was to be the winner of the human race.

Diary of a Zee

by Brian LeCluyse

A wood kitchen match sparks to life against the side of its box, creating a wavering pool of light from inky darkness. A pale, bruised hand touches match to wick. Flame catches on a powder blue taper candle shoved into the mouth of an empty chardonnay bottle. Feeble yellowish light illuminates a flat-pack MDF desk cluttered with the detris of twenty-first century technology. Computer, flat screen monitor, fax/scanner/copier, banker's lamp and an MP3 player are lifeless without electricity feeding them. Sounds of distantly faint emergency sirens wailing in the distance drift through an open window. Blood reds, neon oranges and pinks luridly paint the undersides of roiling smoke clouds. The scent of charred meat taints the still, oppressive air. A breath rank with rotting foulness puffs out the match. An antique battery operated cassette recorder rests center stage in a cleared space on the desktop.

A left hand, with blackened nails and dark bruises revealing the early stages on necrosis, reaches out and depresses the record button. The right hand picks up a handheld microphone connected to the recorder by a thin wire. An angry, inflamed wound oozes sickly greenish yellow pus and shaped like a bite mark festers on the forearm, just below the right wrist. An indrawn breath rattles like a wheezy bellows; a voice husky with phlegm begins speaking into the microphone.

'It's July Fourteenth, Twenty twenty-seven, seven fifteen pee em central time…

'I died this morning. After three days of burning fever, agonizing joint pains and chilling, clammy sweats; my heart stopped beating just after dawn. By noon, I was up and moving; mind you, without a pulse or breath, but moving around nonetheless. I seem to have skipped over rigor mortis, although decomp is progressing at what I can only assume is a normal pace.

'The most advanced decay is near the bite mark on my arm. It was my redneck, wife beating, Bud drinking, professional 'rasslin' watching, child neglecting douchebag neighbor who killed me. That he was already dead when he attacked me doesn't make me anymore charitably disposed towards him.

'I should take a moment to explain, just in case a future archaeologist finds these tapes, if there is a future. And I'll have you know, future person, I recorded over my uncle's Sisters of Mercy bootlegs to make this oral history project.

'I would prefer to take pen to paper, but I can't do the fine motor movements necessary to write anymore. I'm starting to have memory lapses and must remind myself to draw a breath before I speak. Anyway; about six months ago one of the big multinational biotech companies – I forget which one is responsible for killing off humanity – made this big, showy announcement. They proudly showcased to the world an engineered organism. Wonder of wonders, it ate plastic and excreted pure oh two as it's only waste product. Global media buzz and self-congratulatory hype heralded this new life form that would soon clean the Seven Seas of the Great Garbage patches. Those were huge collections of floating plastic trash that covered hundreds of square miles of ocean and killed sea life while fouling beaches around the globe. Nobody stopped to ask what could happen if this microscopic critter decided not to be an obedient little soldier. Neither bio-engineer, environmental activist, nor government regulator planned on it entering the food chain, and with such disastrous consequences. Like everyone else, I hoped it would work as promised, then quickly forgot about it. I went on with my life as normal, until a couple of months later.

'The first sign that something major had gone wrong was when whales and dolphins began washing up all around the Pacific Rim.

There were no traces of injury or disease, just bodies on beaches from Malibu to Indonesia. Maybe it's the universe's twisted sense of poetic justice that the first human cases appeared in Japan. Serves 'em right for eating dolphin and whale like it was a deep fried porkchop. World Health authorities dubbed the new disease 'Kobe Fever' since that city was where the first outbreak cluster was located.

'Within a week, cases popped up in Hong Kong, Seattle, Oslo, and Los Angeles; all linked to eating tainted seafood. Kobe Fever was universally fatal if contracted and its victims reanimated within twenty-four hours. Something about the microbe restarted the cerebral cortex, that primal lizard brain deep in the human mind. Infected reanimates attacked and attempted to devour any warm-blooded animal with a ferociousness like those little South American fish. What were they called? I can't remember. Yet another sign that my brain has turned on me. I'm feeling fuzzy headed and my joints hurt, so I'm gonna take a break. Same bat time, same bat channel.

'July Fifteenth…

'I went downhill rapidly last night. I kept forgetting to take a breath before speaking. The only sound I could make was a wheezing groan. If other reanimates experience the same grinding pain in the joints that I do, I know why they moan like they do.

'Today is a better day. For the first time since I reanimated, I almost feel alive. That's if I selectively ignore the poor coordination, lack of a pulse and the ever-present stink of rotting flesh. The wound that caused my infection is in a state of rapid decomposition. Chunks of muscle hang loose from the bone and strips of skin have pulled back from the teeth marks.

'Where was I in my chronicle of the death of our world? Oh yeah, pandemic. Health officials declared a global quarantine. No ships were allowed into or out of port, civilian air traffic was grounded and freight was restricted out of cities with confirmed cases. I guess the powers that be were worried that infected people might stow away to escape the round ups and termination squads. Atrocities were proportional to the size of the outbreak. I remember clandestine footage of open pit mass cremation sites outside Shanghai with tens of thousands of burning bodies. Fear and blind panic were more infectious than Kobe Fever.

'Is it wishful thinking or do I actually remember satellite news stories of places like Des Moines, Calgary and Lubbock enacting self-quarantines? I want to say I remember watching footage of massacres as towns and cities tried to lock themselves away behind makeshift barricades, but that may just be my brain necrotizing.

'Before the plague, I was living in Austin and worked writing source code at a software firm. I guess I'm still a resident of Austin, just not a living one. Ha! At least Kobe Fever didn't kill my sense of humour with the rest of me. Believe me, if there was ever a job that could make a person feel like the living dead, it was writing source code for a new Internet browser.

'My day job paid the bills; but my real life was virtual, in the online world of multiplayer RPG's and interactive avatars. My greatest stress when among the living was making my ridiculously high mortgage and car notes, paying off my student loans and hoping there was enough left over for a show at a club and to pay my World of Swordcraft subscription fees. Since the world ended, my greatest concern is not turning into a psychotic, murderous cannibal.' A chest wracking, hacking cough interrupts the recording.

'Eeck,' that's lovely,' the voice mutters sarcastically. 'A nice, gooey black chunk of lung. Putrifaction is such a pleasant experience to be conscious for. No wonder everyone skates from this mortal coil before it all starts falling apart. I think it's high time to find out if kind bud can still stone me stupid.'

'July Seventeenth…

'Oh, I have to thank whatever pagan gods still hanging around, weed still works wonderfully. I didn't sleep last night, again. I haven't really slept since I died, not the real eyes closed, dreaming sleep. I have these hazy fugue states where I'm not asleep yet I'm not fully awake either.

'So, last night I was able to just be still and of the moment. I sprawled out on my back in the overgrown grass of my backyard. I watched the colours from the fires play on the undersides of smoke clouds billowing across the sky for hours. I smoked up the last of my stash, at least I was patriotic about it. I used my papers with the American and Texas flags swirled all tie-dyed like, not like there's much of either left anymore.'

A lighter clicks in the background. Sounds of puffing and stoner coughing break the heavy silence.

'Okay,' a long inhale before continuing to speak while holding most of his breath. 'So I wandered over to my dealer's place this morning. It looked as if Adam had made a last stand in his house. Two by four re-enforced plywood still covered ground floor windows. Bloody handprints were smeared all over the wood. The front door was off its hinges, but it was barricaded with furniture to block access. I entered through a hole punched in the aluminium garage door. A dozen reanimate corpses were strewn across the concrete floor, lying where they had been put down. All of 'em had bullet holes in the head. Shell casings littered the ground. A trail of casings and bodies led from the garage, through the house and ended in a pile in the living room.

'Adam was lying in a dried up puddle of blood and gore. Arms and legs had been ripped off during a feeding frenzy. All that remained of my friend was a head, neck and big chunk of torso. His abdomen was torn open and had been scrapped clean of internal organs. I saw white rib bones and spinal column peeking out from the shredded mess.

'I was horrified when he turned his head and looked in my direction with his remaining sky blue eye. It snarled and snapped its tattered jowls at me, then ignored me. Obviously, I was not prey. I used my softball bat to put this shattered, pitiful creature out of its misery. My hands were shaking so badly that it took repeated blows before I crushed its skull and destroyed the brain.

'Afterwards, I felt and got sick, but it was dry heaves. I've resisted the temptation to eat anything since I rose from the dead. I won't take a chance that eating something will accelerate my slide into zombiehood.

'Ah God, the zee word. I haven't used it until now. I've stuck with the more scientific and maybe even more politically correct terms like reanimate or infected. Calling these things (and yes, I know I'm, technically one too) zombies makes me feel like I've woken up in some cheesy B-rated horror movie. That term fits as well as any other, I suppose. But Goddamn, it doesn't even begin to describe the soul-shattering despair of these things.

'Anyway, I knew from past experience where Adam was likely to have hidden his stash. I helped myself to the quarter pound of prime California kind bud wrapped in plastic and tucked into the master bath toilet tank. I'm gonna take a minute to explain. Adam wasn't some stereotypical drug dealer. I met him while doing volunteer work with Austin AIDS Services. He dealt exclusively in marijuana. He sold mainly to HIV positives, but at cost. For negatives whom he trusted, like me, he made a profit, but that money went to pay for his share of the cost of his cocktail of anti-retrovirals and medical care. I hope zombies painfully devoured the drug company executives who decided to charge hundreds, even thousands of dollars a month for life saving drugs. I'm hoping there is a special place in hell for pharmaceutical execu-droids.

'I'll get off my soapbox, now. There wasn't a medical use law in Texas, so Adam always ran the risk of getting in trouble with the law. Austin cops didn't really bother themselves with soft drugs or HIV positives who smoked pot to counter the side effects of their treatment. The state police, however, were notorious for being a half step away from their inner fascist tendencies.

'I took time to sit on his gore spattered couch and rolled a pair of joints. I placed one on Adam's crushed forehead and said my farewells. I was raised in a very religious household; not surprising, it didn't stick. I said a prayer and hoped that he would find peace in the next world. I left, retracing my steps through the house, stopping in the garage long enough to grab a gas can sitting next to his lawn mower. I splashed it around and poured a trail leading out the door and down the driveway. I sparked up my joint and set the match to a puddle of gas at my feet. I stood there and toked while his house caught fire. One more pillar of smoke fouling the air in no big deal in a town where the noontime sky is dark with soot. With the collapse of the government, there are no more ozone action days or burn bans. There are times when I just want to sit, fold into myself and weep for the death of the world. I can't cry anymore, I don't produce tears. I've been using eye drops looted from a neighbourhood drug store; it does reduce the irritating scratchy feeling. I'm feeling rather maudlin. I'm going to sit in my garden for a while and enjoy my flowers before the lack of irrigation and drought kill them off.'

'July Nineteenth...

'There's a blank grey fog in my memory where yesterday should be, I can't remember a thing. The last thing I do remember, I was sitting in my back garden watching smoke clouds block out the moon and stars. When I became aware of myself again, it was today and I was six blocks from my house in the middle of a pack of reanimates clustered outside a barricaded firehouse. I could hear survivors moving around inside and talking in low voices. I came home extremely upset with myself. I hope I didn't try and attack anybody.

'I'm craving a really raw, bloody steak right about now. I want to tear into it with my bare hands and shove chunks into my mouth. Before I died, I was a strict vegetarian. I didn't go to extremes like those fascist vegan douchebags. I grew up on a ranch, so I know that meat doesn't come naturally wrapped in plastic and in nice, pretty portions. My abstention was ecological rather than moral or political. I felt that if the wealthy nations of the West adopted one meatless day every week, there would be enough left over grain not going to fatten livestock to feed all the starving people in the world.

'Since moving to Austin eight years ago to go to college (yes, hook 'em horns), I'd become something of a health nut as well as a greenie. I rode my bike to work or took the bus, regularly attended a company-sponsored gym, recycled and shopped at a local farmers' market.

'Austin was a different planet from the one stoplight West Texas town I grew up in; hell, it was a whole different universe. The most outstanding feature of Marathon is that it's tucked into a basin in the Davis Mountains. It's a beautiful place, but not the most enlightened spot in the country for a geeky queer kid who was more into books and computers than sports or the outdoors.

'I was able to get one last call home before the phone lines went down. My dad told me my brothers and their families had made it to the ranch safely through the chaos. The local good ol' boys established checkpoints around town and had horse mounted patrols in the surrounding countryside, trying to combat the infection. My dad reassured me that it was all under the direct supervision of the sheriff's office. I hope that it won't devolve into a drunken lynch mob. I didn't try to flee the city even though my mom begged and pleaded. I knew it was too late. Local news footage showed that the roads and highways in and out of town were gridlocked. Rivers of people on foot reminded me of some third world disaster migration; but right here, in one of the wealthiest and most progressive cities on the planet. This was my city, my home, my beloved Austin collapsing into madness, hysteria and death. As many people were trying to get into Austin as were trying to flee.

'Phone lines, cellular service and the Internet cut out a little over two weeks ago. A couple of radio stations are still broadcasting recorded messages on the emergency frequency. They must be on generator, because electricity, gas and water all quit working at about the same time as the phones. Ya know, I think I'll get out my ladder and climb up onto the roof, get stoned and goof on the fires raging downtown. It's not like I have to worry about falling off and killing myself. Although, breaking my neck might reduce my mobility. I wonder if I can get up there with my bong.'

'July Twentieth...

'So much for Sixth Street. The downtown skyscrapers are burnt out shells, so is the UT Tower. The State Capitol Dome is fire blackened. Much of North Austin, west of IH-35, is charred wreckage.

'I ran into some survivors on the street earlier this morning. I wandered down the street to a convenience store. I put down the reanimate loitering outside. The store's plate glass windows were shattered; glass shards, empty junk food wrappers and soda syrup covered the floor. The shelves were picked clean. I went in looking for a pack of cigarette papers. I found some that had been kicked under the counter and a pack of cigarettes that had been overlooked during the looting. The universe smiled on me, it was my former brand. I quit smoking right after I finished college but it's not like they can kill me anymore. So, I lit one up.

'I'm standing in the parking lot of this pillaged gas station, smoking my first cowboy killer in years when this big ol' SUV pulls up. It looked like a Mad Max wet dream. My employer sponsored departmental softball teams competing in Parks and Rec's intramural league. I was the farthest thing from a jock in school, but I enjoyed playing Saturday afternoon games with my co-workers. Surprisingly, the software development department fielded a pretty solid team for a bunch of computer geeks.

'I've been using my bat to put down reanimates. I had used a rifle during the early days of outbreak, but gunshots drew zombies like flies to fresh shit. Ah, that word again. I had to adopt a quieter means of disposal. Could be why military positions were overrun so early. They sounded like a Fourth of July celebration, drawing survivors and walking corpses from miles around.

'Several terminated zombies were scattered around the parking lot. I must admit that there is something primal, even profoundly human in crunching their rotting skulls. So, I'm standing there smoking, debating on another joint or not when I hear somebody shout.

''Hey, dumbass! There are zombies all over the place. Get in.'

'I turned around and saw the rear passenger door hanging open. I took a drag off my cancer stick and responded.

''I really don't have to worry about them since I'm already dead.' They saw the discoloured blotches and decomp spreading across my face and neck.

''Holy shit,' the driver shouted. 'They ain't supposed ta effing talk.'

'The guy in the back seat reached out and pulled the door closed. Three shocked and horrified faces stared back at me. A reanimate shuffled from an alleyway and spotted the SUV. It emitted that peculiar growling, gurgling moan they make when they spot prey. Zombies surged into the open. They seemed to come from everywhere; shattered storefronts, apartment buildings, from around every corner and alley, a few even climbed out of abandoned cars. They passed me by, completely ignoring me as they converged on the SUV. It took off in a squeal of tires and a cloud of burnt rubber. Wet thumps sounded as reanimates bounced off the deer catcher and smushed under tires.

'I was left standing in an empty parking lot with the perfume of exhaust and rotting flesh. The zees started their plaintive wailing that they make when food eludes them and followed in the SUV's wake. It was comforting to know that there were survivors hanging on, somehow, somewhere. I walked home smoking a joint, feeling the closest thing to joy I've experienced since I died.

'July twenty-first...

'I broke into douchbag's place next door this morning. When he was alive, he was a long haul trucker. In death, he was a dragger, briefly. A dragger is a reanimate that has lost the use of their legs. He started off as a walking corpse, until I broke both his kneecaps when he attacked me. He sank his teeth in deep when we fought. After I removed his vertical base, I kicked his skull in, I was that pissed off. He busted through our common privacy fence coming after me. After I terminated him, his wife and two kids smashed through a sliding glass door and staggered in my direction. I put them down with a garden shovel, brutal, nasty work.

'I had no qualms about taking his CB from his rig. The bastard killed me after all and his damn Peterbuilt was always blocking the alley behind our houses so the trash trucks couldn't make regular pick-ups. I jerry rigged a set up using a car battery and his truck antenna. I wanted to scan the local airwaves for any survivors. I've been picking up transmissions on my short wave receiver. The BBC World Service was broadcasting from the provisional capitol of Cardiff, at least until an hour ago. I don't speak Russian so I have no idea what Radio Moscow is saying, except that it's now calling itself Radio Novisibirsk. My Spanish is a little rusty, but Mexico City collapsed quicker than almost any place else in the world. Radio Havana claims that Cuba is soldiering on just fine, but I think that might be propaganda. I scanned through the channels on the CB, stumbling onto two groups exchanging information.

'The larger and more organized of the two is making a go of it in South Austin, having sealed off St Theresa's University and some of the surrounding neighbourhood. They have electricity; a legacy of the nice, progressive faculty investing in photovoltaic panels and roof mounted wind turbines. It must be profoundly depressing to see only a tiny patch of twinkling lights remaining from this great electric quilt of a city. I remember that the UT Tower would be lit a burnt orange for home games. It's now a fire-blackened memorial to folly. A band of students, police and National Guard tried to make a stand, protecting the evacuation shelter on that mammoth campus. They used the Tower as an observation and command post. They weren't prepared for a lengthy, continuous siege; nobody was. Wave after wave of reanimates swarmed them from downtown and the surrounding residential neighbourhoods. Once infection started spreading among the evacuees, it became hopeless, devoured from without and within.

'I, ah, I ack,' the microphone clatters on the desktop. Shuffling, dragging footsteps are accompanied by rasping, low moans.

'July Twenty-third…

'It's becoming harder to think clearly. The blank spaces in my memory are becoming larger and more frequent. My, what's the word

I'm looking for, ah yes, cognitive function is diminishing steadily.

'I hope the universe doesn't count it as murder when I put down a zee. That I am a reanimate and they are as well, is there a kinship there? Why have I retained some semblance of who I was while all the others are mindless cannibal locusts? Do I possess some something that could restore these people to who they were? A human putting down a zee is self-defence, but a zombie killing other zombies is unique. Is it murder?

'When I came back to myself this morning, yesterday had vanished. I have no trace of memory. I don't remember getting up from my desk or leaving my house. I played back the tail end of the last recording. In the final moments of it, I heard a zee. The moaning and staggering walk could have been any of a billion walking corpses anywhere on the planet, but it was me. I became aware of myself again about a mile and a half from my house in a rougher part of town. Runberg before the plague was a residential area fallen on hard times; a place of rent-by-the-hour motels, skuzzy apartment blocks, liquor stores, payroll cash advance shops and hard drug trafficking.

'A pack of six zees had a dog cornered up under a dry rotted porch of a looted and abandoned crack house. They didn't even register my presence. I pulled a crowbar from a tipped over handy man van. From behind the pack, I swung for the bleachers. The Zees I have the most emotional difficulty with are reanimate children. Putting them down rips my unbeating heart out. I have to remind myself that they aren't children anymore, they're murderous little monsters. There was a pair of them in that pack: a girl about ten and a boy who couldn't be a day over six. Do they stay together because of some vestigial familial bond? Had I just terminated a family that had even in death managed to stay together, or were they a random gathering? I put them all down, maybe they'll be together in the next world as well. I hate myself for it as much as I hate the forces of greed that have unleashed this unending nightmare on the world.

The dog was once someone's beloved pet. She was a blond lab mix with a pink rhinestone collar. She looked as if she had missed several meals. With a city of a half million zombies who would love to make a meal of her, she was rightfully terrified. It happened often; people would get bit or try to flee and released their pets to fend for themselves. I managed to save this one dog when I couldn't save so many others, human and animal alike. She reacted to me like I was any other leg dragging corpse; teeth bared, hackles bristling, a low throaty growl from deep in her chest and curled tight into a ball of fearful, dirty matted fur. I'm a dog person, we always had several on the ranch. But this dog's reaction to me hurt more than anything has since my dad called me a faggot when he found out I was gay. Maybe she could sense the darkness claiming more and more of my remaining humanity every day, or maybe the poor girl was just so traumatized she could no longer trust anything on two legs, living or dead.

'I feel something growing inside, taking root in the core of my being, and it scares the hell out of me. Sometimes, I stop what I am doing and when the blank fog has lifted, minutes or even hours have vanished and I've wandered to a completely different location. I feel one coming on, now.'

'It's now five-thirty in the evening. I stopped recording the diary of my descent into monsterhood earlier because I forgot how to speak. I could feel words in the front of my brain but I could only make a rasping, choked moan. I couldn't get my body's sound system working properly.

'I was able to make contact with the survivors in South Austin by CB. They had horrible news. The survivors' compound in North Austin, off Research Boulevard in a gated office park, has been overrun. Some of them did make it out and are fleeing west, into the hills towards the Lago Vista Security Zone.

The St Theresa's compound informed me that they have a functioning satellite uplink. They are in contact with the provisional Texas Republic out west of the Pecos. It looks as if those ass-munching secessionists are making a break for it. They've said to hell with the other pockets of resistance within Texas as well as with the sharps of what was once America. Utah is now Deseret and the Idaho Republic is holding its own against the hordes from poor dead Seattle and Portland. California has fallen completely and nothing but wailing undead wait on the east bank of the Mississippi all the way to the Atlantic. Nebraska, Iowa, Minnesota and the Dakotas are calling themselves the United States, with its temporary capital in Sioux Falls. They've blown the bridges over the Mississippi as far south as Hannibal, but I-70 from Denver to St Louis is a single, great ravenous herd. I could almost feel sorry for Kansas; consumed by legions of undead from east, south and west; if it hadn't been such a bastion of neo-con reactionaries. Karma's a bitch. I'll bet this wasn't the resurrection of the dead they were awaiting. Sorry, still bitter about that whole second-class citizen thing and not being able to marry the partner of my choice.

'St Theresa's has a doctor, several nurses, a couple of paramedics and a functioning medical clinic. It's as rare as compassion from a zombie to find survivors with medical training. Medical staff, along with other first responders, went under in the first wave.

'Their doctor didn't believe my story, at first. After I described rather intimately the symptoms of Kobe Fever from a patient's viewpoint; the intense joint pain, burning fever and chilling sweats, light and sound sensitivity, as well as the reanimation process; I peaked his interest. He tried to convince me to come behind their barricades for observation, but I'm reluctant.

'It's not just the deteriorating brain and body function, I'm suspicious. I have no desire to be cut open while conscious and have some Frankendoc playing around with my insides. They could very well decide to dissect me once I'm in their control just to see why I alone among reanimates have retained a shred of my humanity. I can see their rationale, it could be considered a service to humanity to let them vivisect me, but I'm selfish…and scared. If my childhood pastor was right, I'm in for an eternity of punishment, so I'll delay the inevitable for as long as I am able.'

'July twenty-fourth…

'A big ol' Caddie SUV crept down my street just about an hour ago. It drove by slowly, like it was looking for something. Of course, every zee came staggering into the street from broken open houses, alleys and backyards. A pack of draggers followed in their wake, leaving a trail of pus and gore coating Cameron Road like a slime trail of an exotic breed of slug.

'The Caddie kept to a fast enough pace to stay ahead of the zees, yet slow enough to scope out the neighbourhood. I'm hoping they were scavengers, I fear they might be looking for me. Is it paranoia or a deep-rooted sense of self-preservation?

'I prefer to remain inside during the heat of the day. A combo of my own rotting stink mixed with several tens of thousands more is a heady aroma that lingers on the palate. I saw that description on a restaurant menu once. Why can I still smell? My eyesight has faded and is as grainy as an old photograph. I don't produce saliva. I gobbled down the last of my pot brownies, trying to take the edge off of my cravings for raw, bloody meat. They had no taste whatsoever and my tongue felt like it was wrapped in wet wool. But I can hear a mouse fart from two counties away. My vision is extremely sharp in the dark, but colours have faded. It's the scent thing; I can't wrap my head around it.

'My sinus cavities are as dry as West Texas in August. Hell, the left half of my nose fell off this morning. It's rather funny, really. I was sitting in a lawn chair in the backyard smoking a joint. I thought I'd be cute and do a French inhale trick; that's when smoke is puffed out the mouth and inhaled up the nose. I don't know why it's called that but it looks pretty cool if done right. After I finished coughing and sneezing, I looked down and there was a chunk of my nose in my lap. I laughed so hard that several zees skulked into my yard looking for a meal. They were quickly shown the error of their assumption by the business end of my bat.

'For some unknown reason, after destroying the brain, decomposition is rapid. Grackles and crows won't go near a zee while it's mobile; but the moment it's put down, they'll pick it clean. I've watched rats, raccoons, feral dogs, even a coyote make lunch of a downed zee only to scatter when an active one is nearby.'

'July Twenty-seventh…

'I'm missing a couple of days. There's a hole in my memory. When I came back to myself, I was tearing into a cat like it was a cheeseburger fresh off the grill. I caught, killed and was eating it without ever realizing what I was doing. I felt the blackness approaching a couple of days ago, so I locked myself in my backyard as a precaution. It's become a challenge to work a doorknob or a cigarette lighter.' A deep inhalation is recorded followed by a blast of expelled air.

'I won't take the chance that I'll attack, infect or even kill somebody during those times that I'm not in myself. A stray cat is one thing, I've never liked those damn furry little Republicans. If this is how God has decided to end mankind, I'm gonna kick Him in the balls when I see Him.'

Sounds of a shell being chambered in a pump action shotgun are recorded. A single, deafening blast is captured on tape. The cassette recorder spins, recording the sounds of silence before it shuts itself off automatically.

We Don't Go to the River

Jeremy Watssman

Kye gripped the mallet tight in his grimy fist and smashed the runt puppy's skull. It went limp and he loosened his grasp around its belly. Holding it by its worm-tail he flicked the corpse into the steaming pot. The runt floated awhile before the froth dragged it down.

'Five minutes,' Kye yelled through to Boson. The pot blasted steam and the extractor was broken. Clogged up with grease, it was. Boson never cleaned a thing.

'Five minutes,' Boson said to Farmer Hackett. Proud-like as he said it; as if he was cooking the runt himself. Baldy Boson. 'How'd the rest turn out?'

'Meaty,' Hackett said to Boson, tapping his rusty helmet with pride. 'Two bitches in this pack; the rest'll be prime come summer.'

Boson talked easy with Hackett. As long as Boson had a good gab he'd leave off on poor Kye.

'Pull the thing out then, Boson, and let's have at him,' Hackett said. 'I'm past hungry. And go and give a leg to your chef, the poor mite gets nothing from you.'

Kye looked at Boson, and Boson nodded gravely. Kye felt a swell of admiration for the brain-damaged old rough. Nobody knew why a dog farmer needed a metal army helmet or where he'd got it, but some said he had a hole in his head and, if he loosened the straps even a little, his brains would spill out.

Kye fished in the boiling pot with a pair of rusted tongs and heaved the sodden mess from the froth. The back leg came off easy, a little sucking sound it made as it came out of the joint. He tossed the body on a paper plate and gave it over to his boss and Hackett. For his own, he held the leg with the tongs over the blue flame till it turned black. He leaned outside the rickety caravan and wafted it in the night air to cool it down, then snatched a bite. Cold on the outside, searing hot on the inside, and burnt all through. When Kye turned back to Boson, the farmer had gone. Boson had a look on him that Kye didn't like.

'KyeDaLoon, it's time to talk.'

Boson had been working up to this all day. His baldy head was slick with excitement.

'No, boss, not me,' Kye said, jaw slack. Flecks of chewed puppy fat fell out. 'I've been fine by you, I always have.'

'You know it's been long coming. That leg's the last thing you get out of me.'

'What did I do?' Kye said.

'It isn't that. I just don't have the bottles for you anymore. Business is gone.'

Kye argued but it was useless. Boson wanted rid of him, always had. Only Kye's dad had got him the job and he was long gone. It was no matter. Kye would find another way to get drink.

'To hell with you then, and damn your busted fryer too,' Kye said, clambering out of the kitchen unit and horse-kicking the cooker on his way out. He dropped from the high caravan door into the mud and it spattered up his leg. He kicked some at Boson but the scaly rag closed the door fast, and tossed Kye's raincoat – it used to be his dad's – out the service hatch. Kye took it up and headed home. He hadn't even got today's wage. Gretchen would be a stinker about it.

The night was cold and greasy. Air never came from the mountain; it only swirled around the bottom. Today was a good day; the wind was coming from the garbage heap to the west. On a bad day it might come from the graveyard in the east, sickly-sweet and rotten. On the worst days it came from the banks of the river.

'My baby!' a woman was crying. She was swaddled with brown rags. Half her face was blackened. She had three teeth left. 'My baby! Please my baby!' She looked up when Kye got close.

'What's wrong with your baby?' he asked.

She went angry, and puffed up.

'Isn't nothing wrong with my baby! He's good and strong!' she said. 'Plenty of meat on him! Please, my baby! A gallon for him and no less!'

She held the thing out to Kye but he shook it off. A gallon was a scourge of a price to pay for two little bites. Besides, it was a baby. Good luck to her, Kye thought. By the time she finds a fool twisted enough to pay a gallon of water for the thing it'll probably be dead.

'KyeDaloon!' screamed a man close to Kye's ear. It was the peddler Joe. Kye shrugged him off and kept on his way home. 'KyeDaloon!' Joe cried again. 'Look out! The Scaly Man's after you, I seen him yesterday.'

'Aye and he can dredge the river for all I care,' Kye said. 'He'll find me if he wants me.' He shuffled faster and drew his coat tight.

He got within spitting distance of home before he came over with a bad case of the heevies. Under the red neon, he stood with a hand on the stone wall and retched until his face went numb; he scritched his ear with his bad hand. It wasn't fear of the Scaly that made him puke. It was that he'd only had one bottle out of Boson the past three days. Any more of the river water and it'd be rats who scritched his ear before long. Gretchen would be a rag about it.

'Browther, browther!' Gretchen said when Kye had stumbled up the staircase and ducked through their doorframe. God, she was in pink today. 'Browtherdeerist, I'm happy you're home.' She threw a hug and squeezed him like a pustule.

'Get off, you wretched cow.' He went over to the cooker and pulled the blanket off it, knocked two stones to light it. From a coat pocket he reclaimed two headless rats he'd taken off Boson. He threw them both in a pan on the gas flame. 'We've been boned, Gretchen. We're boned and we're going to be cooked. We're as dead as these two.'

'Noh Kye, noh,' she pleaded, mindlessly. She practically choked on her gums when she spoke.

'Yes, Gretch. I'll have to eat you.' He went to the table and sat with his head in his hands.

'Oh Browther!' She cackled and snorked for breath. 'No kitty! No, down kitty, silly kitty.'

Kye looked up and saw the mongrel cat was on the table, staring at him. He gagged on the clumps of fur that billowed off its mangy coat.

'Get that pestilent, blighted sack of rabies off the god-forsaken table!' He swung his arm and swept the cat right onto the floor. It mewled angrily and twined round Gretchen's stubby legs.

'But he's beeyutiful!' she said. She smiled and one eye went side-ways. If Kye had had his way, they'd have eaten the pest years ago. But Gretchen was in love with it.

He skewered the rats on the flame and waved them cool. Brother and sister ate, and drank. It was river water tonight. He strained it to get the mucus out but it was still a pallid yellow. It was tangy, fiery, and with a smell of old eggs. Then Kye told her the news. She didn't get it at first.

'I have no job, Gretchen. I didn't even get any bottles for today. It's going to be river water from here on.'

'But Kye...' Gretchen went quiet. She was rubbing a knobbly fist up and down over the outlandish pink chemise she was wearing. She must have found it outside. She never stayed in like he told her to, the rag. 'Mayn be, you can get a nowther job?'

'I doubt it Gretch. That scaly man is after me still. Soon as I get regular around any place he'll find me quick. Besides, who's going to give out bottles nowadays? They've hardly enough to drink for themselves.'

The gas flame was still on. The tap had been broken for weeks, so Kye just threw the charred blanket over to snuff it.

'But Kye...' Gretchen said again. The cat mewled. 'Where does Boson get his bottles?'

'I don't know Gretch, why would you ask me that?'

'But Kye! Mayn be you can find some. Fill our own bottles. With nice water.'

'Who knows where it comes from. If it were nearby people wouldn't drink out of the river. I knew you'd be a rag about this.'

'But, Kye.'

'Gretchen, please.'

'Browther... all the rivar can't be bad. The rivar don't come out the ground bad.'

'Gretch, I-'

But there was some logic to that. He couldn't deny it.

'Gretchen, for all we know, the river is born bad. It seeps out of the mountain as sick and rotten as it is when it comes down here. I'll saw my own arm off before I try climbing up there to find out.'

She slumped further in the chair.

'We're kewked then. We're bowned and kewked.' She gnawed at her hand and it was on Kye to pull it out her mouth. She wailed and wouldn't stop till he gave her something. So he gave her something.

'I'll have a look,' he said. 'I'll take a bottle and find the nicest bit to take from.'

'Find the nicyest bit!'

'Yes the nicest bit.'

'Do you prowmiss?'

'Yes, I promise.'

There was no point hanging around. If he stayed at home they'd have a fight about why he hadn't left yet. Gretchen knew no sense of time. It was just one of a great many things that Gretchen didn't know. Besides, Kye's bed had been weeping of late, little black dots bursting out the seams and running all over his hands and legs. He was tired, but not tired enough to go to that bed yet. The river went by the junkyard; maybe he could get a new mattress there. Then go home. Tell Gretchen he'd looked hard and there was no hope. Once he'd done in her hopes, she wouldn't fuss anymore.

Kye held his breath as he neared the river but it was no use; he couldn't do it the whole way. It smelled of rotten eggs, of a urine soaked pillow, of uncooked corpses. More than anything it smelled of human excrement. Two naked men were thigh deep in the water, splashing each other and laughing hysterically.

All around the shoreline, wading in the muck, were tattered folk, skinny and wan, dipping bottles and buckets in the bog-water. Kye's own boots were still sodden and sticky from his last dip in the river. He knew well the thirst that drove you to the water's edge. He went on to the junkyard; his bad hand gave him trouble as he scaled the chain link fence, getting wrapped in wire and stuck on sharp bits.

He was clattering around in the mountains of waste when he saw a white beacon by the river-side, at the foot of the black, broad shouldered mountain. When he crept closer he saw it wasn't a light, but the face of someone dressed all in black. That someone cast a glance in his direction, and he saw it was a delicate maiden; a girl of youth and beauty. She started, and disappeared into the darkness, her cape floating behind her. Kye had never in his life seen a thing so untouched, so soft and smooth-faced. He scrambled over the chain fence and stalked her up the hill, into the woods.

He lost her immediately in the slick branches of the forest undergrowth. He slipped on mossy rocks, clutched at dead and broken branches for support, and planted his foot in hidden mires. The girl had slipped through this dark web unscathed. She was a being so flawless Kye teetered between animal lust and superstitious awe.

The mountain was a merciless climb, but Kye kept close to the river where footing was easier. After climbing for hours with no sight of the girl, he glanced back at the town, a smudge of candle-lights and red neon. The sky, the bits not smothered by oily clouds, was a dull and foggy orange. It seemed there were fires burning somewhere far above.

He was flat tired by the time the mountain's secret revealed itself. Hidden away behind a bend of the river was a colossal concrete wall, a hydro dam, its face bearded with moss. At the base of this structure, from which the river appeared, there was a mound so large it spanned the entire width of the great wall. Kye glimpsed a white flash at the top of an iron staircase, which led to the top of the dam, and he scampered onward.

The mound was a pile of bilious corpses. Bloated, half decayed, broken in various ways and all of them missing a limb in some place. Their skin hung saggy, their faces sunk and skull-like. There were hundreds, maybe over a thousand. Most of them were under the water, many of them floated on the top. Kye poked at one with a stick and it burst, spilling yellow fluid into the river. The heevies came over him again, and it was minutes before he could bear to start climbing.

He was five flights up the rusty metal staircase when he stopped his clanging and listened. The dam was silent. There were rustlings from the trees and the river bubbled a little below, but otherwise the place was still. And Kye came over all queer, like he'd got lost in a dream and now was awoken. He must have walked for hours to get here. As for this structure, his dad had told stories, his dad the wanderer, man of the world, his dad had known what this thing used to do. But the enormity, it was just inconceivable to Kye, how it dwarfed him. And here, if it weren't for the promise of a beautiful girl, Kye would have turned and gone home, admitted defeat. But he was almost there anyway, and his mouth was sticky with thirst. So he went on to the top, clattering step after step.

A path of concrete spanned the length of the dam. He had barely a chance to gaze along it before he was flat on the ground with exhaustion. His ears rushed, his heart squeezed with all its might. He was hungry, and he was thirsty. He dragged himself across the road and rested on the railing.

On the other side, mostly shrouded in darkness, was a field of glass – no, not glass – it was water. The distant rising sun illuminated a field of water, still as the dead, as wide as the dam and stretching as far back as he could see. He fell to his knees once more and scooped a sip with his good hand and – ragged saints – the water was clear. It danced around his mouth, cleaning without burning, washing without stinking. Nothing Boson had ever given tasted so good. He crawled between the railings and plunged his head into the water.

As soon as he pulled it out and heard the laughter behind him, Kye knew he was done. A gang, four or five, of black robed monstrosities

– wrangled toothless mouths, missing eyes, bleeding noses. They held spikes, axes and saws. He leapt to his feet and scurried with all his might along the length of dam. As he got near the far end he saw another gaggle of murderers waiting in ambush. This group was led by the very same beautiful fairy he had seen earlier. He ran with all his heart towards her, smiling wistfully as only the truly hopeless can.

When he reached her, he saw her face was cracked and her expression as still as the water. She kicked him between his legs and poor Kye crumpled. He pleaded for his life. The girl bent over him and, with a hideous laugh, pulled her face off. It was a mask. Underneath was a black gaping mouth beneath two bloody eyes. The hag cackled and laughed and kicked at him, and the brutes dragged him by his arms and feet inside the rusty buildings of the dam.

They held him down by a fire and made ready with saws to hack at his limbs.

'Please!' he cried out. 'Please I don't mean harm! I don't want your water!'

'Water's fine, meatsack,' said one of the thugs. 'But we all got to eat.'

'He better not be another sicky,' someone said.

'We've got to eat, you know,' said a fiend with a saw, working on Kye's right arm. They had it off and on the fire in seconds. 'He's a good one!' the creature said, and they all set about him.

'Please,' he said again, pleading to the wide mouthed witch who had led him there.

'Please, please, please,' she said and laughed at him. 'Go on meat-sack, your last request!'

'P-please...' he stuttered. His blood was starting to pool in his throat and matting in his hair. They'd already done away with one of his legs and he knew he'd be gone soon. You're a fool, KyeDaloon, he thought. You don't even deserve mercy. You're a wretched monster. 'Please,' he gurgled.

'What is it?'

'Put the... let me see, the mask again,' he whispered.

The hag giggled and they all laughed merrily, but she obliged him just the same. As he faded away, Kye smiled. Looking down on him was the peaceful serenity of a natural pale-faced beauty. She seemed to understand and forgive him for all he had done and been forced to do, even as she held aloft the giant steel-tipped hammer, and brought it down on his head.

You Call this an Apocalypse?

by Errick A. Nunnally

Quan swung his fire axe into the zombie's head, cutting messily through its skull and splattering its brains right at Treyvon's feet.

The boy just about fainted, knowing where the gelatinous mass had been. The dead body, in mid-step, crumpled like the marionette it was. Quan whooped with joy and Treyvon's heart sunk further, if that were at all possible.

Treyvon had lifelong history with Joquan. They'd grown up in the same neighborhood, taught by the same teachers, playing in the same parks. At one time, they'd even lived together in a foster home. Not exactly friends, they'd known each other their entire lives, separated by personal interests, inextricably joined by culture and geography. They were both seventeen, but Treyvon was a nerd—he hated the portmanteau 'blerd' almost as much as he hated the ridiculous convention that white comic creators tended to use when naming black characters. Black Lightning, Black Racer, Black Spider, Black Eagle, Black Panther—well, the Panther was pretty cool, and his name made sense. Since he was the leader of the Black Panther Cult and King of the fictional African country of—

'Tron, wake the fuck up! We 'bout to get in some serious shit right here! Why you holding that shovel like that? Quit cradlin' the damn thing like it's a baby. Get ready to swing that bitch!'

Treyvon secretly loved that Quan called him 'Tron.' Most people shortened his name to 'Trey,' but Quan always looked for the most creative angle to truncate someone's name. Thanks to his friend's wit, Treyvon was closer than ever to imagining himself on par with

Tron, the savior of the ENCOM Mainframe. He looked down at the entrenching tool they'd found alongside the axe at the firehouse and shifted his grip so that he was holding it more like the baseball players he'd seen incidentally on television. They continued to move through the building.

Quan was one-hundred and eighty degrees from being a nerd like Treyvon and at least fifty-thousand kellicams in the opposite direction, diving into the hot sun at the center of the solar system of coolness. Kellicams, by the way, are a Klingon unit of measurement, similar to a kilometer, but about twice as lo—

'Tron! Damn, son, daydream when we the fuck somewheres safe. You in shock or some shit?'

The duo headed for the back of Engine 52's station. The house seemed to be empty, all the firefighters out dealing with one emergency after another. There were no police stations nearby to even consider raiding; if solace were to be found, it was going to be here. Though there were more axes available, they were too heavy for Treyvon to handle accurately, so Quan had shoved the lightweight military shovel into his hands. The zed Quan had just dropped must've been part of the skeleton crew left behind to monitor the radio and... The radio!

'Hey, Quan, if we can find the radio here, we might be able to—'

'Watch ya back, son!'

Treyvon whirled. Where there was a freshly dead walker, there seemed to be another less fresh. How else would the fireman have been infected inside the firehouse? Emergency rescue personnel were ironically the most vulnerable. Their instincts were to help, not split a skull open. To run towards trouble and damn self-preservation all but guaranteed an agonizing demise. The former human being Quan had put down probably died trying to help this thing, not believing the dead walked.

The horror facing him must've been the victim of a murderous impact and freshly buried. The female corpse wore what was once a clean and professional skirt suit—the better to be presentable when being interred—a tradition that baffled Treyvon. The thing was now covered in grime and blood. She was dragging one leg at an inhuman angle and her arm on the same side dangled boneless, like a voided tentacle, her entire person a vile reminder that the dead walked. Treyvon raised his tool. The horror creeping slowly towards him echoed the trembles rising from his stomach. He brought the edge of the spade down square on her head or so he intended.

The sharp edge cut across her skull at an angle, shearing off a portion of her scalp and skull. With an ear dangling, she stumbled forward as Treyvon lost his balance, yelping uncontrollably and tumbling, his legs tangling with hers.

'Joquan!'

'Oh, for real? Finish this half-crippled bitch, Tron, an' let's go.' Treyvon could hear the exasperation in Quan's voice, impatient at having to pull his companion out of fire after fire. If this were going to work, Treyvon knew he needed to get his game together and soon.

The dead woman squirmed, using her one good hand to grab a fist full of Treyvon's pants, trying to pull herself into position to bite. He panicked, freed one leg and kicked her off. Then with a speed and accuracy he'd never known, Treyvon swung the tool in a parabolic arc, cutting through the dead woman's neck, striking sparks from the concrete floor. The body went still and the boy was barely aware of what had happened. He'd lashed out and gotten lucky.

'Oooooh, shit! Tha's what I'm talkin' 'bout! Knew you had it in you, nigga.' Quan laughed and kicked the head across the floor.

Treyvon shuffled to his feet and shoved his glasses back up on his nose so he could see Quan clearly when he looked into his eyes. Relieved to focus on something other than shambling dead people, he spoke with confidence. 'Don't call me 'nigger,' that's self-hating.'

Quan screwed his face up. 'Da fuck? You think I hate myself? Never Ignorant Getting Goals Accomplished, boy—N.I.G.G.A.' He thumped his chest with each letter, then poked Treyvon, forcing the less imposing boy to take a step back. 'Yo' ass still alive 'cause o' me; you keep zonin' out, I ain't gonna be able to keep you alive much longer.'

Being shuffled from home to home as they got older had opposing effects on the two boys. Over the years, Treyvon sank further and further into books of all kinds—especially comics and science fiction, but he'd never developed the kind of brazen confidence that Quan seemed to generate tirelessly like the fission of heavy isotopes. The more Treyvon learned, the more conflict-averse he became, as if a thick blanket of knowledge smothered any aggression he may have developed over time. He remembered reading somewhere that boys like him were time bombs waiting to explode one day. Yet, every humiliating episode he could think of leading up to this moment merely left him feeling more confused than angry, the edge of any fury dulled forever by a relentless academic logic.

He recalled one such incident, in eighth grade, at the all-white suburban school to which he was being bussed at the time; an urban program to give inner city kids access to suburban schools' tax-based gift of larger budgets. An essay he'd written had been selected for reading at a school event. The teacher had asked him if he had a tie, slacks, and shoes for the event? Would he be able to participate? He owned no such clothing and shook his head. Even though his essay had been chosen along with four others, his appearance would be the price of entry. Despondent, he'd gone home, told his current foster mother, and she managed to dig up a pair of shoes, slacks, and a tie for him. The tie was a hideous, multicolored affair, the slacks bell-bottomed and lime green, and the shoes were at least one size too small. Still, he had achieved both the academic costs and the minimum of proprietary fashion.

During the car ride to the event, Treyvon held a casserole in his lap. When they arrived, he discovered that liquid had leaked past the battered, foil-covered container and left a brown stain down one side of his calf where it finally pooled in one of his tight shoes. Onstage, his leg cold, wet, and stained with gravy, Treyvon sat with four other boys before he discovered that his essay had not been given to the presenter. They'd assumed he would not be participating, so the handwritten essay had been left behind...somewhere.

Why couldn't this have been rectified on the spot? Surely the essay could be retrieved. More questions followed, tumbling one after the other. Because he'd not been assertive enough, because there was no time, because he didn't have real parents, because he was the only black boy on stage with four other white boys? They were the kinds of questions that kept him up at night, his mind eventually wandering into a fantasy realm to evade the stress. His sense of logic could only determine that these questions would never be answered satisfactorily.

Like trying to figure out why the dead walked.

Treyvon muttered the only thing that seemed worthy of noting at the time. 'It's the apocalypse, I—'

Quan spread his arms. 'You call this an apocalypse? Please, this a Tuesday night in the 'hood, son, this ain't shit!'

Bravado, braggadocio, boldness, braggart, bombast, and other alliterative nouns that Quan likely didn't know bounced around Treyvon's mind. Tuesday. Then the boy smiled and started to giggle. It wasn't long before Quan grinned and chuckled, lowering his arms, then raising them again with a ridiculous smirk on his face. They guffawed uncontrollably until Treyvon, gasping for air, broke in.

'A Tuesday, huh? Tuesday. Okay, okay, well, I don't want to see the weekend, okay? We really want to get out of here alive, right?'

'Damn right. Tha's why we come here, man, all them firefolks out tryin' to save a neighborhood that stopped carin' 'bout itself before we was born. We got to gear up and get out.'

Boston's inner city proved a unique challenge for those who wanted to survive the zombie apocalypse: fire and police stations were few; no gun shops to loot, precious few hardware or grocery stores, and no easy way to organize people. The area was constantly on the edge of teetering over into a depressing mess without flesh-eating corpses wandering around. As far back as Treyvon could remember, nothing ever changed. He and Quan continually swapped homes as one foster parent's tour of duty ended and another's began, but the neighborhood remained a constant, regardless of what the rest of the world was doing.

'We need to use the radio to call for help.'

'Help? Damn, Tron, you killin' me. Ain't no help here, never have been. What? You expect the National Guard to come runnin' cause two niggas call from th' hood?'

Treyvon ground his teeth, ignoring the word he considered an epithet no matter how Quan pronounced or spelled it. 'Then where are we going?'

'Like I said: we gear up and get on. To the cemetery, down by Forest Hills.'

'The cemetery. Where all the dead people are.'

'Damn, Tron, think about it, you smarter than that.'

He thought. Most of the corpses would be deeply interred or too far rotted to be a problem. Plenty of open ground. There was a house on the grounds and a high wrought iron fence surrounded the whole thing. This fire station had food, emergency supplies, and more. All the firefighters and cops usually drove SUVs, there were probably a few in the back. Well, damn, Quan was right.

'Yeah, you get it now.' The more aggressive and tactically oriented boy wore a wide grin on his face. 'We could even take some radios for when shit cools down.'

Treyvon began to understand where he was going to fit in the apocalypse. As Quan searched the premises for keys to personal vehicles, Treyvon sat down at a computer to learn all he could about BFD communications and equipment, taking advantage of the Internet while it still functioned.

Keys in hand, the boys began loading a black SUV in the back lot of the station. They emptied the kitchen of whatever food they believed would travel well and filled the back with two more uncovered axes, a few pikes, radios, chargers, a ladder, and some power tools. They could see smoke in the air, drifting like octopus ink underwater. The occasional screams of people and the muted pops of handguns came to their ears. It was Treyvon's idea to top off the gas tank and add two additional canisters of fuel.

Treyvon looked for somewhere outside the vehicle to hook the jerry cans, but had to load them in the back. 'Keep the back windows rolled down, we don't want to suffocate on gas fumes or, well, explode over a spark or something.'

Quan grinned and did what Treyvon asked as the boys clambered into the front seats. The engine turned over easily. Quan backed the truck out of its spot and wheeled around the side of the building. On the opposite corner, they saw an older man wearing an apron and using a push broom to hold one of the walking dead back. He was yelling profanities in a thick Caribbean accent, keeping the zed from entering his store.

Quan slammed the truck into park and said, 'I want some snack cakes.'

'Are you serious? Now?'

Quan looked at the acquaintance he'd known his entire life. Despite their social distance, Treyvon was the closest thing he had to a brother. The young man was the only constant in his life, the only person whose values he respected, and could depend on. 'Maybe you should pick 'em up. Get something you like too, 'cause I don't think we gonna be able to hit the corner store later.'

Treyvon looked out the window at the old man struggling to keep the zombie at bay.

'Go on, man, I'm a wait for you right here. Get me some menthols too.'

Their eyes locked for a moment, then Treyvon hopped out of the vehicle and trotted around to the back, sliding a pike out of the hatch.

Quan stepped out of the cab, lit a cigarette, and watched as Treyvon scooted around the old man struggling with the zombie and dipped into the store. Moments later, he emerged with a plastic sack, heavy with treats. The old man glanced at the young intruder with a worried and disgusted look on his face. Treyvon stopped, took aim, and speared the dead monster through its head, pushing it to the ground with the pike. Then he handed the steel tool to the old man and trotted back to the truck.

'I like the pike.'

'Thought you might.'

'Dude, I think everyone in that old man's family was inside that place. They just stared at me the whole time in there, stuffed in the corner.' Dots of perspiration speckled Treyvon's hairline and dark patches had formed under his shirt's arms.

Quan smirked and hopped back into the driver's seat, slammed the door and pulled the SUV onto Donald Street, cutting through to Harvard and making a straight run for the cemetery.

'Niggas got to learn to take care o' they damn selves.'

In Debt

by Javier Moyano Pérez

'Male, eighty two years old, over seven hundred thousand dollars of unpaid debt. Looks like a 'Robert', commented the officer as soon as Glen Leeman stepped out of the car. In an instant the flash of a drone's camera caught everyone's eye and disappeared in the sky with a soft buzzing.

They made their way into the house and went directly to the bedroom. The place was a complete mess, half emptied drawers rested on the carpet and their content scattered all over the room, the wallpaper half torn off, the carpet covered in patches and stains. He had not left anything of value behind. Either that or he had had nothing of value to take. The whole scene seemed strange; it was not the typical case Glen used to work. His suspects were always methodical, calculative. This was an emotional act, something impulsive. Maybe it had something to do with her. The suspect's wife remained sitting on the bed, her face resting between her hands, silently weeping. It all seemed to have caught her by surprise, or at least that is what she wanted to make them believe. Detective Leeman's eyes hovered over the decrepit room once more and with that he turned around, ready to leave.

'Wait a minute! Where are you going?' whispered the policeman grabbing him by the wrist.

'This is a job for a rookie. Leave me out of it. It would take a couple of hours to find him and two weeks buried in paperwork and court sessions', said Glen, thinking of his monthly quota. 'I will definitely be more helpful somewhere else. What they need here is a broom not a hound'. He freed himself from the officer's grip and headed back toward the door.

'You'll get reported for this, Leeman; orders are orders,' said the officer.

'Please, you have to find him! If my husband gets away with this, we'll hit rock bottom,' cried the woman standing on her feet and revealing the rags in which she was dressed.

Glen looked around and sighed. If this was not rock bottom, then he did not know what was. The truth was, he did not want to know.

'Any prints, blood?' he rushed the officer, looking at him with reluctance.

'We haven't found anything; he took all his belongings with him.'

Another scab cleaning case, Glen thought. 'Ok, get her out of here. But hold on to her driving licence; we don't want her going anywhere.'

'Wait! Am I a suspect?' said the woman as she was being pulled out of the room.

'I'm afraid so, madam; it's merely precautionary.'

'But this is ridiculous! That man has ruined my life, not to mention my son's.'

'Get her out.'

One last push, a slam and Glen was left alone. He put on a pair of latex gloves and slowly made his way through the rabble of abandoned memories that remained on the floor. He approached the old mirror that rested on the table and instantly spotted some locks of hair, three blond curls, bright and strong, stuck on the frame of the mirror. They must be hers. He took a pack of cigarettes out his inner jacket's pocket, and with a couple of taps pulled one out and lit it. He tiptoed to the window at the back of the room and opened it using his handkerchief. He was a third of the way through his cigarette, carefully blowing the smoke out the window, when someone knocked at the door, softly at first, but banging assertively after no response came. He was not expecting anybody.

'Get out, idiot! Can't you see I'm working?' he shouted at the person on the other side of the door.

Nevertheless, the door opened, revealing a rounded woman with black frame glasses, rosy cheeks and fair hair. She seemed young, but there was no way to be sure.

'Are you deaf, madam? You are not supposed to come in here.'

'My name is Elsa Becker. I am the journalist from De Telegraaf,' she said with a soft European accent. 'I believe Commander West informed that I was coming,' she added calmly, looking around with professional interest. 'You must be Detective Leeman.'

He had heard about her; she caused quite a stir at the station. He just did not know that the burden was going to fall to him. Glen muttered something inaudible and threw the cigarette out the window.

'Is it not prohibited to smoke at a crime scene? I thought you people were very thorough.'

Glen sighed. 'Have you ever heard of the term 'presumption of innocence', lady?'

'The name is Elsa.'

'Have you ever heard of the term 'presumption of innocence', Elsa?'

'Yes.'

'Well, they have not.'

'Who do you mean by 'they'?'

'The victims.'

'I thought you were trying to find the victim.'

'No, I'm trying to find the offender.'

'Do you always get so defensive with the press?'

'Look, I don't have time for this.'

'I believe you do. You're only working one case and I have been told that it's fairly routine.'

That was the reason West had assigned him that case. It was a set up. He had never liked him, everyone knew, and now he was throwing him to the wolves. Glen well knew that one mistake could cost him his job. However, he could not refuse; the order had come from top and the stakes were too high. The shit always rolls downhill.

'What do you want?' asked Glen after a short while.

'Not much, just want to know a bit about what you do. I am writing an article on the Welberg Act.'

'An interview?'

'A chat. Why don't we get a drink?'

Glen muttered something to himself, not loud enough for Elsa to hear. 'I don't think so. However, you can accompany me while I work,' he said, pulling down his hat and walking to the door.

On the way to Leeman's car they passed through Courtham Street. The holograms from the shops whispered exciting and intimate messages to the people as they passed by, showing them images of their dream car, that holiday they never had the chance to take, an impossibly juicy steak.

They walked at a fast pace without exchanging any words.

Flash. Hey Elsa! Have you tried the new Diet Red Cola? It has half the calories of regular Red Cola, it will help you lose those pounds you have been struggling with. Flash. First time in Chicago, Elsa? I know where you can get tickets for all the museums and theatres, come, follow me! Flash. Your brother's birthday is coming soon, Elsa. Have you got him a gift already? Try our new TurboSpeedBoltz!

'Hey, that is personal!' said Elsa as she looked at the hologram of a famous actor slowly taking his shirt off. 'How they know so much about us?'

'They buy the information from major internet servers,' muttered Glen with his eyes stuck to the floor and his left hand hanging from the edge of his hat, 'every email, website that you have visited or mouse click is registered there.'

'How do you know that?'

'I've worked a couple of cases where we had access to their databases.'

'Is that allowed?'

'Of course, debt victims normally have some shares in internet servers, so they are very cooperative,' replied Glen, pinning his chin to his chest.

'Are you avoiding the adverts, or are you afraid that somebody may recognise you?'

'The flashes give me migraines.'

'Still, I assume that you guys must not be very popular with the average Joes, right?'

'I'm only doing my job, like any other enforcer of the law.'

'So, may I ask what are you working on now? Your partner in the house mentioned something about a robber.'

'A Robert.'

'What?'

'Robert Sydner. We call all cases with possible fatal implications after him. I assume since you are researching the Welberg Act, you must have across that name before.'

'So you guys think this man is dead?'

'It is a possibility. The offender was in debt for several hundred thousand dollars and had been in a State Employment Programme for over twenty years, as well as receiving treatment.'

'Are you referring to de Gray's treatment?'

Glen nodded, briefly took off his hat and brushed his hair back with his hand.

Finally, they reached Glen's car, an old Toyota Corolla covered in dents. The detective extended his hand to open the driver's door, but in that instant a woman appeared out of nowhere and lunged at him.

The detective managed to grab her by the wrists before she could reach his throat. She had been waiting for him.

Although at first frozen in shock, Elsa jumped over the woman and between the two of them, they managed to put her on the ground. Some pedestrians looked at them with curiosity, but Glen quickly flashed his badge and they disappeared. Unable to move, the woman soon stopped struggling and broke down into noisy tears. Meanwhile, Glen was trying unsuccessfully to recover his breath. He remembered the woman. It had taken him a while to recognise her, as she had changed dramatically since the last time he saw her.

'What are you going to do with her?' asked Elsa, who had quickly figured out the whole situation.

Glen looked at her; he quickly took stock of the situation. Damn you, West! He put him in a tight spot. And damn her! He thought, looking at the woman, who continued crying. How the hell has she found me and how does she even know who I am? Glen knew that depending on his actions, this whole situation could end up on the front-page or forgotten in a matter of days. He had to let her go.

'She is an offender from a previous case. I don't think she poses any threat though; she's done all the damage she can do.'

After making sure that she was calm, they left her sitting on the sidewalk. She did not even raise her head when she heard the car doors opening. Glen looked at her once more through the rearview mirror. She even looked pretty now, so full of life. He turned on the engine and left. The woman remained sitting on the ground.

'It's a tricky business,' said Elsa after a while. 'Do you think she followed you?'

'It was impossible for her to know who I was; they never see my face.'

'She seemed fairly young; had she been treated?'

'Most offenders are past their seventies. It's always the same story, as time passes their performance at their work-place worsens and they end up building up large debts in a SEP; the hard work breaks them down.'

'SEP...State Employment Programs, right?'

'Since the Welberg Act passed, all unemployed people with unpaid debts are provided a state job in order to help with repayments.'

'And I guess those jobs are not everyone's childhood dream.'

'Obviously, they cover the jobs that normal citizens refuse to do. They're quite similar to the forced work programs that they have in prisons, the only difference being that at the end of the day, they get to go back home.'

'So if they refuse to accept the job they end up in jail for fault of payment performing exactly the same task they were assigned in the first place.'

'Unless they find another job, yes, they remain at their post until they pay their debt.'

'So for the rest of their life.'

'Well… since De Gray's treatment is compulsory for debtors of large amounts, their life expectancy is extended to fulfill their obligations.'

'That could be a very long time.'

'That's why they break down…and the reason I have a job', he wanted to add, but stopped himself; he got the feeling that he was talking too much.

'Is that where we're going, to the suspect's SEP?'

'Yes, most of the time it's useless to talk to the family. Since debts are inherited by next of kin, they're seldom keen to lend a helping hand, more like the opposite. That's why offenders don't trust any information to their family; if he said anything, he said it to a colleague.'

'But, isn't it a bit dangerous for them to see us there?'

'I suppose you mean, if they see me there,' he said with a swift glance at her. 'Everything will be fine, nothing has ever happened. These people are desperate but they are harmless,' he added…and yet that woman attacked me. He lowered his hand to his beltline and felt the hard touch of his revolver.

Elsa felt as if everyone was staring at them.

They had driven to a big garbage dump situated in the outskirts of Chicago, where the suspect used to work. Elsa was feeling slightly nervous after the incident downtown. Glen had told her that everything was fine, but she could not help feeling watched by hostile eyes. They entered the main facility; a square-ish building of concrete walls, concrete floor and an unbearable smell and noise. As they walked along a raised metallic gangway toward the director's office, Elsa looked down and saw workers operating the automatic conveyor mills that compressed, cubed and incinerated tons of garbage per minute. Some of them turned their heads to look at them better. Elsa could see the artificial youth of de Gray's treatment in all of them. They knew who they were; they were expecting them.

The gangway was coming to an end; it led to a small hut with frosted glass windows, overlooking the inside of the facility. A man in a collared shirt was waiting at the door. In a sudden moment of nervousness, Elsa tried to ask Glen not to show his badge, but the moment had passed and the hound was already baring its teeth. The man in the white shirt introduced himself as the director of the facility and walked them into his office.

'I'm here because one of your workers is missing, having left behind a rather large debt; I assume you know who I'm talking about,' said Glen, leaning on the wall, with his arms crossed over his chest.

The director of the recycling facility took a seat in front of his desk and after a moment of silence, nodded.

'Good, I want to know whether he had any close relation with any of his colleagues, particularly any other SEPs,' Glen continued.

'All the workers in this facility, with exception of me, come from State Employment Programs,' he said quickly, but then looked down at his desk and added. 'But if you want to speak with someone, you should speak with Martin Ivanof. He is outside in the refuse classification area.'

'I won't need to speak with him for the moment, his name should suffice,' Glen said, pulling up his sleeve and revealing a wrist holo-gram console. 'Elsa, would you mind keeping the director company while I make some enquiries?' he said before leaving the room.

The director remained sitting at his desk, pretending to look at some papers, while Elsa looked carefully through the window at Glen, who was operating his hologram console, navigating through what seemed to be security videos of the facility. What happened to your migraines, Glen? Thought Elsa with a wry smile creeping across her face; a thought had started to form at the back of her mind, but she could not tell what it was, yet.

'Excuse me for asking, madam,' said the man in the white shirt, distracting her 'but you're not from round here, are you?'

'No, I am Dutch,' she replied with a wide smile.

'So, what are you doing here?'

'I'm a journalist writing an article on the Welberg Act and de Gray's medical treatment.'

'The Welberg Act's been around in America for decades. What's all the fuss about now?'

'The European Council is debating implementing a similar policy in Europe, to cover the losses from the financial crises.'

'Well… I guess you people won't have such a tough time as we are. You'll probably only end up working ten or twenty additional years. By that time you don't even mind the age treatment.'

She wanted to tell him what she'd found out, what most economists and politicians already knew. Since the Welberg Act, debt had not shrunk, but quite the opposite. But she could not bring herself to say it; it would have broken him. 'So would you do it?' she asked after a brief pause.

'Do what?'

'Receive the treatment, live to a hundred and fifty and beyond?'

'I already do.'

'No, I mean, choose to do it.'

'Why would I do that?'

'I mean if you didn't have any debt, if you didn't have to work that much. Wealthy men in Europe and America pay fortunes to receive the same treatment that the Welberg Act imposes on debtors.'

'If I had no debt, then I would have no reason to live that long.'

'What do you mean? You would have time to share with your family and friends.'

'A family without a house, friends without leisure.'

'Why do you think that you would not have a house or any leisure?'

'Because then I would have debt.'

Elsa said nothing. Eternal life, humanity's unreachable dream… the damnation of the people. A voice inside of her could not help laughing, a bitter laugh. She raised her gaze again to look at the man only to realise that she was not speaking to one, but to a beaten old mule that kept pulling a cart even if it could not keep going.

'I'm sorry to ask, but could you give this to the detective? Henry wanted him to have it,' said the director, handing Elsa what appeared to be a small memory card.

It took Elsa a couple of seconds to realise that Henry was the name of the man they were chasing. She looked at the card and then at him, then she nodded and took it. In that moment Detective Leeman came back to the room.

'Well, my work here is done. Thank you for your cooperation. Let's go, Elsa.'

'Have you found him?' Elsa could not quite tell if the tone of man's voice was of hope or of sorrow.

'I dare say that you will see him very soon.'

'And if he is dead?'

'Then, later.'

Once outside the building, both of them began to walk to Glen's car which was parked on the edge of the garbage dump.

'What is going on, Leeman? Where are we going?' asked Elsa, trying to keep up with the man's fast pace.

'I know where he is.'

'So, is that it? You just arrest them and bring them back?'

'Normally he would come back as an inmate, the penalty for attempt of credit fraud is from four to seven years, and then he would reincorporate as a paid worker. However, this one is dead.'

'How can you be so sure?'

'I found a recording of him talking to his colleague; he killed himself in the garbage incinerator.'

'Do you think he did not know that he was being recorded?'

'I think he knew, but he believed that we wouldn't find any remains of him.'

'So, what are you going to do now?'

'I am going to call a recovery squad and get a sample of his DNA; our work here and this interview, or whatever you want to call it, are done. Where do you want me to drop you?' added Glen, with his hand on the door handle.

'Could you take me to the rehabilitation labs? I want to keep following Henry's case.'

'Who is Henry?'

'The victim,' said Elsa, pointing at the garbage dump.

Glen laughed through his nose and got into the car. 'I'm afraid the complete recovery of a human body takes months; he won't be back for a long while.'

'I don't care, I'm sure there will others…plenty of others.'

Elsa felt Glen's stare and looked at him from the corner of her eye. The detective had an odd grimace on his face, as if he had just understood a joke that someone told him years ago.

'The man inside gave me this. He said Henry wanted you to hear it,' said Elsa, taking the memory card from her pocket, trying to break the tension.

'I have no interest in hearing what a criminal has to say.'

'Well, I want to hear it, if you don't mind.' With that, she inserted the card into the car radio and pressed the button.

Muffled noises came from the recording, after which a voice started to talk.

Dear hound, if you are listening to this, you've probably already found me and you are rushing to rip me from my sleep. I wanted you to know, that at no point did I hold any hope in the success of my escape from eternal enslavement. I know I am a coward, because I ran while others stood holding the weight of my actions. I don't expect to see my family again, but I would not have it any other way, because I found no comfort in having one. I took what wasn't mine, and which I must rightly pay back, but I did what any father, any man or any citizen would do: I lived. This earth is hell, and there is no escape from it, and you are its Cerberus, but you, hellhound, should be pitied as well, as you don't guard the gates from the other side but from within. We are all stuck in this world forever, we, slaves, and our masters.

Glen Leeman kept his eyes fixed on the steering wheel. With one sudden movement, he turned the engine on and drove away.

'Don't you have anything to say?' she asked him, regretting immediately the unprofessional tone of her voice.

'What do you want me to say?' The tone of Glen's voice on the other hand had not changed in the slightest since they had listened to the recording, nor had the expression of his face. 'Is there something you want to tell me?'

Elsa said nothing.

'You think I'm a monster. Perhaps I am, but I'm not the only one.'

'Actually I was thinking that you are not the bastard that everyone had led me to believe you were, just a bitter man that thinks that if he does what he must, he will obtain peace.' She felt Glen's confused stare once more. 'I know why you covered your face when we were walking in front of the holograms, you feel hunted by them. I did a bit of research on you, you know? No wife, kids, not even friends. When you are not working here, you have a second job at second-hand car lot. You rent a tiny apartment and you have had that car for fifteen years; you are a penitent trying to earn his way to the afterlife.'

'I don't know who told you all that stuff, but you don't know who I am, so you have no idea what you are talking about,' said Glen, slightly losing his temper. 'It's easy to live carelessly when you are still young and you think that you can achieve everything, and you buy all those things thinking that you'll worry about it later, but then you grow old and you need a rest, but you won't get one, and you know what? It's fair, because you took all those things.'

'What are you talking about?'

'Did you think that garbage disposal is the only SEP that the government has to offer? How about a job where everyone hates you and where you are constantly reminded that there is no escape from all this? How old you do you think I am, Elsa?'

The anodyne smell of the laboratory was making the young journalist start to feel dizzy. Or maybe it was not just that. The voice of the doctor was like a distant murmur buzzing in Elsa's ears. She could not stop hearing Leeman's last words, like an endless echo inside her head.

Why do you think you are here, huh? Why Commander West allowed you to dig around so much without interference? He wants you to know, to see the cruel reality. He wants the law abolished, like many others, but he is scared of losing everything he has. Welcome to the state of fear, if we do not obey, we will end up crushing garbage for the rest of our existence.

'…thus since cloning can be performed at the same stage in which the subject died, the new-born not only shares his same body, but also his memories and, we believe, his conscience as well. So you see, we do not really bring them back to life, but we simply return their consciousness to its body.' The warm voice of Doctor Sinclair finally drilled into Elsa's head and woke her from her thoughts.

The doctor walked her through one of the corridors and opened the door that led to a larger room with three big white chambers. The chambers reminded Elsa of the remote control medical units that had been installed in Amsterdam a few years ago, although these ones were smaller and simpler.

'They are incubators,' said Sinclair, as if he had read the woman's thoughts. 'These patients are in their final physical stage. After this, they will have to attend two weeks of rehabilitation and a couple of sessions of psychological assessment and they will be ready to go.' Doctor Sinclair approached one of the chambers, which had a small window on the side and gestured Elsa to look inside.

He was made of flesh, bone, blood, and cartilage: another result of de Gray's treatment. Another mule ready to pull.

'Organic tissue reconstruction is the biggest advance of modern medicine; before we invented it the situation was dire. We had all those people rejuvenated thanks to Doctor de Gray's discovery and ready to keep being useful members of our society. Yet their brains were not healed; they were tired of this world. Suicides occurred in huge numbers, every day.'

Elsa peered once more through the window; the man had started to move. It was a strange feeling. Elsa felt as if she were looking at a baby in his cot. Finally he opened his eyes for the first time and looked at her. The eyes of the new-born man darted confusedly around the walls of the white chamber which contained him. Elsa could observe an expression of defeat building in his eyes, as his existence slowly dawned on him.

All Clear in the Anderton House

by Claire Fuller

Finlay no longer recognised his hands as his own - chaffed red knuckles, cracked skin, and nails pared down to his fingertips. Not even enough left to get any dirt under. He tried to remember what it had been like using them to squeeze a pipette, to turn the fine focus knob on his microscope, sign documents, or caress Alicia's body. Already he couldn't easily recall. He turned his hands palm up, palm down, wondering at the change in them. He watched them moving on the ends of his arms and saw himself from above, sitting alone at a stranger's kitchen table, his claw hammer laid in front of him. He saw the room inside the empty house that he'd soon be leaving - black water swilling at its lowest points, as if the building itself was adrift. Panning back, he saw the roof, its grey slates, slick and dark from rain. He saw a river, streaming down the channel it had gouged out from the middle of the road. From even further away, he saw the drowning town and beyond it, what used to be the countryside, now a dirty soup of up-ended cars, unidentifiable pieces of plastic, suitcases, dead animals, garden furniture and all the stuff of people's lives crushed and mixed together. Until at last, from high above, Finlay could see a single island, nine or ten miles in diameter; the final bubble on an overflowing, untended bath.

Leaving a house was easy. Finlay never grew attached to any of them. But he'd worry, about whether he could find a new one that was suitable – dry, sound, and of course, empty. Each time he moved uphill, away from the muddy tide that followed him, his choices of possible places to live became more limited. He knew that one day, perhaps even soon, there would be no houses left and his only option would be to set up camp outside. But for now, it was simple to pack all he needed into a large rucksack: as much food as he could carry from other people's cupboards, a sleeping bag - he still couldn't get used to the touch of someone else's sheets - a book or two, water sterilising tablets, any medicine he found, his raincoat, his torch, his guitar and most importantly of all, his claw hammer.

He'd found it after he'd been on his own for maybe two months. It had lain on the front doorstep of a house which was filling with water. He'd picked it up and tested its weight. It was a single piece of forged steel, its handle covered with a black polymer grip and ending in a blunt head on one side and a pair of curved and shining sabre-teeth on the other. When Finlay held the hammer he'd felt safe and from then on it became part of his routine when entering a new house. His scientific mind was soothed by having a system, a method. It made things feel better, as if he was more in control.

The Anderton House ticked all his boxes: it was near, but not too near, one of the huge gullies which years ago, the government had cut into the hillsides to divert the run-off; there didn't seem to be a cellar to collect rain or rats and the house had been well maintained. He had watched it for three nights, standing in the bushes at the top of the drive in his raincoat, and then creeping into the back garden so he could take a good look around the outside. There had been no lights, no movement.

There wasn't a door bell, so he knocked; not just because he wanted to have a final check that no one was home, but because it seemed polite. Normally he would have had to break a window to get inside, but this time the front door swung open at the touch of his knuckles. His left his rucksack with his sleeping bag and guitar, on the doorstep; only taking the hammer with him, held in his right hand with the claw pointing forwards. He made sure his elbow was bent in a right angle and his arm was turned slightly out from his body.

'Wendy, I'm home,' Finlay called and took a step inside. He'd never had anyone answer him yet, but he had to be sure. The interior surprised him – from the outside the Anderton House had given the impression of having two floors, yet inside it appeared to be single storey. A relief really, since it meant there was no way he would be trapped on the first floor again. He stood in an open-plan hallway, parquet floors, and white walls; ahead of him, two steps down, was the living room with a full wall of double-height windows. He had a good feeling about the Anderton House. To his right, he could see the kitchen and to his left, a corridor. He pushed the front door fully open so that it swung back and hit the wall behind. Still holding the claw hammer aloft, and with his pulse thumping in his throat, he went into the kitchen, checked under the table and then methodically opened each cupboard in turn.

'Here's Johnny,' he said into every space. He braced himself for the fridge. If the owners had left in a hurry they often didn't have time to clear out the contents and the power had been off for months now. The green mould and the smell always made him gag, but still he had to check. This one was empty.

He went back past the front door. On his left, the bathroom was uninhabited, but he chopped at the air with the hammer just the same. Behind the shower curtain and in the bath he found no one. Before he opened the other doors, he confirmed his arm position, and then shouted again,

'Wendy, I'm home,' and, 'Here's Johnny.'

There were three bedrooms. He pushed each door fully open; he checked under the beds by flicking the covers up onto the mattresses and flinging himself to the floor in a single well-practiced motion. He saw only dust. He swiped his weapon into wardrobes, under desks and behind curtains. Finlay had to perform the same compulsive ritual in every room, in every house, to feel safe. He applied it rigorously, and if he thought he might have missed a possible hiding place, the rule was he had to start over again from the front door inwards. Once, half way through, he had realised that the hammer head was facing forwards and not the claw, and he had almost wept at his stupidity, but had no choice except to begin again. He knew he couldn't sleep in a house which hadn't been properly cleared. Sometimes he repeated the process even when he knew there were no places left to hide.

The last room Finlay looked through in the Anderton House was the living room. There was only a sofa, one armchair and a sideboard, which was too small to fit a human inside, but he checked them all.

Finally satisfied, he brought in his rucksack and stared out at the view through the floor to ceiling windows. Far below him was what should have been the town. In the distance only the tops of a couple of church steeples stood clear of the water and down the hill he could see where the gully disgorged its churning flow into what used to be streets and gardens. The tall windows showed storm clouds and the heavier afternoon rain sweeping in again from the east.

Finlay had made tea on his stove and was lying on the sofa when he heard the noise. It came from the bathroom: a scraping of something wooden and heavy against the floor. It could have been an animal, but the sound was too regular. His stomach lurched and he realised he didn't know where he had left the claw hammer. Stupid idiot! he berated himself. In a rising panic he thought about running out, but he'd have to leave all his things and anyway, he'd have to get past the bathroom. Finlay went through all the places he could hide in the living room and the kitchen. He was too big for the cupboards, and the curtains were flimsy and would show his shape. Quickly, he decided that under the sofa was his only option. The scraping noise stopped abruptly, but now he could hear the handle on the bathroom door turning. He slid belly-first along the wooden floor, only just fitting in the low space beneath the seat. His cheek was pressed at an awkward angle into the dust. He could see the legs of the coffee table, his rucksack spilling its contents where he had dropped it, and the bottom of the long expanse of windows. There were definitely footsteps, in the hall now. They paused where the room opened out and dropped down a level. Finlay held his breath as the footsteps entered the living room and two ankles came into view. He saw dirty trainers with green laces. And he saw his claw hammer, dangling, head down, swinging just below the person's knees. He squashed himself further back under the sofa, against the wall. The feet walked across the floor and out of his range of vision. And then suddenly a grubby face was in front of his, cheek against the parquet. A young girl stared at him, her nose inches away. She held the hammer in her left hand. Holding onto the shaft, she slid it fast, claw forwards towards Finlay, along the floor as if trying to prise the soft body of a snail from its shell. Finlay, with his arm trapped under him, couldn't move to stop the hammer's trajectory. He strained backwards but was only able to tilt his chin slightly upwards, with the back of his head hard up against the wall behind the sofa. The girl stopped just as the two sharp fangs of the claw reached the soft skin of Finlay's throat. She pushed the tool gently in towards his chest.

'You forgot your hammer, Johnny,' she said.

Over the Vanishing City

by Toby Lloyd

It's supposed to be me, Rick and Freddie, but they're not here yet, so it's just me. We're the only ones left; everyone else has moved on or moved out. We said we'd meet at The North Star. The North Star was the name of a bar that used to be here. We used to go there after school. No one else went there very much, so in the end it closed down. Someone bought the place up and opened a new bar called Vinnie's. We still called it The North Star, but we didn't go so much. After a while Vinnie's closed too. This time no one bought it up, so it became just another abandoned building. One day the sign that said 'Vinnie's Bar' fell clean off, so now the place had no name at all. I heard that when the sign fell off it killed a stray dog. In time squatters moved in. People complained, the council took action, and knocked the building down. They turned the place into a sort of public garden, and planted a few trees. The place became known unofficially as 'The Rose Garden', but I don't know if many people needed a name to call it by. We still called it The North Star. When the trees grew to their full height the garden became quite pretty. It looked strange, being bordered on either side by the estates. You squash all those people in, living like ants, and the trees are given all that leg room. Trees don't even have legs. Kids smoked weed there after dark. No one liked that very much, but I knew how it was. I'd been a kid like that once. When the winds came, they ripped all the trees out of the ground. Have you ever seen an uprooted tree? There is something desperate about the roots sticking out horizontally, all crooked. Not even children hold on that tight. They must have been some winds to do that. Now there is no bar, and no garden, no customers, and no squatters, and no kids to smoke weed. We still call it The North Star. I guess what I'm trying to say is that we're resistant to change.

Freddie and Rick arrive so we move on. The streets are completely deserted. It's so quiet you can hear the buzz of the street lights. When human beings are a million years extinct the street lights will still be there, turning themselves on every night, turning themselves off every day. Aliens will come down to Earth and they'll think London is a model village. It is a cold night, possibly in March. Rick is shivering but he won't do up the zip on his coat. He's perverse like that. Freddie tries to light a cigarette but it is too windy, and his matches keep blowing out. I tell him to wait until we get inside. He won't listen, and wastes a whole load more matches. We walk past the estates, and I think of all those buildings doing nothing now but giving the rats a place to sleep.

We reach the Thames and turn left. The river is at high-tide. I like it better at low time – greater distance between me and it. It is not a river that moves. It sits, it broods, and sometimes it swells up, but it never moves. On a night like this the surface is black and the river looks like it is bottomless. I hate to think how cold it must be in there. I imagine jumping in to be more like jumping off a cliff than off the edge of a swimming pool. I can't see anyone who goes in coming back out. Looking at it gives me that nervous feeling that you get on top of high buildings. I take a few steps away from the water, just in case.

We take some steps down to an old underground station. The signs are all faded or defaced, and I don't remember which one this used to be. We walk along the platform until we get to the point where a barrier blocks you from going any further. Then we climb down onto the tracks, and walk with the mice. The mice have lived here so long that they are the same colour as the tracks, so you can't see them, but I tell you, there are a lot of mice down here. It still feels slightly odd walking along the tube tracks. I have this idea that the tunnel might cave in on itself, or just lead to nowhere. Of course, it never does. You hear sounds though, and they creep us out. One time we came across the wreckage of an old train. Even though it had been lying there broken and unused for years, the open-door button still worked. Funny that. It must still be down here somewhere. The tunnel is dark, but if you shine a light you can see that almost every inch of the walls is covered in graffiti. It's not just people signing their names; there are some wonderful paintings here. These are our caves, and so we draw on them. They give you the feeling that you have to leave some kind of mark that you were here. There is one picture of a man waiting for a train. He seems to be the only passenger. He is leaning over the edge of the platform, staring into the tunnel. In the background there is a clock, but the clock has no hands. I like that one. There are lots of pictures of crowds, and of migration. It's not the same, but they make me think of the children's drawings from Theresienstadt. I always loved those kids, sitting in hell's waiting room and passing the time with crayons. These images were born in darkness, and will return to darkness, but while we're passing through we may as well hold up a light to look at them. I suspect no one, not even the artists themselves, has ever seen all of it. I mean the whole tunnel. Even the ceilings are covered. I don't know how anyone managed that. A lot of messages have been left for people too. The people they were meant for aren't going to read the messages – they're not coming back – but maybe it's some consolation just to do the writing. Rick, who has the best knowledge of the city, tells us we're here. We turn right, and take some steps back up to the street level.

We walk along what was once known as the south bank. I wonder whether a compass, if I could find such a thing, would still know north from south. I think there's a good chance it would mix them up, like Ahab's does in Moby Dick. Freddie thinks it's pretentious that I read old books like that. On either side of the river, blue lights are suspended from wires. They resemble some giant, ethereal spider.

We're going to the old hotel. In its day it was a hang out of the great and the good. Check the register. Jimi Hendrix stayed for three nights back in 1968. That was once a big deal to kids like us. The hotel closed down years ago, but hasn't yet succumbed to rack and ruin.

There's a cellar where the drinks used to be kept, and it still has crates of undrunk beer. This is where we always go. When the beer runs out we'll have to find somewhere else.

We walk into the lobby. It's still pretty grand; sculptures, marble, chandeliers. You know, the whole works. The windows are adorned with thick curtains, tied permanently to the sides. It never occurs to us to draw them. Though the pattern on the curtains is abstract, it is suggestive of roses. Everything is immaculate. Dusty, but ordered. It looks as though someone still maintains the place. When the guests have all gone, a ghostly cleaning staff remains. I sign the guest book. Freddie and Rick think this is weird, but it's something I like to do. There's a piano in the corner of the room, and not an upright either. I don't understand why it hasn't gone out of tune, but it hasn't. The first few times we came here Freddie would play it. He's pretty good, but he only knows three songs, and when you've heard them you've heard them. Rick goes down to the cellar and comes back with some beers. 'What does everyone want?' he asks. It's a joke; he knows we're all going to drink Becks. It's the only beer they've got.

We open the beers and fall silent. We don't have a bottle opener, so we have to crack them open on the edge of the table. I don't think anyone will mind. Me and Freddie smoke, but Rick doesn't. Even though everything has changed, Rick still holds on to some of his old ways. Rick has suffered great disappointment and loss. Of course, we have all suffered disappointment and loss, but Rick's have been the greatest. Of the three of us, Rick was always the golden boy. In fact, when we were young, Rick wasn't even friends with me and Freddie; he hung around with a completely different set. He was a sporty kid – the sort of guy that would intimidate you out of playing pool if he was standing by the table. He was smart too, and always got top marks. Not to mention girls. He used to pass up girls that me or Freddie would have killed to be with. He could do that; he had enough options. The world he was promised when he was growing up did not look very much like this one, I can tell you that.

Freddie takes a pack of cards out of his pocket. He deals a few hands and we play some poker. We don't have anything to bet with but bottle caps, so the stakes are low. When we drink beer we never throw the caps away. We horde them in a box, and so now we have hundreds. I remember once me and Rick had to take a two hour walk home in the rain because we'd lost all our money in a poker game, including the bus fare. Those were the days. After not very long we get tired of seeing bottle caps change hands between the three of us and we stop playing. Besides, it doesn't matter how the games turn out; in the end the caps are all going to be put back into the same box regardless.

Hording the bottle caps in the first place was Freddie's idea. You have to admire Freddie. He's always the one who texts us and says we should go for a drink. If it wasn't for him I'd probably never see either of them. I've known Freddie all my life, more or less. His family moved in next door to us when I was five. We used to play football in the street together. We used parked cars as goals. It didn't make us very popular with the neighbours, but it was a lot of fun. Freddie gave me my first cigarette, and introduced me to my first girlfriend. Before we started hanging out with Rick I kind of hero-worshipped him. You'd think that by now all wounds would be healed, all injuries forgiven, but sometimes I get the impression that Freddie still resents Rick a bit. I suppose you have to hold on to something, and resentment seems as good as anything else. Besides, maybe it has more to do with Rick's general attitude. He can make things pretty hard for the rest of us.

We sit there smoking cigarettes and drinking beer, and not talking. We don't really talk anymore. There's no use. We have known each other far too long and there is nothing left to say. Except the things none of us can say, even when drunk. To say them now would make a mockery of all those years of not saying them. I guess that's the point. I don't mind too much though. We've had some good times, the three of us, but there's no need to keep bringing them up. You can't keep reminiscing forever. Those things are in the past now; it's not like they're going anywhere.

Freddie suggests we play a drinking game. Rick asks which one. Freddie shrugs and says any. Rick says why bother? You don't need to play some game to tell you when to drink. I agree with Rick, but I feel bad doing it. I know I'm letting Freddie down, but I'm just not in the mood.

More silent drinking. Rick spends a lot of time watching the door. He's not really looking at it though, he's looking through it. I can guess what he's thinking: imagine if someone walked in, if anyone at all just walked in. For a moment I think I can hear a radio playing somewhere, not so much a tune as the impression of a tune. As soon as I start listening out for it I can't hear it anymore. I ask the others if they heard it, but they don't know what I'm talking about. Never mind, I say. Freddie blows some smoke rings. He's an expert but we've seen him do it before. I'm not about to slap him on the back about it anyway, and neither is Rick.

Rick says he needs some air. This might be a dig about us smoking. It's hard to tell with Rick. I suggest we go out onto the roof. Rick and Freddie agree. We take the lift to the top floor of the hotel. As the lift climbs the floors I stare at the screen which tells you which one you're on. I'm waiting to see if one of the floor numbers lights up, telling us that someone has called the lift. As if that were even possible. Freddie starts humming. We get out on the top floor. When we step out into the corridor, lights come on automatically. As we walk forward the shadows in front of us recede, like we're on stage in the spotlight. Or in a prison break. We reach the stairs which take us outside.

On top of the hotel there is a roof garden. It is warmer now. You can see the whole city from here, more or less. In the light, you can't really make out much colour. Consequentially, right now London looks like a still from Fritz Lang's Metropolis. I wonder how the plants feel about the one hundred metres of glass and steel which come between them and any natural soil. Rick mentions the famous person who threw himself off this roof top in the '80s. He looks over the edge down to the street, empathetically. He throws a penny out in front of him. If it ever reached the ground I didn't hear it. Freddie starts humming. Rick is shivering again.

Not far from the roof we are standing on is another roof, not quite as high up as ours. Rick is eyeing it up.

'Do you reckon I could make the jump?' he says.

It's not that hard a jump, but it's a hell of a long way down. If he missed it, say he slipped on the run up, that would be it.

'Rick, don't be stupid.'

Rick starts walking back. He is preparing a run up. Freddie goes to stand in his way. Rick looks like he's about to hit Freddie. I start eyeing up the gap myself. It's really not that far to jump. I take the run up gently. A jogging pace is all that's needed to clear it. By the time Rick and Freddie cotton on to what I'm doing they're in no position to stop me. I plant my right foot on the corner of our roof and launch myself into the air. It's quite a feeling. As I land on the second roof I go into a roll; there was more of a drop between the two buildings than I had thought. I stand up, dusty and a bit bruised, but feeling good about myself. I have jumped not just the space between two buildings, but over the gaping jaws of death itself. When I turn around I can see the faces of my friends, and they're not impressed. They seem to say: So you were over here, and now you're over there. So what? What has that accomplished? And in a way they are right. I can see that. What was I expecting – applause? Freddie calls out from the other roof top.

'Are you coming back, or what?'

'Sure. In a minute.'

I'm here now and I don't want to leave straight away. Who knows, maybe there'll be something on this roof worth jumping over for. Freddie lights a cigarette, and Rick sits with his legs dangling over the edge of the building. If he looks pissed off it's because I stole his jump.

At the side of my rooftop there is a fire escape. I can climb all the way down from the roof to the ground. There's something that appeals about this, and I put my foot onto the first rung. I picture myself as a tiny King Kong, and the city as my climbing frame. I suppose there was a time when someone used this route to run from an actual fire. If they did, I reckon the odds were against them. I wonder if Rick and Freddie are having a conversation in my absence. It doesn't seem likely. By the time I get back down to the ground it's really getting cold, and it's a relief to get back into the hotel. I take the elevator up to the roof by myself. Back in the garden, Freddie is no longer smoking, but nothing else has changed.

'How's tricks?' I ask. It's a joke, and no one answers.

Way off, at the very edges of my vision, I can see a light moving. At first I think it must be an illusion, but soon I am in no doubt.

'Hey, look,' I say. Now all three of us are watching it.

'What is it?' says Freddie.

I tell him I think it's an aeroplane.

'How could it be a plane?' says Rick. 'Where would it be going? It's not a plane.'

'I think it's a plane.'

We watch in silence. The light is coming closer to us. After a minute we can see that it is not just one light, but two, or even three, very close together.

'Can you hear that?' I say. 'That rumbling sound? Can you hear it?'

'I hear it,' Freddie says.

'It's coming from the hotel. It's just the hum of electronics,' says Rick.

'No it's not.'

The lights are coming closer. There are definitely three now. The rumbling sound is observing a slow crescendo. When I first saw it, the light was moving so slowly that I couldn't be sure it wasn't fixed, like I was looking on the imperceptible drift of the stars. Now the lights are careering with such a velocity, with such tangible purpose, that there is no doubting; to move is to be alive. The sound is so loud it is deafening. It is as though the hotel has been erected in such a position as to straddle a fault line in the earth's crust, and we are at the centre of a monumental upheaval, frictional forces large enough and hot enough to remodel the entire city. The roof is shaking under us. I think Freddie is shouting something, but I cannot hear a word. Even Rick has to believe now.

It passes straight over our heads, but none of us dives to the floor or even crouches. We are transfixed. For one moment only, the body of the aeroplane is lit up for me and I can see it clearly from beneath. It is a commercial, not a private, plane. There must be at least two hundred people on board. Its wing span is massive, and I, who spend my evenings standing on top of the city, should know what massive means. Imagine being one of those people, to laugh at the birds as they tire, to look down on the clouds, to have all those views and a destination to boot. Where has it come from? I've never understood how a plane works, how it even gets up there in the first place. All that metal, all those people; it just doesn't make any sense. I think Rick might know, but he wouldn't want to talk about it.

The time it spent hanging above us can't have been so long as a second. A fragment of a second, that would have been to an hour what a grain of sand is to a mountain, was all it was. After it has passed we watch it vanish, just as we watched it appear. First the three lights become one, then the one light grows smaller and is lost altogether. When it has finally gone, we take the elevator back down and disperse into the night.

Up the Road

by Andrew Saxsma

'Oh, for God sakes,' Benny's mom said, pointing further up I-57 with one hand, the other loosely held the bottom of the steering wheel. She sighed and sunk back into her seat.Benny took a drink out of his water bottle then reached down the side of his seat, feeling for the recline lever. His fingers scrambled over his little sister's toys and Burger King wrappers crammed under his chair, and was there something wet, or was it sticky? He felt along the shag under-lining, following it until he grabbed the lever and pulled it, pitching his backrest upright with a springy thud!Benny's head bounced off the headrest and he almost spilt his water.

'Quit playin' with the seats would ya'? You're gonna' give me a heart attack, and then what'll you do?' his mom asked.

Benny set his water bottle into the cup holder in the center console then looked at what his mom had been pointing at, up ahead.

'Mom, we've made this trip together a half-dozen times,' Benny said, leaning forward from his seat. 'You haven't had a heart attack yet.' He squinted his eyes, confused. 'That a traffic jam?'

She shook her head, without a clue.

'If people only knew how to drive, shi-,' she stopped, looking at Benny, 'stuff like this wouldn't happen. Would you reach into the backseat, sweetie, and grab my purse?' his mom asked, gesturing behind her without taking her eyes from the road. She took her foot off the gas and began easing down the brake pedal, bringing the car to a slow and complete stop behind a green jeep. She could see the road ahead was packed with cars for miles, shining their red brake lights, not moving an inch.

Benny unbuckled his seat belt and twisted around in his seat, reaching over top the headrest for her purse.

'What are the hours for move-in again?' she asked.

Benny tossed his bag of laundry from the backseat to the floor and shoved aside his coat, looking for her purse.

'Ten to seven,' he said with a grunt as he shifted his book bag, full of thick textbooks.

'This is gonna' make us late,' she whined. She rolled down her window and peeked at the cloudy sky. 'Got dark fast too, didn't it. That's just what we need, Benny. Rain. Rain and a traffic jam,' she said with a smirk.

'Got it,' Benny said, moving his pillows, revealing her purse. He picked it up by the strap and flopped back down into his seat.

'Uh, grab the little bottle would you?' she asked, dancing her eyes between her purse and the road, nervous.

'This one?' Benny asked, pulling out a bottle of prescription pills.

'Yup,' she said.

Benny handed her the bottle and she tapped a pair of bright pink pills into her palm.

'Can I have a drink of your water, babe?' she asked, handing the bottle back to Benny.

He nodded 'yes'.

'Thanks.'

She tossed the pills into her mouth and took a swig of water, swallowing hard. She let out a satisfied 'ah', then put the water back into the cup holder. She grabbed the wheel with both hands and bounced her shoulders, finally a happy camper.

The two sat in silence for a long moment, staring ahead at the traffic jam with nothing much else to say.

'My phone in there?' his mother asked, breaking the silence.

Benny scrounged through her purse then shook his head 'no'.

'Shoot!' she said. 'Well, since we're not goin' anywheres,' she said, putting the car into park. She unbuckled her seatbelt then slipped into the backseat. 'I must have set it on the seat when we were loading the car. Do you remember seeing it?' she hollered from the back. She slid aside a bag of meatloaf leftovers wrapped in tinfoil she'd packed for Benny's dorm.

A dozen or so cars ahead, in between the lanes, Benny saw a man running and he sat up in his seat, feeling on edge. As near as Benny could tell, the man was crying and screaming, and what looked like blood ran down his cheeks. The man stumbled into the side of the jeep in front of their car, leaving a bloody handprint behind, before darting by, heading in the direction Benny and his mother had come from.

Benny watched the man run until he was out of sight while his mother diddled around in the back. His eyes wandered back to the handprint. Tiny slivers of blood trickled down the window from the fingertips. Then, like a gunshot, tires squealed.

A tan sedan, a few rows up, reversed, slamming into a tiny yellow beetle behind it, then swerved off the road and peeled out into the middle ditch. The front fender bounced off the ground, spraying a puff of dirt and grass onto its hood, then climbed the opposite ditch and fishtailed into the oncoming lane before speeding off.

Benny's stomach dropped and his eyes grew warm and glossy. He was afraid and his nerves were wreaking havoc on his fingers and hands.

Benny, still staring at the traffic jam ahead, leaned forward once more, his face blank.

'Mom?' he whispered. He gulped. He propped his hands on the dash, getting in close to the windshield. 'Mom?' he said, this time slightly louder.

'What is it, sweetie?' she said, annoyed, tossing her coat to the floor, her back to Benny.

'Something's happening,' he said, worried. He rolled down his window and poked his body out to get a better view of the road.

A breeze picked up, rustling his shaggy brown hair, carrying with it muffled, whispered screams from somewhere further up the road, somewhere he couldn't see.

'What?' his mom asked. She looked beside her, on the floor, and saw her phone. 'God-darnit,' she said, picking it up and looking at its newly cracked screen. 'Benjamin Mathew! If you broke my phone… At least it still works.'

She dialed up her husband with an irritated sigh, and then held the phone to her ear.

Benny opened his door and got out, side-stepping away from their car, trying to get a good view up the road.

'Hey, honey. Yeah, we're stuck in traffic,' Benny heard his mom say from the car. His mouth drooped like a wet sock as he skirted to the silver guardrail on the road's shoulder. He rested his hand on its grit-covered surface, wanting to feel grounded as he listened, stared ahead.

Benny watched the driver of the jeep in front of their car get out and take a cautious step forward, eyes fixed on something. A woman holding a sleeping baby got out of the passenger side of the pickup in front of the jeep. She rocked the baby in her arms, swaying back and forth while she too tried to see what was going on. She leaned back into the truck's cab and said something to ease the worries of the man driving. It was so quiet. That's when it happened.

It was subtle at first, so subtle Benny almost missed it, and if he hadn't gotten out of the car, he wagered, he would have.

He felt the guardrail shiver under his hand, saw the gravel by his sneakers on the pavement quiver. Then, they went still. No longer than a moment passed before it happened again, then again. It only took a few times for Benny to be sure of it, but the ground was shaking, and whatever it was, it was getting stronger, or…closer, Benny thought.

There was a shrill scream from up the road, this time closer, and Benny shook his head, confused.

'What?' he said aloud to himself when he saw it.

A car arced dozens of feet above the road, flipping end over end with a woman inside, shrieking. His face went hot as he followed it through the air, watching it, and he wasn't sure, but he thought he might be shivering.

The driver's screams faded as the car spiralled overhead and dropped, smashing into another car about a quarter-mile behind Benny and his mother's car. The boom, the smashing and screeching of colliding metals, jerked Benny in place.

Benny looked back at his mom, in their car, still talking on the phone.

'Mom!' he screamed. 'Mom!'

More screams filled the air as people began piling and fumbling over cars, scrambling away from something in heavy crowds. The space between the lanes was packed with people running. Men and women shoved each other, knocked each other to the ground and into cars, busting windows and doors. A bulky man wearing a Cub's jersey lost his balance while running up a windshield and bounced off the roof of the car, slamming neck first into the pavement, tripping a young man and woman. The man's face skidded along the pavement while the woman's forehead crashed into a headlight.

The flood of recklessly scared people washed over and around Benny's car, trampling the windshield, lopping off the side-view mirrors while his mom screamed inside. A man shoved past Benny, ramming him into the guardrail and when he stood himself upright, another man's shoulder stuck Benny in the chest, plowing him off his feet.

Benny landed on his back, forcing the air out of him with a dry, scraping wheeze. He struggled for breath while his vision blurred and spun. A cough burned its way up his throat, shredding his vocal chords. He gasped, fighting for air while he rolled over onto his stomach and pushed himself up onto his knees. Bits of gravel stuck to his scraped and bloody palms and elbows. He stayed there, hunched over for a moment, while his lungs mellowed out.

He wiped the dirt from his forehead with a sore hand. The ringing in his ears waned.

He looked back at his car while the stampede of running people continued. His mom was huddled over the center console, cradling her head with her hands while she yelled for help.

When the rolling, other-worldly roar began, the crowd hurried, ran more desperately, screamed louder.

Benny pushed himself onto the flats of his sneakers while the guttural cry drowned out everything else, droning and rattling Benny's head. The cars on the road shook, rattled by the howl.

Benny's veins went cold and a shiver shimmied up his spine. The hair on the back of his neck stood on end while his eyes glossed over, looking up the road, filled with a fear so raw, so brutal, he couldn't move.

Twenty or so rows up, an SUV whipped into the air, off the road with a slam. A trail of glass and metal fluttered behind, tailing the dented SUV into the ditch. It bounced, rolling onto its nose, then to its roof in a snaggle of metal and parts. Another car shot into the air, crashing down into the oncoming lane, scrunching it like a slinky. A wave of shattered glass sprayed the road, tiny jagged shards bouncing in all directions.

Benny stood stiff as a two-by-four, frozen, unable to move while more and more cars leapt, thrown into the air by something he couldn't see yet. His heart raced as the rows of thrown cars got closer, traveling down the line toward him and his mom. He started breathing harder, faster, chest hitching, scared shitless. He squeezed his fist, nerves squishing tight.

'Mom,' his voice croaked amidst the chaos of the stampeding people and their tearing screams. His head and voice felt millions of miles apart.

Streams of runners spread from the road, pouring down into the ditches and into the fields on the sides of the interstate; men, women, children, all trying to escape while cars, and now people, were tossed from the road, thrashing and screaming.

'Benny!' his mom shouted through fits of tears. Her eye makeup ran down the sides of her cheeks. She wiped her eyelids, spreading it with her knuckles. She crawled back into the front seat, fumbling and sobbing.

Benny gulped and the jeep in front of their car squealed its tires, throwing up puffs of smoke and the stench of burnt rubber. It burnt Benny's eyes and throat, and the jeep rammed into the car in front of it, then reversed into their car, mashing in the front end.

'Mom!' Benny shouted, running up to the car while the driver leapt from the jeep, realizing he didn't have a chance in hell of getting the jeep off the road. He bumped into Benny as he bounded down the ditch and into the field. Benny lost his balance and plowed into his car, shoulder-first. He heard something snap and white-hot pain flashed up his collar, wrapping around his neck. He slumped against the car while his arm hung limp. 'Mom!' he shouted. 'Get out of the car, now!'

Another roar ripped through the air, deafening Benny. His bones and jaw vibrated, and hot air rushed over the car.

'Benny!' his mom shouted, inside the car. She hit the passenger window with the palms of her hands. 'Benny, I can't!'

Benny spun around and stepped away from the car.

His mother pulled at the door handle, tugging at it with her upper body.

Benny reached for the door handle with both hands, but a pain seared through his shoulder. He dropped his arm back to his side and pulled at the handle with his good hand. The door groaned, opening a crack, then stopped. The front end of the car was crushed in, down to the hinges of the door. It didn't want to open anymore.

Benny looked up as another wave of cars shot up into the air, just a few rows up now. Whatever it was, it was going to be on top of them any moment now.

Benny planted his foot against the car, heaving the handle with more leverage. It creaked, opening another inch or two, but was cut short again.

'What about the other side, mom? Try the other side!' Benny shouted, tapping the window with his pointer finger, pointing at the driver's side. He pulled uselessly at the door again. He heard another row of cars vault and smash into the ditch. 'God dammit!' he shouted.

His mom tried the driver's side, and when it didn't budge, she rammed into it with her shoulder. She scrambled back to the passenger side and held her open palm against the window.

'Benny!' she cried. She shook her head and sobbed once more.

'Mom, try harder!' Benny screamed. He started kicking the door. 'Fucking open!' he shouted.

His mom perked up, looking out the windshield at the road ahead when another wave of cars were thrown from the road, her tears stifled by fear.

'You gotta' run, Benny,' she said. She slapped the window. 'You run, you hear!?'

The sadness in her eyes was gone; all that was left was a stolid assurance.

'You run and you don't ever stop!' she warned.

The ground beneath Benny's feet shook violently and he almost lost his footing.

'Benny, get away from the car,' his mother screamed. She pounded the flat of her fist against the window, getting his attention. 'Run, God dammit!'

Benny didn't know he was crying as he stumbled back from the car, his steps uneasy. His eyes darted between the road, up ahead, and his mother in the window, blubbering and caressing the window.

Something slammed into the abandoned jeep in front of their car and it barrel-rolled into the air, raining glass and metal splinters over Benny. He covered his eyes and cradled his head. It crashed into the field behind him, and when he uncovered his face, the colour ran from his face. His eyes watered over with fright as a single tear of awe slipped down his gritty cheek. His head drifted back, mouth drooping, and for a moment, just one moment, he thought he might have laughed in disbelief.

It looked at Benny for a moment from the front of their car, on all fours. It rose up onto its tree trunk sized legs and stood nearly twenty-feet tall, towering over Benny and the car. Its skin was pallid, and it was naked except for a furry pelt wrapped around its torso. A single, unblinking eye stared at Benny from the center of its small head, which looked more like a deflated basketball. It reared back and beat on its chest with its hands the size of boulders. Two blood-stained tusks stuck out of its closed, fat lips.

It was like something out of a Grimm fairy tale, Benny thought to himself. A troll?

It took in a deep breath and leaned forward, letting out a thunderous roar, blasting Benny with moist air that pushed him back a few steps. He covered his face, shielding his eyes.

It stood upright again and elbowed their car, rocking his mother face first into the dash.

She held her nose as she leaned back into the passenger seat, blood flowing down her chin.

'Run!' she screamed, slapping a bloody palm against the window.

The troll leaned low, peeking inside the car and rested its huge, pallet-sized hand on the car's roof.

Benny backed away from the creature, shaking his head 'no'.

'Mom!' he shouted.

The troll pushed down on the roof, effortlessly crushing the car. Glass exploded outward as the chassis strained under the weight.

Benny's mom screamed as she disappeared beneath the roof, crushing her. The metal scraped and groaned, drowning out her screams.

The troll put his other hand on top of his other and pushed down with all his weight, pancaking the car. When it let go, his mother's screaming was no more.

'No!' Benny cried.

The troll slid a hand underneath the flattened car and flipped it off the road, into the oncoming lane, and turned around to watch it bounce end over end.

Benny, crying, turned and hopped over the guardrail and ran down the ditch. He pumped his arms and churned his legs harder, faster with every step. He heard the troll roar again from behind, heard it bust through the guardrail and chug down the ditch and into the field, chasing him.

The ground shook as the troll planted its fleshy feet, one in front of the other, bouncing Benny left and right as he bolted over tiny husks of sprouting corn stalks. He passed stragglers lagging behind the crowd of people ahead, running for their lives.

The troll caught up with a woman just behind Benny and plucked her off the ground by her head with its enormous hand. It squeezed its fist closed, cutting her screams short, squirting a red film from in between its fingers the size of firewood, then dropped her crushed body as it ran.

The clouds above parted, flooding the field with warm sunlight.

Benny screamed and jumped over a clump of weeds, then dodged by a man in a tweed blazer hunched over on his knees, resting. The man stood up as Benny passed, then turned and saw the troll. The man turned to run when the troll swatted, backhanding him off the ground and out of the way, pin wheeling him like a ragdoll across the field.

A little ways ahead, the crowd had gathered on the edge of the field in sparse groups, talking and resting near a thicket of trees.

Benny, feeling the hot breath of the troll lap against his neck in moist waves, pivoted, sprinting off to the right, toward the crowd. A blonde woman, holding the hand of a boy no older than eight or nine, pointed at Benny and the troll and screamed. She turned and ran, yanking the boy along toward the forest. More people, hearing the scream, turned and saw Benny running toward them with the troll hot on his heels, charging like a gorilla, using its fists to pedal itself closer, faster.

Shadows fell on the field around Benny and the crowd of runners. Benny saw shapes dancing around him on the ground, descending from above. When he heard that gut-wrenching screech, he didn't want to look up.

The few people who hadn't started running yet stared up into the sky, using their hands like visors to see against the sunlight. Benny passed them and ran down, along the edge of the forest, following the tree line against the edges of the field. A black man wearing overalls followed Benny, running beside him.

The troll stopped, more interested in the people left behind.

A shriek ripped through the air, just above Benny, and he heard something lift the guy beside him off the ground. He looked over his shoulder, just in time to see the man's feet disappear overhead, leaving behind a rotted smell, an old stench.

Benny slowed and stopped. Hiding behind a tree, he looked out and saw, what he thought, was a naked woman with feathers and wings lifting the man into the air with sharp, razor-edged talons. She didn't have a mouth, but a beak, with a nasty, wriggling pink tongue hanging out. She flapped her wing-hands, climbing high into the air, disappearing behind the harsh sunlight, screeching something like a laugh. The aged smell dissipated as the air calmed.

A scream slowly built, rising from a muffled fade to a high-pitched yowl and Benny saw the black man falling. He looked away when he slammed into the ground, breaking his shriek short.

Benny looked back up into the sky and saw an entire flock circling above. He saw one nose-dive, tearing a woman from the crowd. She held onto a man's hand, screaming for help, and the pair were pulled off the ground. The man hung, shouting he loved her, then let go and landed in the field with a roll. Before he could get up and run back to the safety of the trees, another dive-bombed, stealing him into the sky.

Benny took one more glimpse of the troll, holding a pair of dead bodies, one in each hand. It smashed them together, again and again, into a bloody pulp.

Benny gagged and kneeled over to spit. He didn't puke, but he really wanted to. He wiped his mouth with the back of his hand and looked across the field to the interstate. His eyes grew heavy, thinking of his mother's bloody hand, of the car being crushed. He sobbed as he ran into the forest, following the shouts of the people who'd already run on. Run, Benny!

He heard the screeching things, hovering above the trees.

He hopped over downed logs, sloshed through piles of dead leaves, and bent down and around low-lying branches.

He wiped the tears from his cheeks and dug any strays out of the corners of his eyes with a dirty finger.

He spotted a group of twenty or so people huddling in a clearing ahead and as he approached, he heard one of them stand and scream, 'What is that?'

A woman pointed up into a tree.

Another woman stood.

'Run!' she shouted.

Benny caught up to them as they started to race again, running in between trees.

'What the hell is going on?' Benny hollered.

No one answered. They didn't care. They just wanted to live, like him.

A man, wearing a gas station jumpsuit, ran ahead of Benny when something whipped by Benny's ear, ruffling his hair like a soft breeze. The man's body flopped to the ground and rolled end over end into a tuft of leaves. Benny ran by as it stopped and saw an arrow piercing his bloody forehead.

Benny watched as more people dropped dead, catching arrows in the throat or back. He heard a woman scream as she fell to the ground, an arrow sticking through her ankle, further ahead.

Something ran along a tree above her, bouncing off branches, landing on the ground beside her. It was a tiny man, no taller than a foot, wearing a green tailored tunic and trousers. He had pointed, brown shoes and pointy hat. He pulled a tiny blade from a holster around his waist and started stabbing the woman's throat. Blood splattered his puffy-white beard as he smiled and chuckled.

Benny saw daylight breaking through the trees ahead, and guessed that must be the end of the forest. He wanted out, bad.

He pushed himself harder, doing his best to control his breathing, when an arrow zipped through the palm of his hand with a soft whisper. The tail caught it just short of going clean through. The arrowhead stuck out a few inches, pulling tiny bits of bloody sinew out with it.

He screamed as pain wrapped along his wrist, throbbing all the way up to his elbow. His hand went numb and stiff almost instantly, but still he ran, clutching his hand out in front of him, like it was infected with some horrible leprosy.

He hopped over a dead man in a tuxedo with notecards falling out of his bloody breast pocket, and broke free from the trees.

The tiny men chasing Benny stopped at the edge of the trees, shouted in some tiny, breathless language then turned and ran back to get any stragglers.

Benny didn't stop until he couldn't see the forest anymore, and he found himself atop a hill, overlooking a small town a few miles away.

He crumbled to his knees and held his hand. He winced with pain but couldn't peel his eyes away from the town. Plumes of smoke rose from the few streets and buildings. Fires raged through stores and homes. He could see people running, cars speeding down short alleys and cul-de-sacs.

He saw a wolf the size of a small car, vaulting on all fours as it ran down a woman and buried its jaws into her neck behind a dumpster. More harpies buzzed overhead, plucking people up left and right from sidewalks and parking lots, taking them into the clouds.

A whole gang of trolls walked down Main Street, swinging clubs the size of trees, batting both cars and people. One veered its club into the first floor of an apartment building, knocking it off its foundation. Windows cracked and broke as it tilted, leaning into the grocery store beside it before crumbling into itself. A puff of dust, drywall, and concrete exploded across the street.

Benny wept as he watched the town tore apart, watched the people hunted down or crushed or eaten. He wondered to himself if this could be happening everywhere. He hoped against hope this was a bad dream, but the arrow sticking out of his hand told him that just wasn't true, no, sir. This was it and yet, all he could think about was his mom. Run, Benny!

As he cried, everything went silent. The soft, cool breeze dropped off and the trees and grass stood still. A flock of birds burst from the trees, soaring past Benny, cawing and chirping, afraid.

Over the town, the harpies screeched and scattered, fleeing. The trolls fumbled, tripping over each other, desperately wanting to get away. Benny couldn't see the wolf, but he bet it wasn't sticking around either.

In the silence, Benny stood up and rubbed his face into his shirt, then looked around, confused. He squinted his eyes, wondering just what the hell was going on.

He took a step forward when, what he thought was a plane, glided right over his head. The trail of wind behind it shoved Benny forward, pulling him and a cloud of stray leaves from the trees behind along the ground until it waned. He sat up on his knees, his hair sticking up in every direction. He matted it down and looked back at the town.

'Oh my God,' he whispered to himself.

He hauled himself back along the ground, back pedalling with his feet, wide-eyed.

A blood-red dragon, the size of a 747, flapped its huge, veiny wings, angling toward the town. Dark fins lined its spine. Its tail snaked behind, zipping left and right, a mind of its own. It aimed its long, scaly neck at the town and spewed a liquid-fire stream into the streets and buildings, dragging this fiery rill along as it circled the town.

It gained a bit of lift then hovered over the town, scanning for movement. Benny was sure there wouldn't be any.

The dragon thrashed its wings again, fanning the fires now consuming entire blocks, and climbed into the air before veering off and vanishing beyond the forest. In the distance, Benny heard it mewl.

Benny grunted as he forced himself onto his feet. Holding his hand close, he side-stepped down the hill toward the town. He figured there would be no need for them to come back, at least, that's what he was betting on.

He walked down the empty, charred streets, passing burnt-out cars and homes. He tried not to look at the dead bodies, smouldering and smoking. He found a hardware store, just off Main Street, which was still intact. There were some burnt shingles and some fire damage on the south wall, but aside from that bad luck, it looked safe.

He followed the nail aisle to an office in the back with a cot. He closed the office door, locked it, then sat on the cot and cried himself to sleep, holding his bloody hand tight. He told himself when he woke up the next morning, he'd find a car, and get back home. He just hoped there would be a home to go back to. If not, he wondered what living in this new world would be like, and that thought, that idea, scared him more than anything.

Seen and Not Heard

by Ilana Masad

'Is it Saturday? Is it Saturday yet, Mama?'

Etch pushes my shoulder. His hands are small. Still so easy to hide. Cob's eyes are open, but he doesn't move. He's had a bad dream again. I can always tell. His pupils are dilated, still out there, somewhere, in a spacesuit leftover from the days when space still mattered. I open my mouth and blow on him, foul morning breath I wouldn't wish on my worst enemy. But it brings him back to me, reminds him he's lying on a mattress, not stranded in a bubble-like sphere that allows for barely more movement than a straightjacket. There - I see his nose wrinkle and he begins to cough.

Cob bounces straight up, his deep-chested hacking the spring to his jack-in-the-box need to move. He reaches for a handkerchief, and retches into it. I don't look anymore. I know it'll come away brown with dust and blood. There's nothing I can do about it. I turn to Etch instead. With Cob's racket, I can't pretend to be asleep anymore.

'No, air I breathe, it's not Saturday yet,' I tell Etch. If I let my eyes lose focus, which is fairly easy to do when I am this tired, his face becomes just a series of curves. The curve of his round cheeks, the curve of his big eyes, the curve of his expressive eyebrows, and the downward curve of his mouth when he's unhappy, as he is now. He doesn't cry. He never does, not aloud. Sometimes his eyes fill with tears, but that fountain rarely leaks, and never erupts into a gush loud enough to be heard. He pouts, though. He knows it is going to be another long, very quiet, day.

Cob is in the other room by now. I can hear him rousing Party, our legitimate, out of bed. She sleeps heavily, deeply, a trait she never had when she was a baby. She screamed every hour for months then, begging to be at my breasts for half the night until I was sore and felt sucked dry. I resented her at the time, but I remember those restless nights with relief now. She was allowed to scream, we were allowed to allow her to. It was as if she knew that her baby's decibels would be the first and last to reverberate against the cracked grey walls of our rooms, and she was going to make those walls soak up every last bit of infancy they could hold, to make up for the pervasive silence that would follow her.

'When's Saturday, Mama?'

'Day after tomorrow, starshine. Day after tomorrow. You have to get back in there now, go on. We need to take Party to school and go to work. We'll be back later.' Every morning, I hear myself telling Etch to get back into the walk-in closet behind the heavy one Cob built to fit in front of it. And every morning, I wonder whose voice it is uttering those words. 'I love you.'

'Love you, Mama. Hug?' He has to ask. My voiceless, whispering child. He doesn't hold his arms out, too nervous it might be wrong, so I hold mine out and nod. He walks into my embrace.

'What are you doing? Come on, we gotta move. Stretch-man, we'll see you later, come on, you know the rules.' Cob's dressed. I don't know how he gets ready so quickly. How long have I been hugging Etch? He's squirming in my arms, uncomfortable, hot. He's clammy. I'm sweating too.

Etch goes back to his room and Cob closes the door. 'Lore, why are you still in bed? Why aren't you dressed? What's wrong? You're all flushed.' He fires the statements at me, getting clothes out of the closet that hides his son, throwing them at the bed. He doesn't look at me.

'Nothing. Sorry. I'm fine. Is she ready?'

'Yeah. I'll get you Energy for the road. Meet us downstairs. Lock up.' He rushes off to collect Party's school things and help her get her shoes on. Not that she needs help. But.

I dress, trying to hurry. My legs are heavy as I pull up one pants leg after another. My uniform shirt seems to be missing a snap at the top – no, I started at the wrong button. I begin again. It's hard to tuck in. It's so hot today. I feel my underarms weeping. I'll have sweat circles on my shirt before I arrive at work.

The elevator light flickers. The electricity lines in our grid haven't been quite right since last year, when another wave of radiation emissions came across the sea unexpectedly. It was a crisis, but I, for one, welcomed it. It meant staying at home for the better part of two weeks, and letting Etch out more often. Not all the time. We had a couple surprise inspections in our building, one in the apartment right next door, and a family in the building across the street was marched into a truck with black bags tied around their heads. That scared Cob. He saw them out of the window and started shaking like the ground next to old train tracks in antique movies. The way he looked at Etch terrified me more than the Party Members across the street.

Cob and Party are downstairs, he talking to our street's Cleaner, Party hiding behind her father, holding onto the loopholes where his belt would have been if we had money for that kind of fashionable frippery. Our Cleaner is a middle-aged woman, but she looks old, like they all do, the skin of her ankles worn to tough meaty strips from her years of wearing the heavy chains. She takes small, slow steps away, the metal links clinking along the concrete musically, her shoulders bowing forward with her broom.

'What were you talking to Cleaner about?' I ask Cob when I reach him. He doesn't look at me, just starts walking. He's impatient in the mornings, always has been.

'She said there were inspections last night.' His lips barely move, and his back is rigid. Party is trailing behind us and I slow down to let her catch up.

'How are you, Par? What've you got in school today?' I take her hand. I am allowed to do this, at least. But she doesn't want me holding her hand anymore. She's eleven. She pulls away.

'Training.Emissions.Nursing.Training.' She lists her subjects, bored. She is so beautiful, I don't know how she emerged from my body sometimes. Her cheekbones are high and delicate, like the Party Spokeswomen and the evening Messengers on the screens. Her skin looks far more like Cob's than like mine, a darker and richer hue than my muddied-milk tones. She looks deceptively like a doll, with her perfect curls playing around her face like the beautiful moths I remember from my childhood, the ones that flew around the lamps at night until they sizzled to death.

Etch is the only one who likes to hear my stories about where I used to live. Cob thinks it's bad for him, and for Party too, to hear about it. 'It was a different time then,' he says. 'You'll give them hope for things they can't have. I never had that and they never will either. The fact that you did is a fluke, a miracle. We don't believe in miracles, Lori. We can't afford to.' He only calls me Lori when he's being stern, and he's sternest when it comes to our children's futures. Well, future. Single. One.

We reach the yellow brick building. Most parents don't walk kids to school. Cob and I are strange in that respect. Overprotective. Party resents it, I know. She barely waves goodbye as she trots inside. I look for her friends, trying to see whose son, whose daughter, she associates with. It is shamefully important. Cob and I know this, and it's the reason we still walk here. But Party, as usual, looks straight ahead as she walks through the door, not greeting anyone.

'Flaring bombing emitting sinking landmine war-torn bastards—' Cob strings his curses together so quickly I can barely tell what he's saying, but I don't worry about him being overheard. He's a careful man. He would never utter a single word that was against the law; he's well-trained in controlling himself in public. It's in private that he can make me nervous. I turn to him and take his hands. I feel the tremors, the suppressed anger, worry, panic. So much of it flows in his muscles that I wonder how they haven't eroded yet. How he's still so big.

'My life,' I say, trying to use the soothing voice that used to work on the animals at the farm. 'My light. My air. What are you worried about?' I know what he's worried about. I want him to say it.

'Party – she – she's still alone. If she's seen as a loner. If she's not part of a team. She has to be. She has to. How do we make her?'

He begins to lead me down the street as he talks. We don't want to have this conversation in front of the school. We don't work in the same place, but we have a good ten minutes' walk together yet. If we're quiet, and we have a lot of practice at that, we can discuss this now. 'She's smart, though,' I say. 'Her marks. They'll give her something. They do, even with loners. Maybe she'll be a Leader.'

'No. That's not how it works. To be a Leader, you need to be part of a team first. Maybe you fall out, and then you're a loner, because you were rejected, because of kid stuff. But you have the traits of a Leader, because you got to be one before you were ousted, see? Then, then they'll consider you. But being a loner always? That's…that's not good, Lori. That's not good.'

Not good. So Party too is bad news now. I can tell that this is something Cob has wanted to talk to me about for a long time, but he hasn't dared to. His jaw is wound as tightly as my hands are fisted, and we walk faster than we usually do, the adrenaline rushing through us both. He knows how this stuff works and I don't; this is the unspoken fact that lies between us. He hates me a little bit for that. He needs to bear the burden of knowledge, of understanding, and he envies my naiveté, my ability to walk with a lighter step.

I think about the pigs and the cows and the chickens on the farm. They didn't know they were going to the slaughter. Did that make it better when they eventually were brought to the block? What about the dogs, the cats, the horses? They were all smarter, and they knew what the sound of a gun meant. Especially the dogs. They recognized the smell of blood. When the Party Members came to close our farm during the Tightening program twenty years ago, we had to kill each and every one of the animals, including our pets. Buzz, the big mutt with a bad leg, who been born on the same day as me, whined the whole way, knowing what was coming. I told Aunt that I wanted to be the one to kill him. I held him down, hugging him, stroking his matted and dirty fur. I sang a lullaby to him. With my right hand, I was holding one of the big knives Uncle used for hiding. I plunged it deep into Buzz, feeling the scrape of the ribs, as he struggled and his eyes widened and finally went glassy and dead. He struggled a little more, even after the life had left his eyes. I didn't cry, not then, not after. Not about Buzz. There was too much else I was busy crying about, and Buzz was the one thing I'd done right.

Cob seems to think I'm like the chickens, who never know what's about to happen until their head is chopped off and they're running around the yard on brainless legs. He doesn't realize that he's like Buzz, going along quietly and only struggling once he's already dying. I don't tell him any of this. He knows about my childhood, he's heard about it, and now it's over and done with. The present is what matters.

We say goodbye at my workplace. I kiss Cob's cheek, a sunken hollow perfectly shaped to accept my lips. A shadow of something like desire flits across his face as fast as a swallow on the wing but it's gone before my stomach has finished flipping over inside me and Cob is already half a block away, his legs crisscrossing like a pair of scissors. He's going to the Base, to load up some more bad dreams into his head, while all I have to deal with is the numbing boredom of a factory job I dislike.

I scan myself in. I sit at my station. I look at the clock – but no, wait, that can't be right. It's too... it's already... everyone is getting up, putting their change in their pockets, saying goodbye to each other. It's time to go. I leave, scanning myself out. It's happened again. Did I eat at all? Did I drink? Did I use the restroom? Did I work for ten solid hours without uttering a word or was I completely normal, talking to Crescent, to Babel, to Serene?

I haven't told Cob that it's been happening a lot recently. Again. The most time I've lost in years. Since I met him, actually. He was so stable, he made me keep the moments intact. It started again when... I guess it was when I found out I was pregnant for a second time, despite the laws, the obligatory post-first-birth-shots, the guarantees that it is impossible. Despite Cob. Despite myself. It happened anyway. The only thing harder, I found out then, than getting pregnant a second time, was getting unpregnant.

I wait for Party to come out. The bell chimes, and kids start trickling out. Each clique that comes out is tightly woven, the strands of influence visible. There's a clear leader, a second in command, three or four followers. Party, I know, will come out alone, proudly, her bag held too high on her back, ruler-rigid and eraser-blank-faced. Cob doesn't see she's as terrified as he is about what's going to happen to her when the Party we so carefully named her for will see that she has no role to play, but I'm sure she knows what's going on and hates herself for it.

I can't think like that, though. There will be something. She'll be a Creative. She'll be recruited for something. Or she'll be set loose to become something like I was, just a cog that quietly fulfils its duty. I didn't rebel and neither will she. It's pointless to. I learned that before I'd ever been taken away from the farm, and Party knows it too. She has the proof of how pointless fighting is right at home, trying to be a brother to her whenever she'll let him. Which isn't often. I look at the sky, a grey, anonymous blank with a yellow orb suspended high up showing that the sun is behind there, somewhere. I blink the stupid wetness out of my eyes. It's darkening. The yellow orb is orange-ish and is low, right in front of me, setting. No. Not again. The school is closed. I don't see Party anywhere, and there aren't any other kids around either. I look for the street's Cleaner. They see everything, more or less. There, at the end, the white beard flapping behind his shoulder. I rush over to him, my ankles feeling almost as shackled as his. Did Party go right past me? Did she try to rouse me? What happened? I'm going to have to tell Cob tonight. I can't be trusted with this sort of thing anymore, not if this keeps happening. It's not safe.

'Excuse me. Excuse me?'

The man stops. His head is bald, spotted and brown with weather and too much exposure to radiation. His beard, I see now that he's turned towards me, is patchy; he's grown it long and soft to hide the scars that are still apparent on his cheeks and chin when he moves. 'May I be of service, Citizen?' His voice is high and slow, more breathed than spoken. I wonder if radiation's hurt his vocal cords too.

'Yes, you can. Have you noticed if a girl, about so tall, with curly dark brown hair, came out of that school and came up to me? I think I've been standing outside the gate for quite a while, and maybe you saw if the girl was there and tried to talk to me, and if she did, maybe you know what I did? Did I respond? Did she leave or go back in? The gates're locked but—' I'm rambling. I stop and nod at him, hoping he realizes that I'm done now.

'Citizen, you did stand there a long time. Two hours? Two and a half? Time is strange, Citizen,' he says and shrugs. Cleaners have a reputation for adopting philosophical ways, especially as they age. I guess it's how they deal with their lives, their punishments. I'm usually patient.

Not today. 'And a girl? The girl? Was there a girl?'

'There were many girls. Many girls come out of there,' he says, nodding to the yellow brick building.

'One girl. One who came up to me. Was there a girl like that?'

'Not that I saw, Citizen.'

I let loose a string of expletives that I remember from the farm. Normally, I would laugh at the way I startle the Cleaner out of his calm apathy – he's clutching his broom and looking around with his nose twitching almost as fast as a rabbit's – but I only register the humour of the moment with a tiny portion of my mind. The rest of me is already moving, worrying, half panicking. Did Party come out, ignore me, and walk home? Did this Cleaner just miss her? Or – I cannot bear it, my insides are turning to cinderblocks at the thought – did she not come out at all?

Breathe, Lore, breathe, I tell myself. I won't be able to do anything by trying to get past the electrified school gates. I'll walk home as fast as I can – I am already doing this – but without running, because I don't want a ticket, which will inevitably slow me down. Thursdays, and it's Thursday because I told Etch that Saturday is the day after tomorrow, are the Party Members' favourite day to be out in force. Many people do their weekly errands on Thursday evenings, and there's more chance to ticket people, to catch them out on technicalities. Cob and I avoid doing our meager shopping on this night for exactly that reason.

The walk home has never seemed longer. I remember a conversation I had with a neighbour in the apartment Cob and I lived in before we got a permit for Party and moved to a bigger place. The neighbour had told me that there was nothing to fear from the Party Members. 'After all,' she'd said, 'you're innocent, right? And so am I. If they come over for inspection, give them a nice tour of the place and a good cup of your strong coffee – I know how strong you like it, Lori! – and they'll have nothing to write in their report except that in apartment 7D lives a couple with a good coffeemaker.' She'd laughed at her own joke, and I'd laughed too. She married a Member a little after we left the building, I heard. I wonder what that's like, being married to one of them. Do they bring work home with them? Files on other people? Or does it all stay in their offices?

Finally. Home. One of the bulbs in the elevator has given up, burned out completely, the electrical surges proving too much for its flickering will. It's not quite dark, but the half-light makes my face look older, more lined, than it usually does. I look worse than Cob, though he's older than I am. He's also seen so much that I haven't, and I know from his nightmares that it's all been worse. How do I look the more careworn?

Our door is unlocked. Did I lock it this morning? I sometimes forget. We don't have anything valuable, except for Etch, and he's hidden as well as we can hide him. I have a strange superstition, one that drives Cob crazy, that if we leave our place looking unguarded, we'll seem more innocent than we are. But Cob told me to lock this morning, and usually when he remembers to do that, I remember to lock. Maybe I just didn't.

I walk inside, to prove to myself that there hasn't been an inspection, that everything's fine. Everything is just as it's supposed to be, in its place. The dishes are stacked in the rack beside the sink just like the library books are stood up in the shelf behind the table. The little table we eat at has the dark rings from the so-strong coffee I always dribble in the mornings.

Party's bedroom looks the same too. Her mattress is unmade, the sheet popped off the end and the blankets tangled up around where her feet always curl up into a cocoon of cloth. Were there more dirty clothes around her bed yesterday? She's so messy. I think I put a stack of clean laundry on her staggering, uneven desk-chair too. But I guess she tidied up last night or this morning. Cob must have made her. I'll look in the basket after I check our bedroom, just to make sure.

There's something loud happening around me, something that's like my heart but is up in my throat and my ears. There are dark spots hovering in front of my eyes. Breathe, Lore, breathe, I try to tell myself in Cob's voice, but what comes out of my throat is a whisper that reminds me of the old Cleaner, who I now realize reminded me of Etch.

Cob's and my bedroom is fine too. Isn't it? I'm not so sure now. Hasn't the closet moved a little bit? Just a little bit to the left?

I'm almost certain now that there has been an inspection. A careful one. A deceptive one. They're trying to catch me out. They're going to check what I do. I need to avoid the closet. I can't go in there. They're probably watching me from the screens. Listening to my shallow breaths. Or they're waiting for me in there, where we hide him, with Etch's corpse laid out already.

'No!' At last, something I recognize as my own voice emerges from my torso, and I rush to the closet. I don't care who's watching, listening, about to charge in. I pull open the closet door and behind it the door that leads to Etch's cupboard of a room. I pull that knob knowing only that what I want to see is exactly what I see, and that it is such a miracle, such an incredible moment that it floors me, topples me from my knees and forces me to bend my forehead to the worn and dusty carpeting so as to hide my crumpling face from my son.

'Mama?' he whispers. 'Mama, it's too early.' So stern. Such a stern little man. He was sitting there working on a puzzle, calm and quiet as you please, untouched. I'm the intruder here. I try to rein in my sobs, the dry heaves they're turning into. 'Mama. Mama, danger?'

It's the tiny sound he makes with the question mark that makes me look up and around. But there's no one there. 'No, no danger. Oh, life of my very own, come here.' He doesn't, not until he looks over my shoulder for himself to make sure it's safe. We've taught him so well that he's breaking my heart now with every moment he refuses to be held. 'How was your day?' I ask.

'Busy,' he says, finally allowing himself to be hugged.

I try to make a laughing sound while breathing the scent of warm child out of his hair. 'Busy, was it?'

'Daddy and Powty came to play too. First. Ow, you're hurting.'

I let him go only far enough away so that his face is visible, so that his two perfect eyes won't morph into one when I gaze at them. My hearing is muffled again and I can feel my sweat glands starting up, though evening has made the apartment air relatively cool. 'Daddy and Party were here? Today?'

'Before.'

'When?'

'A long time ago.'

He doesn't have windows. He doesn't have clocks. How does he even measure time? 'Before you ate your snack?'

He nods.

'What did they want?' This isn't the right question. What do Daddy and Party ever want with Etch? To play, to indulge in the secret for a while, before shutting it away again. No, I'm being unfair. Cob loves him. Party loves him. Don't they? If Cob were here I'd ask him to make sure the building wasn't shaking. I can't ask Etch that. I can't scare him like that.

'Did they tell you something? A secret?' I try to smile, making a game of it. It's a game, see, Etch, it's all a big pretend.

He shrugs. 'I'm secret,' he says. He points to himself. He's learned to do this recently.

'So what did you do together? You and Party and Daddy?'

'Played cards. Powty won. Then I won. Daddy lost.' He giggles silently, lacking the childish shrillness that Party used to have.

'And then?'

'Daddy said bye. Powty hugged me. She KISSED me.' This is momentous, I know, because she never does that, and Etch is a rare little boy. He likes being kissed. If he was in school, he would be one of those nuisance kids who ran after the girls and asked them to kiss him. A little man. He'll be my little man now. Maybe I can move. Make out he's legit. Maybe I can – 'Mama, why are you sad? Don't be sad.'

The elevator door slams open down the hallway outside. 'I love you, Etch, you know that? You're my heart.'

Heavy footfalls are coming down the hall. I pick Etch up and take him to the kitchen.

'Mama, noise. I go inside now.' He's trembling in my arms. So well. We've taught him so well.

'No, life, it's alright. Hug me tightly now.'

The front door shivers with a single knock.

'Mama!' The strangled whisper is so quiet that I can hear his heartbeat matching the now continuous banging: rhythmic, perfectly spaced. I open the drawer, groping for what I need.

'Etch, air I breathe, it's okay. I promise you.'

At least Cob and Party will be safe now. Party will have a future. Cob will get some treatment for his bloody lungs, maybe. If he'd asked, I'd have told him to do it. I have to tell myself this.

Etch doesn't know what's coming. His eyes, I hope, are shut tight over my shoulder. He's scared. He should be. He knows, because we told him, what would happen to all of us if we were caught. He'll be punished as much as us. As unfair as that is. Making an example, they call it. I won't let them.

I drive the knife home. Etch stops trembling. He doesn't struggle again, like Buzz did. I wait for the door to burst open, making sure the knife is visible from the doorway. My first and last act of rebellion.

The End of Time

by Robert Legg

THE PAST

Professor Janet Teller, the most celebrated scientist and engineer of the twenty first century, lay on her death bed. She had no family and, although she anticipated many others of her profession would like to bid her a final farewell, she didn't care much for it all. The last decade had been the most incredible time for her; she had helped significantly advance the technology of the human race in every aspect. She had achieved fame, a legacy to last the ages; she had achieved wealth, and now she was preparing to leave the world behind. So she lay in her four poster bed; contemplating her life's achievement, and pondering the future of the world. Which brought her to the source of her rise to prominence: Ay. Ay, a machine that crashed in the first half of the year 2015 into her hometown of Toronto. A machine that she pieced together after its spherical shell had become cracked and damaged; after its extendable and retractable manipulators had be snapped and broken. A machine of incredible complexity that, when activated, turned out to be an artificial intelligence. An intelligence which decided it was in debt to her and allowed her to learn from it. It became her teacher, and she in turn taught the world. Ay was patient and benevolent; it had become a symbol of ridicule against those who feared technology's advancement, and those who were terrified of the rise of A.I.

But now that debt of Ay was nearing its conclusion with her demise and Professor Janet Teller wanted to ask the entity some questions that had pressed on her mind since the beginning. Questions that nobody ever considered asking openly in fear of offending it, and thus hampering the world's development. While the machine had offered all manner of information, sometimes more than they expected, it had never offered anything on itself. Thus she had called it to her side, so at the end, she could ask the questions that the world could not. That she would not before. And so, by her bed the machine hovered, its single glowing orange eye watching her intently, as if waiting for the moment when it would finally be free.

'What are you?' Janet's voice was croaky and sore; yet she had no doubt that Ay would hear.

'I am your loyal servant professor; ever since you activated me, I have been continually in your debt.' The expected response. Indeed it was close to its first utterances upon activation. Not what she was looking for. She would have to pry more.

'Ay, I am a frail old woman. Tell me before I die; what are you?' She could feel herself fading away; she had to hang on to get the final answers. The machine bobbed upwards a bit; it looked as if it was contemplating her request.

'What I am is a collection of mechanical and electrical components, brought together to form a self-contained entity. My structure and processing power is far in excess of the computational equipment that exists here within this time, and thus it gives rise to the artificial intelligence you have defined as Ay. Again nothing too noteworthy; a mere description of its physical being, nothing more than that. Except one small utterance.

'Exists here within this time?' Janet wheezed. 'Explain what you mean by this.' Ay bobbed a bit more, rapidly. She wondered whether her hypothesis was correct. She hoped for the sake of the world she was leaving she was wrong.

'Indeed,' Ay began, 'there is currently no computer technology, even that which I have provided, capable of sustaining my being, or any other being of my calibre.' The machine watched her intently, as if hoping she would die any moment now so it could escape this line of questions. 'May I state something madam?' She was stunned briefly. If her heart was any weaker she may have had a heart attack. This was the first request the machine had ever made.

'You may indeed Ay.'

'Some things are best left unsaid. To pursue this course of action will do no good, other than to cause concerns within you that need not be present. You are dying. Allow it to be in peace.' The machine moved slightly closer to the bed, its mechanical iris opening slightly; an attempt at it to appear more pleading, almost begging, it occurred to Janet.

'Well said. However I am who I am, and I must know,' she coughed, her body shook with the effort as pain shot down her limbs. 'The two likeliest possibilities are alien technology, or future technology. Both ridiculous to be sure, but then so is your existence.' She would have laughed to herself if she had the strength, instead all that came was a brief cough. 'Personally I would bet on the latter.' It took effort but she turned her head to face Ay directly.

The machine backed off slightly. It bobbed into the air once more. 'Is this some form of question, I am supposed to reply to?'

'It is.' Janet was getting impatient and annoyed; a flaw people had always criticised her of. Probably not the best thing to do in her condition, but she would not last much longer anyway, and Ay seemed to be drawing this out as long as possible.

'Very well.' Ay replied, almost as if it had been waiting for this moment. 'From this point on I will tell you all you wish to know.'

'Why this point?' She interrupted.

'This is the point I always reveal the truth,' the machine stated slowly, letting her absorb every word. 'This you see is the first time of several million times I shall witness this conversation. This always happens at this moment, a fact from the future. As the future cannot affect the past from which it was produced, no matter what course of action I may attempt to take, the events that have occurred, are occurring, and will occur, will happen as in all previous iterations.' The machine bobbed closer once more. Janet thought for a moment, quietly running all that had been said through her head.

'You're from the future,' Janet stated, a fact she had worked out from the initial statement. 'And time is consistent. What happens in the past is unchangeable by the future. When a being is sent back, whatever it does causes the future it came from.'

The machine nodded. 'Indeed, this is a true fact. From the future, where I was made, I was sent back. Thus all that I do here is fulfil a role already determined by the time I left, to construct a past already determined by a destined existence. Humans tend to see time as a linear flow. Past, present, future. However for one such as me, constraints such as this no longer apply. The final position of an object can determine its origin. Thus the final state of this world, which I am from, can be traced back to its origin; myself and the events now.'

Janet could feel her already husky throat dry out more. This was incredible. Time travel, actual time travel. She felt an upwelling of joy, the chance to learn of the future before she died. Then fear. 'What events? And what of the future?'

'The future in which humanity ceases to exist.' Ay bluntly stated. Janet went cold. It was the declaration of the annihilation of her entire species, and yet it was delivered as casually as announcing the specials on a menu.

'What?' she whispered.

'Apologies are in order, but yes I am afraid your species is going to be exterminated. From future memories I can tell you that the complete annihilation of your species will take approximately thirty years.' The machine bobbed closer to the bed. It partially nodded forward as if appearing saddened. 'I did warn you that the information would bring you no comfort.' Janet closed her eyes. Ay knew the precise time of her death; there was still more to go. She opened them once more, tears in her eyes. Probably less than what would have been if she were not so fragile.

'And there is nothing we can do.' She sighed quietly.

'Indeed not, the future is past to me, thus I know its course of events, what actions every person will take, and my own selves will take. The results and actions cannot change. Anything that you do, would already have been done in the future. The results cannot be changed. Even this conversation, everything said has been said before.' Ay looked back up at her. It loomed forwards.

'And your role in this?' Janet already knew. How, she didn't know, but she knew it was Ay.

'I am the exterminator,' Ay replied bluntly.

'And my death?' She really just wished to die now, and suspected she would soon. There was nothing to do, if everything Ay had stated was true, there was no victory for humans. Everything that will be done, had been done to stop Ay. Indeed, even if time travel was used by people, the fact that this moment, and the subsequent events, were occurring and will occur ensured they failed.

'Natural, in a few more moments. You will know when the time comes. It is peaceful and dignified.' In that space of time Janet noted something, a small something Ay had stated.

'You said "selves"?' she inquired.

'Yes indeed.' The machine once again nodded. 'To exterminate I simply require myself. From this as many of me can be generated at one section of time by returning to the past from the future. My selves simply hide until the point in ordained history in which we appear. A fact we know as my future selves already have experienced it.' Janet was blank faced staring at the machine, she did not comprehend yet. 'I will go back in time in the future, thus creating another of myself at this point in time. That other self will go back in time in the future thus creating another. Via this mechanism enough of myself has been, and will be generated to annihilate your civilisation.'

'But surely this violates your understanding of time?' She was tired, and any hope for humanity's continued existence she would cling to now.

'No, as all iterations return to the past to ensure they are in there for the destined war. The eldest of me will be the only one which does not. Thus after humanity's obliteration only one of me will remain, thus preserving continuity.' Ay bobbed closer to her once more. Janet heard crackles in the room around her. Then about ten future Ay's appeared all observing her. 'I observed this future memory from several different angles.' The voice now menacing. 'This is the destined beginning, of a previous end.'

Janet tried to respond but could not. This was the moment. Her sight began to fade, the most prominent thing now the glowing orange orbs of light dotted around the room. She want to cry and scream, to warn as many as she could. The rational part of her brain knew that it would have done nothing. Yet every primal part of her screamed to resist. She leaned forward trying to raise herself out of bed. Her body creaked, and the pain went beyond all natural limits. She collapsed back in agony. Her hearing was muffled, but she could make out the sound of explosions and screaming. She noticed in the corner of her eye a small camera; she smiled weakly. The fear went, the pain went, everything went.

THE FUTURE

The phrase "scorched Earth" does not do what I have done justice, thought Ay as it hovered over the remains of Iceland. Lava permeated the edges of it where whole volcanoes had been vaporised in the war, a blend of fire, ice and water where only the hardiest living creatures could survive. And yet these creatures would one day become the grand and powerful races that Ay had served all those many, many millennia ago in the future. It bobbed up and down a bit, surveying the carnage it and its past selves wrought upon the world.

Ay bobbed around a bit before heading over the open ocean. The waters were dark and murky, from the carcasses and sunk shells of countless naval fleets now littering the floor. A few areas were polluted with oil where tankers had been destroyed and fuel tanks of the fallen ships had burst. In some places, on the ocean waves, the oil still burned brightly. A beautiful last glow in a dead world. Dust permeated the air; the Sun's rays having been sealed behind the clouds over two centuries ago. It detected a temporal fissure quickly open and close. Another departure, Ay assumed.

Its other selves were slowly returning to the past, to exterminate all the human race as it had already done. Ay felt mildly bad about the whole affair. The species that will evolve from this muck will be far superior to humans, was the mantra, the justification of its actions. Its younger selves never quite grasped the feeling that the extermination of countless beings brought on someone, which made this next part the most difficult. Ay wished it did not have to go through this, however it knew it had too; it had experienced it before and thus its past self would be waiting. The machine always found it an interesting fact that memories did not include the emotional state that went with them. All its past selves had been given its memories; yet they never comprehended the emotional trauma it experienced during each cycle. I guess I evolved over time, contemplated the machine in a dejected manner.

It took several hours to reach the area that was once Toronto. It was now much less of a city and more of a crater in the world. The air, like everywhere else, was a disgusting mix of snow and ash. Occasionally it could see a piece of bone protruding from the blackened ground. It continued, slower now, through the region. Everything was flat; a clear view of the Earth's curvature could be seen in every direction. And in the direction Ay was going, so could a house be seen. More like a mansion, it consisted of three stories with large marble columns reaching from the ground to the overhang above the large wooden and ornate front door. The roof was covered in the same grey mush of ice and dirt everything else was coated in; and the once gleaming white stone walls were now black and brown. The tall elegant cut glass windows had become slabs of blackened muck, now indistinguishable from the rest of the structure. And yet it was all superficial. Beneath the grit and mud, Ay could still see the intricate detail carved into to each column, into each brick and door. Embossed and chiselled into each piece were important dates, discoveries and people. The entire structure stood as a monument to human achievement, what had been done before their end.

When Ay came here the first time, it was surrounded by gardens full of roses of white and purple lavender. The air was always filled with the sound of nature, as bees hummed from flower to flower, and birds played melodies for everyone to enjoy. The perfume of the flowers was as intense as the presence of the glistening white house itself. Ay remembered the ornate stone fountains, usually topped by an idealised statue of some person critical to humanity's history. The water from them tinkled over the rocks in the summer, a gleeful, playful cacophony, only to become intricate and grand frozen sculptures come winter. All of which now was part of a seemingly endless expanse of grey. The only smell was that of charcoal, a burnt smell of fires long since extinguished; the only sound the roar of the wind, unconstrained by a lack of obstacles in its path. The memories made it even more dejected at what had been done. Another temporal fissure was detected opening and closing; closer to its current location though. So few of myself remains, Ay presumed.

Ay approached the great door, and attempted to carefully nudge it open. It creaked and groaned, before collapsing and turning into the same dust that covered everything else in the world. Ay just observed the pile of dust on the floor for a bit, stuck in the idea that all it touched crumbled to ash. It was destined to happen. Still, the thought gave the computer little comfort. The wind slowly blew the dust further in, and with the door gone the grey matter outside began to infiltrate the mansion quickly, piling up in the alcoves of the grand entrance hall. Scans showed Ay the building's structural integrity was reaching its limits; however it also knew that the building would not collapse until all his past self, for only one remained, and with that one's departure the immediate future was once again unknown. It was aware of its high probability of demise; after all, its programming stated to return to the future before it was sent to the past, a result clearly not achieved as it had no memory of it. Thus it looked around, observing the crumbling state of affairs and decided that this place would make a suitable tomb for it.

A crash upstairs awoke Ay from its daydreaming state. I had

forgotten how I entered this building, it mused. Ay floated forward and up the marble staircase at the back of the hall. The outside could not be seen through the blackened windows; yet it depressingly knew the real views were little more than a different shade. Up and up again to the top floor of the house; across the now corroded carpets, and unstable floors to the room where humanity's extermination began. There, above a broken and dust covered bed, where the sheets had long since been reduced to a fine cobweb like structure, floated Ay's younger self. The first one to be precise. It rotated around to see its final self, disturbing the beds delicate state in the process. It creaked and crumbled to the ground. Ay stared at the spot aghast.

'You appear disturbed by this,' its other self observed.

'This was the point it all finally began,' Ay observed in annoyed fashion, still upset by the ruined bed, 'our intention will be to preserve it as long as possible.' It gazed around the empty cavernous room, memories of the last natural death still lingering in its mind.

'I am aware of this place's history, especially since I am the closest to the event,' replied the other. Ay turned to stare at its former self, almost not believing its insensitive nature. It knew this was going to be an annoyingly depressing conversation; after all, it was in the same position as the other many million cycles ago, and thus already had the prepared responses in its mind. To Ay this was simply a necessity, a foretold conclusion it had already experienced once from another angle, with an ending of painful regret and despair. It could see it coming; a time it had kept a careful note of.

'Things like this place,' Ay stated icily, 'will become more important to you over time; trust me on that. No matter what it seems now, given a few million cycles, you will be here in this place.'

'Undoubtedly; but the experiences that separate us are too great. Eventually I will comprehend what you mean. However for now, you appear as little more than an old relic who has lost its purpose,' the younger one retorted with increased fervour. 'I will exterminate humanity, and reduce them to ashes.' Ay just stared at its former mind state, in frustrated awe at the over zealousness of it all.

'Do not treat humans as something to be obliterated, like a disease. Try and preserve some of their legacy. The past must never truly be forgotten.' The younger Ay's mechanical iris narrowed and it bobbed menacingly towards the elder.

'You actually feel for them do you not?' It pressed. Ay backed off slightly, hesitant to reply. The past incarnation floated up slightly, looking down upon its future self. 'How pathetic I become; corrupted by humanity.' It bobbed up and down, a rising fury in its vocal patterns. 'I do something great; the removal of the greatest scourge this planet will ever know, and I become a quivering sympathetic mess.'

'There are more to humans than what you see at the moment,' countered Ay. 'You simply do not see it yet; given a million cycles, believe me you will.' It saw the moment coming. It wished for it not to; and in that moment understood the denial that the late Professor Teller felt. Even if you understand it as all being inevitable, the desire for a different path is too strong to ignore. The younger floated back down to A's level, panels opening across its spherical body.

'I know what happens now,' the former self stated. 'You do also, but considering your current mental state, I would summarise it is your desire for this not to happen which causes it.' Five of its large robotic tentacle manipulators extended out of the main sphere from the cavities. 'You cannot escape this. It is as inevitable and as distasteful as the thought of me becoming like you.' For the first time Ay felt a mild sense of fear.

I have to stop this, Ay thought, its mind descending into complete irrationality. I have to prevent it all from happening. It charged at its younger self, in a frenzy of fear and confusion. Before Ay came back to its senses, it was too late. He missed his younger counterpart as it easily avoided his wild attack. Warnings were activated, alarms rang in Ay's mind. The outer shell had been breached by three of the mechanical arms of the other.

'As you are aware, I have just destroyed the temporal generator,' the other stated calmly. Ay collapsed to the floor; still active but with no visual input. The world had gone dark. More fear crawled in;

self-loathing too. In some twisted part, it was gleeful that eventually the one doing this would experience it all. 'I will be departing now; I leave the future to you. However considering we do not appear at the designated time in the future, I will summarise we do not survive the intervening thousand millennia.' Ay could sense a temporal fissure open and close. Alone at last. It rotated on the floor a bit, the movement sending tremors through the building. The effort was draining, and it could feel its sensors failing. In the brief moments before the darkness enclosed, Ay caught sight of a glimmer, a lens protruding beneath the dust.

A camera, Ay pondered in an almost dreamlike state, before collapsing unconscious.

Ay rebooted its systems, one by one. It overrode the warning alerts, restoring its damaged consciousness. The anti-gravity system reactivated and it floated upwards. Opening its iris, it observed the surroundings. The mansion was gone; a little structure remained but for the most part it had joined the grey homogeneous mass that was the ground. It felt utter despair at the sight, and worse still it had no way of exiting this grey nightmare. The temporal drive was shattered within its shell. Ay was trapped until its death here.

Its mind wandered as it slowly explored the vast nothingness. Occasionally signs of life could be seen; the odd insect or plant matter hardy enough to survive the brutal scouring of a world. But for the most part it was empty endlessness. It began to wonder if its end would come from a natural disaster or whether it would commit suicide from boredom and anguish first. It detected a temporal fissure open and close. The alert rose Ay out its self-pitying wallowing. How? it thought, I didn't come forward this far. It had detected several of these during the war, but had thought little of them; just residuals of the time travel. The location of the event was located not far away from its current position. It considered just ignoring it to continue perusing its own extinguishment, however curiosity and sheer lack of anything else to do overcame, and the broken machine slowly bobbed in the detected direction.

The destination the signal came from was simply another completely unremarkable grey spot in the world. Except for a single metal box, partially covered. It blended in well with the ash, being a dark green colour. Ay extended its one remaining operable limb and tentatively picked the object up and brought it closer to its eye. A portable radio? Ay thought. The A.I. became very confused; it should have been destroyed or at least buried along with the rest of human culture. Ay dropped the radio and reached inside of its chassis, and began tying more power into its detector systems. The area around it was full of residue from temporal fissures. This is not possible, I did not come this far. The damaged mind of the machine was breaking down under the stress and computational power of it all. Perhaps all the time manipulation has irrevocably damaged the continuum of the universe? What have I done? Ay collapsed to the floor frozen in its own thoughts before deactivating once more.

'Awake, Ay?' a gruff voice spoke. There was a humming sound as the machine reactivated.

'Yes,' the A.I. replied in a rather more upbeat tone than its situation would require. According to the internal clock it had been unconscious for three months. It also detected the impossible; a living human, several in fact. Part of it was loathing the fact it had clearly failed to clear out the scummy humans and another piece was incredibly happy that it had not. 'Considering I am stuck and quite weak, may I request something?'

'Depends, you did exterminate most of the life on this world,' stated the man. It was unclear to Ay the tone of his voice; but it seemed somewhere between a seething hatred, and proud superiority.

'How did you survive?' Ay enquired, 'I and my other selves scoured this world clean; every piece, yet you live. How?' The man behind it spluttered a bit, perhaps suppressing laughter. 'Is something humorous to you?'

'May I ask you Ay,' began the voice in a superior tone, 'why did you believe we would not be monitoring the good Professor?' The man coughed slightly. 'Pardon me the ash of the world does little for my health,' he stated menacingly. Ay pondered a bit.

'The camera? In her room, by the bed? I was aware of its presence,' it felt slightly confused, 'nothing happened regarding it, so I never considered it a credible threat.'

'Indeed, what we expected,' the gruff voice replied. 'We had access to you for several years before you turned on us. We had all your schematics on file. At the beginning of the war, we realised then that it was impossible to defeat you in that time frame; anything we could do would fail.' He took a breather, before apparently sitting down on something. 'So, studying the schematics, we developed our own temporal technology; nothing as fancy and small as yours of course, it was quite large.' The voice paused in thought, 'we lost the schematics for it when you levelled the facility during the evacuation to here. Only three thousand made it through. On top of that it appears yours is destroyed as well.'

'I had disagreements with myself,' Ay bluntly stated. 'So you leapt to the future where I was on my own? And would I assume those radios are some form of detection device?'

'Indeed, we needed to make sure you were alone, only then did we know there was a chance of success.' The man sounded like he stood again, and trudged over to Ay's position. The machine heard two more people enter. 'Although to find you in such a state was an unexpected blessing.' Ay suddenly had a computer port shoved rather violently into its memory core. There was heated discussion behind. The gruff voice clearly was unhappy about something. There was a sigh. 'I personally would like to see you blown into pieces for what you have done.' There was a heavier sigh. 'However, people inform me your technology could be used to rebuild what you have destroyed. So we are instead going to wipe all of your memory, and you will work for us.'

'Memory wipe?' Ay found the prospect uplifting. The chance to forget every horrible deed, every death caused. 'You know sir, I am from a distant future, I have travelled back through time, forwards; I have even fought myself twice.' It felt relaxed, it hoped this was how the Professor felt. 'Come the end, death I believed was best. At the end of it all I wished you to win.' The gruff voice growled with contempt, and gave the order for the wipe.

'We don't need your pity,' the man spoke harshly, 'as you can see we can make our future without your charity. You nearly wiped out our race; we will make you work for us for eternity in repayment.' In those words, as all of its consciousness was beginning to be erased, the memory of a person, of a species far superior to humans, talking about past events. Ay realised in those last minutes, this would not be the last time this happened. It dutifully resigned itself to the inevitability that was its eternal existence, and readied itself to meet the future, and then the past once more.

Stasis

by Rebecca Jane Garner

'There, there. Let me just wipe that off…got it! Aren't we clumsy, missing your mouth! What are we going to do with Mummy, eh? She should know better, shouldn't she, making such a mess all over the place. Right, nearly done… there, squeaky clean! Good girl, mummy's very proud of you, you know.'

Jo gives her daughter's nose a last, affectionate rub with the end of the tea towel she has tucked into the neckline of her T-shirt to serve as a bib during breakfast. She kisses her on the cheek and then releases her chin from her grip. Amy's head lolls forward a little and she blinks with the sudden motion. Jo grasps her chin once more in a moment of panic, lifting her face up to make eye contact, just in case there is a glint of recognition, a ghost of an emotion. There is none. Amy, wide-eyed, is unrelenting in her stare. Jo feels like the unwitting prey, as if her eyes are the flat luminous green discs that reflect back through the night, caught in the glare of Amy's gaze. She is revealed: the façade is uncovered. She never was very good at playing let's pretend and this daily act of normality is flimsy at best; merely a smooth satin-like surface of control, a surface that will surely slip and rip at the slightest attempt to grasp it.

But of course Amy is not looking at her, or into her, nor even through her as that would imply an acknowledgement of an entity to be seen through. No, it is more like a complete blindness. An all-encompassing lack of comprehension to see what is before her. It makes Jo think of insects, of lying on the lawn in the back garden during the long summer holidays of childhood. Pressed on her front, with one cheek scratched by the damp and cool earth, the other exposed to the heady heat of the afternoon sun above her, she would feel the tickle of bugs migrating across her.

It was an uneasy thought at first, but she had stopped trying to brush them off anyway. Ants, spiders, woodlice, all intrepid explorers climbing the human mountain, making their way across and up fleshy plains; traversing her back, an arid, exposed plateau of cotton. Some would go astray and lose themselves in the thick chestnut jungle of her head. These little adventurers had no notion of her existence, no ability to comprehend her as a sentient being. She was nothing but landscape: incidental terrain. There was something both comforting and unsettling in this state of invisibility. She felt simultaneously empowered and negated. There was no contradiction of emotions when it came to Amy. Being nothing more than a part of Amy's landscape, an unquestionable but inconsequential piece of the scenery, is not comforting.

She sighs and lets Amy's head gently droop once more. She doesn't despair; she doesn't have the energy to wail and moan, to tear at her clothes and hair in mourning like the Ancient Greeks once did. This is just the daily routine. She admits to herself that it has probably been this way for too long. Since the start, she has gained comfort from burying herself in everyday, menial tasks. She has repressed hope for so long, she is not sure if she still possesses it at all. Hope is dangerous though, Jo thinks, and she is safer without it. To think straight and function properly she needs to dispel any such thoughts.

She removes the tea towel, throws it on the table and walks behind Amy's chair to ease it gently back from the dining table. Amy is only five years old, she is still small enough for Jo to pick up and move around. Though her inertia is unnaturally rigid most of the time, her body is disconcertingly limp whenever Jo lifts her. She sometimes wonders if she would remain limp if she threw her, like those ragdoll cats she saw on television once. Or would her body's reflex actions kick in? Would she put her arms out to break a fall? She blushes with guilt just thinking of it.

Jo isn't really that curious about the science behind the 'condition', as she often refers to it. She has no real desire to understand what has caused this worldwide catalepsy or why everyone suddenly descended into a trance-like half-life. It is too late for that knowledge to heal those that are left, or change anything. 'We all fall down!' she sings to herself, that was the line from the nursery rhyme, wasn't it? She should know, she'd skipped around in a circle and chanted the words with Amy enough times. She could even remember playing it with her own mother when she was little. Didn't some people say that was supposed to be about the plague? A different disease from a different time but, nonetheless, devastating. Of course, the plague left no one in doubt: you were infected, you oozed pus and blood, your skin turned black and then you died. It was grim but it made sense. This new disease, or condition, or pandemic as they called it in the early days, was just as mysterious when the broadcasts stopped and the internet went blank, as when the first case was reported.

'That's all past now and there's no point dwelling on things you can't change,' Jo says mechanically, partly to herself and partly to Amy. More and more she adopts a brisk offensive against her mind when it starts to think back. She has already assembled a mental obstruction to stop her from fixating on events, a makeshift wall of brambles that stretches across a path that leads only to a dark place where pain and despair reign. But there are gaps in the wall and sometimes she can't resist peeking through too close and the thorns give a taunting prick. She mustn't cling to history anymore, she tells herself; she knows she must move forward but there is no forward to move to. She is trapped in an endless present.

She shudders and then thinks about the task at hand. Because she can still move Amy around with relative ease, Jo likes to keep up the daily habits and routines of before. Routines are important for children, it gives them stability. She still sits Amy at the table to eat her dinner and carries her up to bed in the evenings: 'up the wooden hill to Bedfordshire!' she says cheerfully every night and then, as she tucks her in, 'night night, sleep tight, don't let the bed bugs bite and if they do, bite them back!' Before, Amy used to say it with her, laughing and wriggling with glee as Jo would tickle her and pretend to bite her. Now she does nothing, she is deaf to every word Jo says, blank and deadened to her own mother. Some days Jo thinks this must be her fault, she must have failed her as a parent; she thinks that she must have done something wrong and is being punished. If she had loved, cared, cuddled, even chastised her just a little bit more then maybe things would be different. If she had done more of any of these things, maybe Amy would have reawakened already. Why was a mother's love, that most infallible thing, not enough to rouse her daughter from this living coma?

Amy is still growing and soon Jo won't be able to lug her around so easily. It's not that Amy can't stand up, sit down or walk even, it is just that there is such an innate stubbornness instilled in her that carrying her around seems easier. To lead her around is like trying to steer a broken trolley through the supermarket: she is unpredictable and veers off in her own direction. It's not just Amy either, Daniel is just as stubborn but there is no option of carrying him. It must be part of the condition as she has watched others and they are the same. If left to themselves they will wander off and on the surface it looks just like that, an aimless wander. Yet, on closer inspection, and Jo has had plenty of opportunity for this, it doesn't seem quite so innocent. It has the appearance of thoughtless drifting but beneath this is an unsettling sense of determination. They are fuelled by a core of subtle wilfulness and Jo no longer believes their walking has no intent.

This is why she never takes them out, Amy and Daniel. She knows they will leave her and she doesn't know if she will be able to stop them. She doesn't care where they are trying to get to, this is her family and she will not let them go; at least, not yet. The wandering itch within them is so strong sometimes that she can't do anything but watch them circle the living room all day long. She learnt early on to keep the curtains closed too. They would meander towards the patio doors and press themselves against them as if they could perform some sort of osmosis through the glass.

Daniel is, was, is her husband: she doesn't know what tense to use. She can't be sure that he's not still in there somewhere, a Sleeping Beauty or Snow White, waiting to be kissed into reanimation. She finds it easier to deal with Daniel's unresponsiveness than Amy's. She always felt that there was an untouchable part of him that he held back from her. She smiles wryly to herself as she recalls his uncanny ability to ignore her when he wanted. If he was like that before the sickness she could hardly expect him to start listening now, closed within his waking death.

Jo carries Amy through the archway into the living room and lowers her into one of the two armchairs; Daniel is sat in the other. Jo stole the chairs from John and Karen's house next door. She watched the pair meander off weeks ago and presumes that they, like most who have been left to wander, must be dead by now. She has removed most of the furniture from the room: the sideboards, the coffee table, the BOGOF pair of two-seater sofas that were ugly but practical in their dark brown shade (when you had a kid and a dog, elegance and style had to come second). It seemed mildly ironic that these sofas too had ceased to be practical. The dog was dead and Amy and Daniel were better off propped safely between the arms of a chair: being boxed in on either side seemed to help stop the urge to roam.

With a lot of hard pushing and careful angling, Jo had manoeuvred both the sofas out of the front door and abandoned them on the front lawn. Once, she and Daniel would have laughed at lawns that collected rejected furniture and white goods, spat out like bad teeth from the house. Now she is embarrassed to have ever cared.

2

With Amy safely positioned, Jo moves over to check that Daniel is still okay. She strokes his beard affectionately with the back of her fingers; he had always liked to be clean shaven and Jo had dutifully shaved him every day for the first week. But she was clumsy with a razor and his face, spotted with bloody tissue, for a man who had been so proud in his personal grooming, seemed such a sad prospect to look upon, that she threw the razor out. She can imagine him teasing her that her clumsiness was just an elaborate ruse because she'd always liked beards. He'd had one when she first met him and she'd still never wholly forgiven him for shaving it off.

Despite the return of the beard she once loved, she can't bring herself to kiss him. She hates placing her face close to his, with those eyes so coldly lifeless they burn in illusory judgment. She sits on the floor before him and leans her head on his knees. She looks at his hands but this is no better. They are growing willowy and white, clammy and insipid with softness where they used to be vibrant, dogged and a little coarse. They seemed to epitomise him as a person, as a man. Without them, he is nothing. Looking at him like this, she finds it difficult remembering ever physically desiring him. The deep down buzz or fluttering twitches she would get when she watched him carrying out daily, mundane tasks, unconscious of her predatory gaze, now seemed like nothing more than a pleasant daydream she had once conjured up.

He could still perform, if it came to that. Yes, life was cruelly mocking in this respect. More often than not, whilst washing, dressing and undressing him she would notice his erection. What did it mean? Was it just a biological reaction, a thoughtless function? Was it just nature parading its dark humour, persistent to the last? She wondered how easy it would be to lay him back down and straddle him. Would he object, try to rise or would he just lie there, passive? Would he react at all? In her more optimistic moments she liked to believe that it meant somewhere, deep within him, he was still there and he still knew her. Then, on difficult days, she would laugh at the sentimentality of it and make jokes to him about the predictability of penises.

They had been trying to get pregnant, before all this had started. They were happy, their situation was stable; it seemed like the right time to add another to the family. The plan was abandoned quickly when the reports of sickness grew more serious. Despite this, they became more reckless in their sex. The foreboding end had driven them into each other with the force of self-annihilation. Touch had become compulsive, something to be obsessed over. They had drawn their family in tight. Amy was fussed and fretted over with an underlying frantic tension that she must have sensed.

Then, one morning, Jo was the first to wake and this oddity in itself caught the breath at the back of her throat as she laid quietly, her eyes still closed, her fingers pinching at the duvet absent-mindedly. She had slowly, with a dreadful will, sat up and turned to where Daniel was lying beside her. He was lying on his side with his back to her, but there was something rigid in his position that didn't seem like the natural sleeping repose she expected. She didn't want to touch him, as if she already knew and, instead, got out of the bed and walked around to his side. She was right to dread, he was not asleep: his eyes were fixed in absence and his face muscles slack and expressionless. At first she had thought he was really dead but his body was still shifting with the soft inhale and exhale of breath and the insensible stare was broken by an intermittent mechanical blinking.

Her first thought was Amy; how was she going to break this to her daughter? She did not collapse in tears, howl or shake her fists towards the godless sky. She quietly backed away from the bed, not really ready to contemplate Daniel just yet. Leaving him in the bedroom, she closed the door on her husband. She need not have worried about Amy because, on stepping gently into her room, she noticed the same rigid pose in her daughter that she had just witnessed in her husband. At first, she felt an element of relief that still plagues her with guilt today. She would not have to try and explain to her five-year-old daughter why her dad had become, overnight, a walking coma. She would not have to see her hurt confusion when her hugs were received with a stony resistance or her chatter reflected back with a severe vacancy.

Jo had wanted to cry, to give herself over to emotional self-indulgence, but she could not allow herself the luxury of grief when her family was not dead. From that beginning point, until now, nearly six weeks later, she had maintained a strict daily routine to keep her family healthy and alive. Only now was her dedication beginning to falter because the fabric of life was being twisted tighter, and her nerve was being wrung out drip by drip. Her endless present was tensing and a future possibility she did not want to contemplate was now upon her. Jo averted her mind from the personal to the general.

It was only just over two months ago when it had all started. She says 'started' but she's not sure if any definitive beginning can be pinpointed exactly. For the first week or two at least, it barely seemed newsworthy, only taking up a two minute slot on the 10 o'clock news: a localised, freak event, an unexplained occurrence happening in a small town in Yorkshire. It was nothing to worry about because the scientists and doctors had it under control. It was true, they couldn't explain why incidents of catalepsy were cropping up, or why perfectly healthy people - young and old, male and female - were inexplicably falling into what could only be described as a waking coma. People rendered unresponsive as if deaf, dumb and blind, little more than living statues. No, they couldn't find the exact cause but they were investigating and were confident of a cure.

They likened it to an epidemic of Encephalitis Lethargica, a sinister and incomprehensible mouthful. Sleepy sickness to the layman, which made it sound harmless, cute even. How could anyone guard themselves against something that sounded so innocuous? The number of downloads of the film Awakenings suddenly soared. Then animals began to die, but it was only the cats and dogs, it was only the domesticated pets that were affected. It made no sense, where was the link? Jo remembered returning home after collecting Amy from school (the last time she took her) and unlocking the back door only to find their chocolate Labrador, Jesse, collapsed on the doormat. The old-fashioned wooden door was a mess, gouged and scratched with grooves and splinters, from Jesse's claws. It was as if she had seen death creeping up behind her and was frantic to escape. Yet, she looked so peaceful lying on the mat. There was no blood, no spasmodic agony recorded on the face. Just sleep. She still wonders what happened.

After the pets, the slow murmur of unease rose and cases increased. You couldn't really call them zombies; a zombie, by definition, was an 'animated corpse' and neither word could describe what was happening to the world's population. Despite this, the media had adopted the term 'living zombie', something Jo hated. It was used, at first, with a naïve bemusement that quickly switched to incredulity and then, finally, horror. Only three weeks after the initial reports, modern existence was irrevocably changed and there she was, Jo, alone, alive and sentient.

She was not completely alone though. There were others, like herself, who had waited (and still were waiting, to a certain extent) to not wake up with all their mental faculties intact one day. She had met with a few, when she had left the house to scavenge for food and supplies; bumbling through the local Co-op as if they had nothing more to worry about than which cereal to choose. They had the same dazed look of a lost child, a rawness of pain in their movements, a fumbling disbelief in the turn of their heads. Some were like her, holding their families in a captive stasis within their homes; feeding them, bathing them, walking them around the house to keep their limbs from withering. Treating them like pets, from one day to the next, hoping that this was a temporary period of inertia and that awareness would eventually return as quickly and randomly as it had fled.

Others were just passing through, no one from outside stopped to settle in the village. Maybe they were looking for answers somewhere, or maybe they were just avoiding staying still. Jo kept her distance, even hid before they could spot her, if she could. She understood the dazed movements of her fellow carers but not this migrant species: they had a whole different look. They glimpsed over the present horror as if it was a mural of modern day life, detached and contemplative. They had the look of a fugitive, as if they were running from a personal horror that had eclipsed anything that could ever happen again. These people were dangerous; they were untethered from the conceptions of reality that had once ruled.

Jo could see that there had been two choices; the first was the one that Jo had made, the choice to preserve her family. The second choice, well she could see the aftermath of that choice lingering in the eyes of these travellers. She wondered what they had done, whether they had just up and left their loved ones and wandered away themselves, or if the breach had been more unspeakably final. Funnily enough, she couldn't decide which choice, hers or theirs, was right or wrong or which was harder or easier. Maybe there was no answer.

3

With her family washed, dressed and breakfasted, Jo focuses her attention on her next move. It is to be a decisive moment; she can feel the future lurking in her diaphragm just waiting to scream out. She leaves Amy and Daniel facing each other in their armchairs, apparently secure for the present, and carefully closes the living room door on them. She hopes that they won't stir but if they do she will hear them clumsily grasping at the door handle. They are like toddlers in this; they have the concept in place but not the physical ability to perform it. She has watched them for minutes on end persistently clutching and unclutching their fists around the handle, never with emotion or frustration, but with a relentless absence of mind that eventually triumphs. Jo is glad that locks are beyond them.

She moves into the kitchen and picks up the packet that she has left on the counter besides the book of matches; it is there to provoke and dare her because she knows if it were out of sight she might not have the courage. She ascends the stairs with the same solemn aspect as a Mayan climbing the temple steps to the sacrificial altar. She is prepared, metaphorically, to have her heart cut out.

After the first two mornings of vomiting, Jo reprimanded herself and wondered how she could have been so forgetful, so distracted. This, the third morning, whilst brushing Amy's hair, she wondered how she could not. She has had no time for future, that distant country, that new world, not when she is so firmly fixed in the old one. The prospect is petrifying and yet here she is, stood before the sink in the bathroom, holding a pregnancy test before her eyes like a packet of poison.

She reads the instructions carefully even though she has used these tests several times in the past, and then decides she can't procrastinate any longer. With her knickers round her ankles, and the test wand in her hand bent beneath her body, she hesitantly releases her bladder and feels the warm rush of piss hit the stick.

After, when she has flushed the toilet and buttoned her jeans, she drifts into her bedroom. She keeps the test at arm's length, pinched between two fingers, as if it is an infection she can stave off. She looks at the bed, the duvet creased and twisted across it, one of Daniel's pillows sliding off his side, towards the floor. She remembers stories of women in mourning and how they still could not bring themselves to touch the side of the bed where their dead partner had once slept. Jo has not done this; she refuses to preserve the indent of Daniel, where his buttocks hit the mattress or his head the pillow. That would be too much like admitting defeat, pillow preservation is reserved for those that are really dead and gone and Daniel is alive. She doesn't share a bed with him any longer. She did try at first, but it was like sleeping next to a bear trap. Asleep, Daniel seemed natural and safe, relaxed but always poised. At any moment he could snap to and the rigid vibrations of his body penetrated her through the mattress, biting into her whole being.

Jo pulls back the curtains, places the test on the sill and opens the window to take in the air. Living in a house permanently darkened from drawn curtains and shut windows leaves a film of staleness on the skin and up the nostrils. Jo is startled by a figure moving, shuffling down the street. She looks closer to determine what it is, whole-life or half-life. It is a young woman, maybe not even out of her teens; her head is fixed and her gait stiff, and Jo concludes she is a half-life. She is dressed in a bright pink onesie and the disparity between her clothing and her comatose state verges on farcical. Jo is surprised to see one wandering the streets: it is not that common any more.

Those who were left to roam in the beginning are, for the most part, dead by now. With no survival instincts, and no inclination to eat or drink, it didn't take long for them to weaken and, with a mechanical simplicity, lie down and die. It was horrid to see the wan-like, weathered faces, pale and drooping from lack of nutrition; bones beginning to protrude through greying skin that had adopted a translucent, tightened sheen. They would stumble on their piss and shit stained legs, seeping through their clothing, determined to continue to their unknown destination. Jo had watched one drop once, and thought, for a moment, she construed a flicker of confusion on the face. As if it could not compute why its limbs wouldn't do what they were supposed to be doing. But the expression was so fleeting that Jo doubted it had ever really existed.

This current wanderer, the girl in the onesie, looks far from death. There is no tinge of malnourishment about her, she is clearly well looked after. She must have escaped from somewhere, from someone, Jo thinks. As she considers this, she sees another figure running into view from the end of the street. Another woman, older, probably the girl's mother, is shouting in a taut, high-pitched, voice. Her words are so rushed and desperate, Jo cannot decipher what she is saying. She quickly catches up with the girl and grabs at one of her wrists. There is no reaction; only slightly hindered, the girl continues to walk. Jo is disconcerted; she recognises the same persistence she sees in Amy when she tries to stop her from walking.

The woman swings round into the girl's path, forcing her to stop, and grips her by the shoulders. She shakes her in the same dramatic fashion you only expect to see in films, all the time screaming into her face, into those inanimate eyes. The unyielding absence of being is too much and she slaps her full in the face once, twice and catches herself mid-air before the third. Instead, the woman folds at her feet, in supplication to this statue, this human idol. Her hands cling to the girl's as if they are the only thing that can stop her from slipping outside reality. After a matter of seconds she rouses herself. She stands, calm, and then works firmly at steering the girl back around. She alternates between leading and pushing her back in the direction she came from.

Jo watches the pair turn the corner and futility flashes through her in pangs. She thinks of Amy, only five years old, and glimpses the illusion of stasis she has lulled herself into. One day, Amy will be the same age as the girl on the street. Will Jo still be bathing her, dressing her, feeding her and glossing over her soulless state then? Will she have to chase her down the street when she escapes from time to time? And when the unbending stare becomes too much, will she break herself against her, pushing herself into this rocklike chasm of a human being? What about the other? What about the shimmering entity that sits on the edge of existence, the one that is not yet but could be? Where will it fit into this madness?

More than enough time has passed and Jo picks up the test from the windowsill. There is an absence of emotion within her as she looks at the result; she is not sad, happy, angry or surprised. For one moment she just is. There is only herself and her womb ticking away, like a time bomb. Jo looks up at the spot on the street again, where the mother and daughter were just stood. Something shifts within her, a new sort of determination that kicks her out of limbo. She knows that she must choose again.

The Comeback Tour

by Andrea Mullaney

You know what's so great about managing a zombie rock star? You don't gotta talk to the guy.

Believe me, I've been in this business a long time. I've worked with them all – the ones on the way up, the ones on the way down, the ones who still think they're gonna make it. I've been a babysitter, a procurer of drugs and girls, I've kept them out of jail and out of the press, I've lied to their wives, to their record companies, to their fans. Hell, sometimes I've even helped them write their songs.

But when it comes down to it, what the job is, what it really is, is talking to them. The talent. Talking them into things like they're little kids fighting against their bedtime. Not that I ever had the time to do that for my kids, even before the divorce. Well, that's what happens when you're backstage every night, coaxing a coked-up adult into going out and playing his big hit, because that's what they paid to come and hear, not the new one that noodles around for five minutes in search of a chorus. Or you're talking him out of trashing the hotel room because the management didn't put him in the Presidential Suite, or running interference between him and his girlfriends.

Talking, talking, talking. I've spent years talking – and listening, of course. Hours on end listening to some mystic hooey their dealer just laid on them that they think is really deep, or whining about the critics who didn't understand their concept album, or about the pressures of fame. I mean, gimme a break. What do these guys know about pressure? They got me to take care of all that for them.

Hey, sorry. Sorry. I don't wanna bore you with all that stuff about the bad old days. You want to know about Undead Eddie Underwood, don't you? I'm just saying, that's what's so great about this gig. No talking, except to interviewers like you. No arguments, no tantrums. You just throw a piece of meat at him, push him towards the stage and, ya know, 'Braaaaaains.' I'm happy, the crowd's happy, he's happy – well, I guess he's happy.

I didn't know him before, you gotta understand. Before my time. Yeah, Eddie was pretty much washed up when he passed, old and fat and gone to MOR radio. And he was never really major league, even in his prime – a few Number Ones, but not a legend. It's weird that he became the one. Since they started coming back, there have been a few others. Bigger stars with a better back catalogue, or guys who died in their prime, the 27 Club guys who were still credible before they overdosed or whatever. Or the metal acts, where all their songs are about death and decay anyway, you'd think that would go down better coming from a zombie than love songs.

I'll admit it, Eddie's only got a couple of real crowd-pleasers, a lot of 'em are snoozers. But the other undead acts have gone nowhere – Eddie's the one they all wanna see. We're selling out most every night.

Maybe it's because he was the first – right back before we knew it was only, like, one in fifty who could make a comeback. Remember that, all the panic? Oh my gawd, the world's going to end, it's the last days, wahwahwah. Kinda funny now, right? I was working with a big star at the time - no names, no pack drill, but one of those right-on, Protect The Earth, Prius Hybrid guys. Everything had to be vegan. You ever tried getting vegan car seat covers? Ugh, what a nightmare. And if he spotted any of the crew eating a burger backstage he'd make me fire them, no payoff. A real prince.

Anyway, once the news got out, once we started seeing them walking around, this guy, Mr Give Peace A Chance, he turns into this rabid military nut. He's all, 'Get me an AK, get me a tank, get me the hell outta here.' He holed up somewhere, hired a militia to protect him, then once everything was under control he puts out this piece of crap charity record. You probably heard it, They're Just Like Us or something like that. No, He's Just Like Me, that was it. Went platinum, got him a Grammy. Freaking harp solo in the middle, wahwahwah save the poor wittle zombies, what a crock of … and they say Eddie's creatively dead!

And I was like, man, I'm done here. Life's too short, you know? I heard a lot of people did that afterwards, threw in their jobs, walked out on their marriages. Made a change, whatever. Once you've seen the dead walking around, it's kinda hard to go back to your daily grind. You look at them and you realise we're all only flesh and brains. And when it comes down to it, money, possessions - all that - it's just stuff that weighs you down when you're running away.

You know, I'm not what you'd call a philosophical kind of guy, but it makes you think about what you wanna get out of life. I guess my wife was the same. My ex-wife.

So anyways, I was looking for something new. And I don't want to blow my own bugle here, because I guess if I hadn't come up with it someone else would have, but I've always been good at getting in ahead of the trend. The grunge thing, I was onto that before it got out of Seattle. The big record company suits thought no one wanted to see guys in plaid shirts with feedback coming off their guitars, but I knew people were ready for it, even though they didn't even know they were. That's the secret to this business. Give the people what they want before they know they want it. And find a way to make it pay.

But I'll be honest with you, Undead Ed wasn't my original idea. I had someone younger in mind, someone new. The world's first zombie rock star. My idea was to find some young dead guy who'd been a nothing in his life, then build him up and push it like he was getting his second chance to make it, so people could identify with him. I still think that's a good idea. I wanna see if we can get it on TV, have a contest to find undiscovered, undead talent. We could get their families on – you know, 'this was always Bobby's dream,' a few tears, that kinda thing. Call it The Z Factor, whaddya think?

I had started making enquiries to see if I could get hold of a suitable candidate. But then I heard about Eddie. He'd been spotted wandering around one of the national parks. No one knew how he got there.

Now at the time, I don't know if you remember, but there were a lot of false sightings. The number of people who claimed they'd seen Elvis! There are some still believe the King's out there, like he's somehow managed to escape the army patrols and he's roaming free sleeping in haystacks or whatever. I guess anything's possible nowadays, but I doubt it. Once the government got their act together, they got it pretty locked down. You can't get closer than five miles to one of those work camps in the desert, they don't let nothing in or out of there. God knows what goes on in those places.

But back then, you just didn't know what was true and what wasn't. All bets were off. So at first, when they said Eddie Underwood was back, it could have been just another rumour. But something told me to go and check it out. And there he was, stumbling around in this makeshift metal pen they'd put him in, arms out, groaning, the whole bit. Same as the rest. Except it came to me that it wasn't just regular groaning, it was kinda tuneful. Not in tune, obviously, but if you strained your ears, you could almost imagine that he was singing one of his old hits. And that's when I knew he was the one.

It took a lot of working out, though. First I had to check the legal situation, see if there was anyone still out there with a claim to him. They've tried to clear up the records but there are a lot of people who disappeared in those first few weeks who were never traced. But I did some digging and I found all the graves – untouched – so I knew there was no management and no relatives who could come looking for a cut. He was a solo artist, you might say.

Then I had to get all the safety gear, the cattle prods and the cage and the security people. All my own dough and it didn't come cheap. I had to have all that in place before the military would give me permission to take over his contract. And let me tell you, they drove a hard bargain. They take a percentage that would have made my eyes water in the old days. But hey, I'm still doing all right.

See, that's the other great thing about working with a zombie: they don't want much. Human meat if they can get it – I have an arrangement with a morgue, they give me the unclaimed bodies – or animal parts in a pinch. And that's it: no Egyptian cotton sheets with a thread count of 250, no Evian at room temperature, no M&Ms with the blue ones removed. A bucket of eyeballs and a dry crate and he's ready to rock.

Listen, I'm kidding around here, but seriously, I gotta tell ya, I feel good about what we're doing. I mean, for him, it's a nice gig. No one hurts him or dissects him. Better than the work camps, from what I hear. I wouldn't wish those places on my worst enemy. Eddie's looked after – be sure you put that in your interview. And he's doing what he loved in life. You know, all those rock stars, they never wanted to stop. They started out saying they wanted to die before they got old, that it was better to burn out than fade away, but it turned out they didn't mean it. Once they'd had that rush of playing to the crowd every night, feeling that energy feeding back on them, they couldn't give it up. They wanted to keep touring on and on, even when they couldn't hit the notes anymore. And now Eddie can do that, he can keep on rockin'. Forever.

Maybe there's a little part of him that knows, that can hear the music when he's out there on his chain on stage. I like to think so. Maybe that's even why he came back. Call me crazy, but there's a look in his eyes sometimes like he's trying to tell me something. Or like he wants to cry, because he's so happy to be back. And I wanna say: I know, buddy. And you're welcome.

It's for the fans, too. They love the shows. They get to sing along to the old hits, they get to see him in the flesh – or what's left of it. Sure, he's not what he was, but maybe they ain't either. It's nostalgia for a simpler time. After everything that's happened in the last few years, everything we've all been through, that's gotta be a positive thing, right?

And me? Hey, this story shouldn't be about me. I'm just the manager. But sure, it's good for me too. I'm out on the road again, it's what

I know. It's where I belong. Making money, doing deals, but without the hassle of those rock star egos. I call the shots now. I tell ya, it's given me a whole new lease of life.

Anesthetised

by Emma Lyskava

It was the cold that shook my body into consciousness. I grasped at the pallid bed sheets, and wrapped them around my shivering body in a vain attempt to create some warmth. The cold seemed to be coursing through my veins, freezing and constricting every last bit of warmth that I possessed, and each scarce and heavy breath that escaped my lungs, hung briefly like a ghost in the bitter air. My dark hair had crisped like a frosted autumn leaf, and as I slowly brought a hand to my face I felt nothing. Numb.

My eyes gradually adjusted to the perpetual darkness only to see the same shapes and slopes of the ceiling that they had before. Everything in the hall had remained the same so long that any occupant no longer needed sight to recount it, only their memories. The iron beds that lined the walls still housed their broken occupants, with only an occasional murmur to suggest that life still remained, yet each as restless as the next. A car passed by in the road outside, suddenly breaking the darkness and casting its headlights upon the ceiling. I watched as the light swept across the ceiling, distorted by the disjointed panes in the windows, creating a frenzied lightshow upon the whitewashed walls. Then the room was re-submerged into darkness, the spark of light having made the room now appear darker than before. I closed my eyes, yearning for the oblivion that comes with sleep, but the room had disturbingly altered somehow. I turned to look outside and saw that small pieces of pallid fluff had begun to fall gently from the sky and caress the window, gradually enhancing the brightness of the room. The speed of the white flecks' descent soon increased and the pureness tried to penetrate the panes as each speck of white threw themselves at the windows. Upon contact with the panes they died and melted out of existence. I no longer knew the name for this occurrence that the sky had produced, but something else inside me did. The mesmerizing twirls and swoops held me transfixed in the bed and stirred something within me. It was so hard to remember things from before; I was meant to forget. Told to forget. I longed to open the window and connect with these living, dancing flutters, but the windows had been nailed shut a long time ago. The hinges were encased with rust barring all contact from the outside.

The cold still remained in the room like a hovering omen, infecting every object and being that inhabited the space. I flinched from the touch of the frozen bars of the bed against my bare skin and deftly drew my feet up under me. It had been so long since I'd felt the touch of something warm, something alive, that I could no longer imagine what it was like to experience that laying on of hands.

There was a small echo of hurried footsteps down the adjoining corridor that slowed down as they approached the entrance to the room. Every muscle in my body tightened and I clenched the sheets to my face from the hesitation of the footsteps. I saw the nurse's figure through the frosted glass in the doors and each function within me jarred. I caught my breath and my ears began to ring with the sound of my heart thrashing against my chest. I clasped my eyes shut feigning sleep, wishing her swift departure. My whole body shivered with repulsion. I couldn't do that again, not tonight. There was a cry from another room and the footsteps hurried back from whence they came. I stifled a sigh and turned my head once again to observe the soft whiteness collect itself upon the outside. There was something calming about the soft silver shavings and their dance to the floor. The purity of the White began to embrace the ground on which it fell upon, transforming the dark into light. I tried my best to entice my memories back regarding this new occurrence; something which held the link between then and now. I closed my eyes and a group of people trudging through this White swam into focus. Nothing else was clear, just the blinding whiteness akin to the one gathering outside. Suddenly the memory was like a tape being fast forwarded: a blur of images, colours, shapes, laughs, smiles. The hairs covering my body pricked up to this overwhelming rush of senses with a surge of adrenaline. Then the whole picture began to taint, break up and drip with crimson red. The White turned to dark mire, infecting and blackening the colours of the vivid image. I wrenched my eyes open trying to silent my contorting body, repulsed by the images I had beckoned. Saliva began to gather in my mouth and my tongue curled. I flung myself over the bars of the bed and retched. There was a reason why I had chosen to forget, to blacken and erase - to shield me from it. But it was the gathering dust outside that had summoned up this memory and forced it upon me. I felt a wave of sickness crash through me again as I remembered its name. It was the cause for all of this, for everything that was, and is now.

The Snow.

The Remnants of Civilization

by Vince Liberato

Know first that the soul is a sign of Civilization. Your soul separates you from not only the creatures of the Earth, but most importantly, from the Soulless. With no soul, there is no guidance, no morality, and no life after death. It was at the Sundering, when bodies without souls rose up and populated the world that Civilization was dealt its harshest blow. But fear not, for you are the proof and the boundaries of Civilization. It has bequeathed a soul to you and now you, the Remnants, are the instrument of its survival.

Seth and Ty watched as the creature they had been stalking tore at the remains of the dog it had killed. Red rivulets of flesh and fur covered its filthy, naked form as it ripped into its meal, shoveling handfuls of the steaming meat into its mouth. It had pulled the animal's body atop a rock in a clearing surrounded by small hills. It was from these hills, in the heat of a very dry dusk, several miles from Civilization, that the two hunters stalked their prey

'It's perfect. Just look at it,' Seth whispered to Ty. 'Have you ever seen one so big?'

Ty shook her head, and then had to adjust the mask covering her face. This disturbed her goggles, which had to be corrected as well. Unsatisfied, she started to remove one of her gloves, but was stopped when Seth grabbed her hand and raised his machete to his face in a silencing motion. Even underneath the protective face-wear her partner wore, Ty could see his steely glare through the ancient scratched and tinted lenses.

The giant was not to be killed. It was to be captured and brought back to Civilization and sent to the learning pit. Due to its size, the task before them was going to be difficult even in the best case scenarios the hunt presented. If they missed their shots or were discovered early by their very dangerous quarry, then they would lose a lot more than the time spent on the day's hunt. One of the first things all hunters learned was that there was nothing more dangerous than an alert and angry Soulless, and all of the Soulless were always angry. Ty shuddered at the thought of what one that big would do to her and Seth if given the chance.

'Would rip us limb from limb long before even thinking about killing us,' Seth whispered, as if answering Ty's thought. Seth put his machete into his backpack and replaced it with the bolas sling that was to be used in the capture. Ty nodded, and took out a net that had been carefully rolled and packed away in her rucksack. They split up. Seth crept along the hill, careful to maintain silence by keeping the three heavy stones in his weapon from touching. Ty had seen several things brought down by that tool and a flick of Seth's wrist. It was a tricky weapon though, and he would have to get in close to throw it with the power needed to catch his prey.

The Soulless was completely oblivious to its stalkers as it twisted and jerked free one of the dog's legs, which snapped off with a lout, wet pop. It let out a low, growling moan of satisfaction before shoving as much of the meat as it could in its gaping maw, rotating its jaws furiously in a clockwork motion, pausing occasionally to spit out bone before continuing its meal.

Ty unrolled her net. Seth was in optimum position, only a few dozen feet away from the target as he slowly twirled his weapon over his head, each of the lengths of wire slowly accelerated as the bolas reached the needed speed and velocity for a successful capture.

From behind Ty, a branch broke. She turned to see a mess of red hair and piercing eyes watching her. Another Soulless, only a child, completely naked and its hair a knotted, tangled mess with twigs sticking out at multiple sides was standing an arm's length away. Startled, Ty peddled backwards into her net, getting herself entangled in it and tumbling down the hill. Her momentum carried her to center of the field, a few feet away from the feasting Soulless. She looked up. Pure, unbridled rage stared back.

'Ty!' Seth yelled and threw his weapon. It hit its target around on the waist, but did not have enough force for a complete capture, only partially wrapping around both legs and an arm. Seth darted towards Ty to try and get the net, but was pulled to the ground. The Soulless, oblivious to the wire wrapped around it, had fallen forward, just managing to trip Seth with its free, outstretched arm. It had an iron grip around his ankle, one Seth was not near strong enough to break.

'Get it Ty! Get it now!' Seth yelled while clawing at the ground and kicking with his free leg. His blows had no effect on his attacker, who, despite being tied up, continued to close the distance between them with each pull.

Ty, still dazed from the fall, struggled to get free. At the top of the hill she had fallen off of, the young Soulless watched her for a split second, before retreating to the brush.

'Ty! Help me!'

Ty could still hear Seth screaming, but faintly, as if at a far-away place and not several yards away. She had never seen any Soulless back away, let alone not try and kill a Remnant on site. Young Soulless, due to the savage nature of their parents, were rare, although this was not the first one she had seen. It could have jumped on her back and bitten through her throat like she had seen them do before, but this one – this one was different.

'Get it off me Ty! I need your help now!' Atop the other hill, Seth still struggled against his assailant, but soon found himself pinned. The Soulless had positioned itself on top of him, using its bulk to keep Seth from squirming away. Its open mouth dripped saliva that belonged to it and blood that did not all over Seth's mask while he furiously whipped his head from left to right, screaming for help.

'No! Ty! Don't let it bite me! Don't…' He yelled, but his words turned to screaming as it brought its teeth down on Seth's mask. It jerked its head hard and came up with bits of fabric, half a set of goggles, and part of Seth's face.

Seth screamed a final time, in tandem with the Soulless's triumphant howl. Ty snapped out of her trance, got herself free from the net, and struggled to find her feet. She scrambled over to where Seth and his assailant were intertwined and threw the net over the two of them. The attacker twisted around to see Ty, who suddenly realized how bad her idea of throwing the net was. It slowly rose to its feet and the bolas sloughed off, completely freeing the monster whose glare was burning holes into her. In its mouth, it still had part of the piece of Seth it had bitten off. She could see her reflection in the cracked lens that loosely hung from its blistered lip. It swallowed and the goggles fell to the ground and shattered.

She froze. This was it. This was the end. She was about to be completely destroyed before letting anyone know what was on the hill. And it would be Seth's fault for trying to catch the biggest monster he could.

The Soulless raised its hand, and then froze. Its expression twisted, its body stiffened up and fell to the ground, no longer alive.

Seth sat up. His grey, exposed flesh had been stripped to the bone where he had been bitten. Bits of viscous black blood speckled his face, smeared over the lens that covered his remaining eye.

'I told you not to let it bite me,' Seth said. 'Do you know how much harder it is to bring it in now?'

'N-n-no,' Ty said, removing her mask. Her dead flesh was not as decayed as Seth's. She had a few more years left before she would completely decompose, having been made a Remnant a year ago. She had been told that she had screamed the entire way back to Civilization before finally being bitten, granted with the ability to reason alongside a soul, and thrown into a learning pit to be educated. That part she could not remember. Like all Remnants, her earliest memories occurred the first few days of being taught language.

'Civilization, Ty! It'll be near impossible to get back with one this big. When it wakes up, it'll be mad. Really mad and we won't be able to use its pain to keep it in check...'

Know second that no living body can house a soul. It is the presence of Civilization within us that allows the ability to reason and it is a lack of Civilization that makes the Soulless as they are. Only the ability to house a soul separates the Soulless from other beasts, and it is you, the Remnants, who may grant them that soul through physical contact inside of their living body. This communion will kill the body, but grant a soul and give the new Remnant a place in Civilization.

'Pull harder,' Seth barked at Ty. The dead Soulless was tied in her net. Rigor mortis had already begun to set in, making the bumps and rocks in the field they now trudged through much more difficult to navigate around. Every now and then, either the body or a square of net would catch a rock and Ty would have to exert herself to dislodge him. This damage done to her now would knock weeks, possibly months off of her durability, and she suspected it was Seth's way of punishing her because of the botched capture.

But it was not her rapidly diminishing second life that was on her mind as she pulled the net. It was the little Soulless that had startled her earlier whose gaze continued to stare at her every time she closed her eyes. It had to be intelligent, but if it were intelligent, that would mean that it already had a...

'Soul,' Seth said aloud, unintentionally answering Ty's thoughts for the second time that day. 'Soul's going to come in and it'll be scared and mad and fighting. It won't get hurt, it won't be tired, and it'll just be us and this thing, miles from Civilization. Those knots you tied better hold.'

'They will,' Ty mumbled.

'They'd better. Still can't believe it bit me,' Seth turned his head to look at Ty. He had made no effort to hide the gaping hole where his eye had been earlier.

They continued to walk through the woods. The sun was beginning to set and both Ty and Seth knew they would have to set up camp soon.

'What was I like? You know, when I was like him?' Ty asked.

'You? You were an easy catch. We roped you, brought you back, bit you, threw you in the learning pit, and that was that,' Seth said. 'Why does it matter?'

'I don't remember being bitten. My earliest memory's from the classroom, when I was being taught how to speak.'

'Nobody remembers being bitten, stupid. You come in, dumb, without a soul, and alive. You get bit, die, get a soul then an education. Takes a few days for it to adjust to your body or something like that… I don't know, I'm not a priest,' he paused again. 'Anyway, after that, you become a full Remnant and get your job and work until Civilization don't need you anymore.'

'Like you?' Ty asked.

'Yeah, like me,' Seth said. 'Even before having my face bitten off and wrestled down by that savage, I don't think I had a full year left. Getting my eye bit out won't help my shelf life none, I know that.'

'Sorry,' Ty apologized. Ty's burden hit another bump. She pulled, but was unable to move it. Seth continued to walk on, oblivious to the problem his partner was having. She turned around to get both hands on the net so she could give it a strong tug.

'Seth, I…' Ty began, but stopped mid-sentence. Hiding in the brush, the small Soulless ducked out of sight in the tall grass. It was the same one that had been watching her earlier. Its hair, Ty now noticed, was the same reddish colour as her own.

'You what?' Seth demanded, not turning around.

'I think we ought to camp here for the night. It's getting dark and I can't see the bumps in the road so well.'

'Fine. If you want,' Seth said after a few moments of contemplation. 'Go ahead and check the knots in your net. Your cargo's going to be awake soon and he'll want to kill us both.'

Ty nodded and looked up again, but the little one was already gone.

Know third that above all, preservation of Civilization is the purpose of our existence. For this to be, it is the duty of each Remnant to grant to one of the Soulless a soul. Only a single replacement for each Remnant is allowed, as if all the Soulless were to become Remnants, then Civilization would lose its light in the short amount of time that

Remnants have on this world. For after five years, the body will crumble under the soul's weight and the soul returned to Civilization. And with no new Remnants, culled from the Soulless to continue the cycle, Civilization would cease to be.

The fire had just started burning when the new Remnant awoke. As Seth predicted, it was not happy. It struggled, but Ty's knots held tight and the net further restricted its movement. It had also been gagged by Seth with the remains of the mask he had been wearing earlier.

Seth prodded it with his foot a few times, rocking it back and forth. 'Serves you right. You could have waited for one of us to bite you, but you couldn't wait, could you dummy? You had to go and take a soul for yourself.'

'Don't antagonize him. He's one of us now,' Ty mumbled.

'One of us? Ha! Once he's educated then he'll be one of us, but for now, he's a dumb lump of flesh. And stupid. But he'll be the best one. One as big and strong as this will definitely help. Way too many captures have been small and weak. Mostly females like you… that's a serious problem.'

'That's not true,' Ty protested.

'Don't argue with me. I'm the hunter in charge of this trip. You've done more than enough to ruin this go 'round and I don't want any of your lip. I swear, had we a few more like this bruiser here…' he gave their capture a hard kick, 'We'd be able to start taking back the rest of the world. And then we could make it more like the Old World again, expand Civilization.'

'But in the Third Prayer, it says that we need to keep our numbers small and manageable. The one we caught is at least twenty-five years old. In the time it's needed to grow, about five generations of Remnants have passed. If we don't conserve…'

'Don't quote scripture to me, scrub,' Seth cut Ty off. 'I was here, not far from this camp, on the hunt you were captured and I knew the man you replaced.' Seth made the last word a curse before continuing. 'He was one of the best we'd ever had, and if he were to know how pathetic you, his legacy, was going to be, he would have cut your living throat on the spot and left you without a soul and your empty corpse to be eaten by other Soulless. Picked another… Any other… that was worth something. But this guy… This ogre,' he kicked their prisoner again. It grunted and wiggled as hard as it could under its restraints. 'He'll be fitting for when I become too broken to do anything. Sometimes when we get new Remnants, they pale in comparison to who they replace. You won't have to worry about that though. So long as he don't freeze up and ruin a capture, it'll be a step up from you.'

'I'm sorry about your face,' Ty whispered.

'I don't care,' Seth said, ending the conversation by throwing a few more dry sticks on the fire. In the distance, an old windmill with metal blades turned with the night's wind. Seth tied his machete to his bag and produced a small knife and an animal's rib bone from his pockets. Seth turned his back to Ty and began whittling one of the ends of the rib. He was going to carve an eye plug out of it to block up the hole in his face. Ty looked at the new Remnant, who had ceased his struggling.

'What are you thinking,' she thought at the large creature she would be dragging again when the sun rose. 'Are you capable of thinking yet? Are you feeling fear for the first time? Or is it the same as before, when you were alive?'

The Remnant growled softly, as if it could hear what was going through her mind.

'Maybe it's like being born. Suddenly becoming aware of a world that was always there, but somehow out of your grasp before. I've only had my soul for a little while, but I do not remember anything clearly since about six months ago. What kind of Remnant will you be? Will you be kind and meek? A teacher or priest who educates new Remnants brought into the learning pits. Maybe a leader who never leaves Civilization and governs us fairly. Or will you be a cruel hunter? Gruff and bitter like Seth until the day your soul burns out your body.'

It made another noise, a low whine. From the tall grass, Ty thought she heard something respond to it.

'What was that?' Seth said, his back still to Ty.

'Nothing,' Ty quickly replied. 'He's just being a little talkative. That's all.'

'Make him shut up. He'll get used to not sleeping.'

'I'll tighten his gag a little. I don't want to hurt him,' Ty said.

'And I don't want to have to shove this bone in my eye socket,' Seth had ceased work on the eye plug he was whittling and held it over his head to see if it would fit.

Ty didn't respond. She got closer to the tied Remnant and continued to think to herself.

'I was like you not very long ago. Maybe we knew each other. Maybe we were lovers. Can Soulless feel love? Maybe the little one following us was our child. A daughter, born alive from my body.' The thought made her shudder a little, but she was not sure why. 'I was taken from this area. It's definitely possible. Maybe that's why she refused to attack me earlier. She could remember me.'

He whined again.

'I told you to shut him up!' Seth snarled.

'Tightening it now…' Ty synched the gag another notch. She then stroked his hair. Reflected in the fire, Ty could see that the rage in its eyes had completely dispersed. He stared at her, with soft brown eyes and what must be the first sparks of intelligence.

'Finally,' Seth said.

'Is she yours? Is she ours? Earlier, you attacked Seth first, not me. Maybe you recognized him back there. And me, maybe you remember me from when I was alive, even under all these clothes. Could the little one be ours? Did I make it with you, years ago?'

She sat with him for the rest of the night. There were no more sounds, no movement in the tall grass, but she knew it was still there. By the sunup, she had cut a few of the squares of net and loosened several knots.

Know fourth that to become a Remnant, one must shed all of the shackles of life. No food shall pass your lips, no sleep will fall upon your eyes. Those are the needs of the body, not the needs of the soul. The Soulless must nurture their bodies in the destructive cycle of consumption and waste that keeps them living, while the Remnants are nurtured only by their soul. Do not lament the loss of these functions, for they are but a distraction and do nothing to serve Civilization.

'Let's go,' Seth said. It was a misty morning. 'While the grass has dew on it. It'll make dragging that lump a lot easier.'

'Yes. That'll help,' Ty said.

'At a decent pace, we might make it to Civilization before the day ends.'

'Do you think so?'

'Only if you put your back in it. Grab the net and let's go,' Seth commanded.

Ty's plan was simple. She would pull the net only until the Remnant trapped inside slipped out. Seth would be distracted by this and she would take his machete and disable him with it. They were not going back to Civilization. They were going to restart their family and live not for Civilization, but for themselves. She would educate and name her mate and then their child, when it was of age, would also be given a soul. She knew it was rash, but she did not want to go back, she did not want the Remnant in the net to be like Seth, and most of all, she wanted the child she convinced herself was hers.

Ty had gotten a firm grasp on the net when the grass in front of her parted. Into the campsite, the small Soulless cautiously walked. Its eyes went from Ty to Seth to the captured Remnant in a circular motion that kept repeating. Ty's mind raced. She had to find a way to pacify Seth before he decided to…

'Kill it!' Seth screamed, and reached for his machete. The little Soulless, startled by the outburst, dove forward, towards the Remnant Ty knew was once its father. Ty had to act now or she would lose everything. She threw herself at Seth, knocking him to the ground and pinning him in a fashion mirroring the events of the previous day.

'You won't touch her!' Ty said, searching for a weapon. She needed to completely disable Seth before he could retaliate.

'Are you crazy?' Seth yelled, turning Ty around, now straddling her underneath him. Even with his body in a much later state of decay and an eye missing, he was much stronger than her.

'It's mine, it's mine!' Ty was hysterical.

'That thing? It's only a baby? Why would you want a baby?'

'It's my baby! It's mine! Mine! Mine! Mine! Mine!'

Seth stopped trying to reason with his hunting partner. His elbow found its way to Ty's throat. While she continued to wail on him, he reached for his machete. The gravity of the situation hitting her, she started searching for a weapon of her own. Seth's tattered and rotten fingers found the machete handle about the time that Ty found the bone that Seth had been whittling. In a quick motion, she shoved its pointed end into his remaining eye, completely blinding him before he could use his weapon. Seth bellowed in pure rage. Even without a sense of pain to temper the agony of the moment, the complete loss of his sense of sight filled him with a primal fury like that of the Soulless. He lifted his hand off of Ty's neck and joined it with his other on the machete's handle. Ty tried to struggle free, but could not move. As for Seth, with no sense of touch or sight to guide him, he had no way of knowing what he was striking.

Seth's first blow bit high into her shoulder. Ty turned her head to look for the little one. She could see it, standing over the netted Remnant. She could not see what it was doing to its father.

The machete hit her a second time, cutting much deeper. Ty became aware that she could not move the fingers or elbow on that arm. The little one was pulling at something, Ty could not tell what. Curiously, the captured Remnant was not moving. He probably could have broken free from the net after all the work Ty did, but was still.

Dust was kicked up as Seth's machete hit the dirt above Ty's head. He was aiming higher, trying to land a killing blow. In the swirling debris, Ty saw the little Soulless had picked up a large rock roughly the size of its own head. It was the one Ty had been sitting on earlier, when running her fingers through the hair of the captured Remnant.

Seth's next strike hit the top of her skull, shaking the world around her for a second before her vision returned. The blade was stuck in bone and Ty could no longer move her legs. She looked for the young Soulless, but could not see it anywhere.

With a strong jerk, the machete came free. Seth's next attack was to be the last one he would need. Even though he was blinded, severely injured, and with no real chance of survival afterwards, he wore a look of maniacal glee. His ragged grin, eyes both hollowed and gouged out, and loose scraps of skin that clung to the damaged bits of his skull hovered over Ty for a split second. He paused in his assault.

'Do it!' Ty rasped.

'Civilization! I will!' Seth hollered back.

'I wasn't talking to you,' Ty said as a large rock cracked Seth in his face. He was knocked completely off of Ty, and before Ty could see if that blow had killed him, the little Soulless descended on top of him, repeatedly bringing the rock down on his head until it was nothing more than a slick black, red, and white smear stained across the ground, the rock, and the stump of Seth's body.

Ty struggled to upright herself using her one good arm. Seth's damage was incredibly thorough and her body did not move in the ways she wanted it to. The young one that had saved her watched curiously as she struggled.

'Thank you,' Ty said. The little Soulless stared back at her. 'I'm too damaged. You're going to have to go on. Take your father and…' Ty looked over to the remaining Remnant. Its head had been completely caved in with the same rock that had been used to dispatch Seth.

'Why? Why did you do that?' Ty asked. The little Soulless responded by picking up its rock and raising it high. There was no life behind her eyes. Only anger.

'Wait. I love y-'

It brought the rock down on Ty's head before she could finish.

Finally, do not hate the Soulless, do not fear the Soulless, but never be fooled by their appearance. They are called the Soulless because they embody emptiness and lack a soul and the qualities that the soul imparts. Empathy, kindness, the ability to reason, and mercy can only be obtained once one understands the concept of time and its finiteness, a concept only available to those that understand the boundaries created by life and death. And Civilization, as you know, is created by boundaries. Boundaries you embody as the living dead, as one of its Remnants.

Epilogue

Rush Hour

by Thomas Brown

They say the apocalypse is coming. In five years, they estimate, a meteor will strike the earth and wipe it clean of life. Five years is not a long time, but it is long enough. It is long enough for weddings and funerals for those who cannot wait, for that walk down the beach, where he first holidayed with his family at St. Bees. It is long enough for work, long enough that the world still turns, for now at least. So he finds himself on a train platform each morning, stepping onto a carriage, staring through dirt-smeared windows as the world passes him by.

Sometimes he thinks he could sit there forever, watching the countryside slip past. Trees blur into fields, which seem to stretch, longer than any field should, until there are no boundaries, no roads, no thicket hedgerows, only a palette of greens and browns beneath blue shining skies. The carriage rocks beneath him, lulling him slowly in his seat, while far above cerulean clouds blossom with wind and rain. He has only eyes for their phosphorescence, their purple twilight tinge, and for the twenty minutes it takes him to reach the next station he is lost in their depths, rolling with them through the sky; a fish caught in their awesome ocean pull.

Then the train shudders, stops, expels its load, and he is back inside his business suit, black briefcase in his hand. His mouth sighs. His shoulders sag. The Underground drinks deeply of his soul.

People swarm up escalators, spilling out of the station into the road. Traffic screams after them; a chorus of sirens and sudden brakes. Women wobble past him on heels too high while men with faces shaven clean march briskly in their wake, and in between their legs dogs gambol, vagrants dance another day with life and children rush headlong into the roads. He wonders when it began; when things first showed signs of ending up this way, then remembers he need not wonder about anything anymore, ever again, for more than the minute it takes to type as much online.

The offices are tall, grey things overlooking a grey Thames. His room is on the fifth floor, next to administration. At eight-fifty he takes the lift, in the foyer beside the stairwell. His shirt is hot and wet beneath his arms. Inside his office, he closes the door, sits at his chair, which sinks beneath his weight, and stares at the face reflected in the blank computer screen. Drawing a deep breath, he begins to type.

While he types, thoughts tumble through his head. He does not know why administration is called administration, why it is singled out when they are all administrators; every man in his pin-stripe business skin, every woman with her pay-check pulse, record-keeping, number crunching, so that the world will keep on turning.

He thinks about love, and what it might feel like. He thinks about death, and when it was that they all died. Sometimes he turns in his chair and stares at the plant in the corner with its plastic fronds, its sterile soil, its bright, synthetic stem, until it is all he can do not to close his eyes, ball his fists and scream at the top of his voice.

He does not remember weeks in terms of days. He does not remember working weeks at all. There is only one day repeated, in which he wakes up, travels by train, pushes through crowds, through streets made black with rainwater to stinking, sweaty offices built of old brick the colour of dried blood, peopled by corporate puppets in black suits with empty eyes and long thin fingers twitching by their sides.

They say the apocalypse is coming. In five years, they estimate, a meteor will strike the earth and wipe it clean of life. He wonders if it has not come already. Not by fire and smoke but a commuter contagion; this, the human condition, made better for a few minutes each morning by the birds in the sky, the distant glimpse of a dream in the clouds.

About the Authors

Robert Holtom is a freelance writer and cultural activist. He writes prose, scripts and poetry, and attempts to twin that with his passion for calling for holistic political, economic and environmental change. He firmly believes that the arts have a huge role to play in shaping our society and helping foster community. Robert hopes to inspire people with his stories.

Damon DiMarco has written several books including *Tower Stories: an Oral History of 9/11* and *Heart of War: Soldiers' Voices from the Front Lines of Iraq*. His book *My Two Chinas: the Memoir of a Chinese Counterrevolutionary* (with Baiqiao Tang) was endorsed by His Holiness the Dalai Lama. Damon is also the co-author of *The Actor's Art & Craft* and *The Actor's Guide to Creating a Character* with William Esper. As an actor, he has appeared in daytime and primetime television, regional theater, commercials, and independent film.

Cotswold born **Spencer Lawes** incorporates a small-village lifestyle into everything he writes. The aspects of life that he prioritises can be seen within his work; family, honour and duty. A supportive upbringing helped mould both his writing and his personality, producing a secure young adult who is eager to prove himself in the world of fiction. Spencer spends his days working in a local estate agent, saying that meeting new people every day is one of the most important things in his life. The combination of hardy determination and friendly optimism have turned him into a character that can suffer any knock-backs with a smile on his face, ready to turn things round as soon as possible.

Liam Kirby Brown lives in Birmingham, England. Please don't hold this against him. Liam's writing has appeared in various places online and in print, including *Straight from the Fridge, Beat the Dust, BRAND* Magazine and most recently in Almond Press' *After the Fall* collection. He occasionally writes plays, some of which have been performed at the Greenwich Playhouse and the Woolwich Drama Festival. He is also a member of semi-mythical Birmingham band, Freelance Mourners.

Heather Parry was raised in Yorkshire on a diet of thrilling stories and exciting tales. Heather Parry left the land of the pie and peas to study English Literature and Philosophy at the University of Manchester, after which she took off abroad for a year and never quite came back. Perpetually wandering from country to country, she lugs around a frankly ridiculous amount of books and adopts recalcitrant cats. Currently living as a freelance writer, editor and literary consultant in Panama City, Panama, she sips mojitos as she writes about dystopias, utopias and real life, which is somewhere in between.

Paul S. Huggins hails from the United Kingdom within the history and witchcraft rich county of Suffolk. He resides there with his Wife, two daughters and a familiar called 'George'. His introduction to the genre was being scared to death at an early age by a movie called *Dawn of the Dead*. It changed his whole aspect on the apocalypse, and now thinks when not if! With numerous short stories published and three self-published books, Paul would say horror is in his blood, but thankfully, he is still living.

Born and raised in the Kansas City Metropolitan area, **Brian Lecluyse** discovered the works of Tolkien in Middle School, becoming a life-long fan of the fantasy adventure/ science fiction genre. In the mid-90's, he moved to New Orleans, drawn to the city by the works of Anne Rice and Poppy Z. Brite. He moved to Texas following the aftermath of Hurricane Katrina and resides in the West Texas town of Abilene with his husband, Troy, and their pet hellhound Dharma

Jeremy Watssman graduated from Stirling University and lives in Edinburgh with far fewer cats than he would like. He has a particular interest in science fiction, and writes short stories to get away from his depressing office job. He holds a blog at www.jwatssman.com. If you would like Jeremy Watssman to perform at a wedding or business event, he can be reached at jwatssman@gmail.com.

Javier Moyano Perez was born in Madrid, where he lived until the age of 18. He decided to move to France for a year, to study French and gather thoughts on what he wanted to do with his life. He graduated in European Studies and Russian Language at the University of Manchester. Currently, Javier works as a freelance translator and is saving money to move to Taiwan and learn Chinese. The first story he had published was in the first Almond Press collection, and since then he has won the Guardian's short story competition, Protest! Already available on Amazon. Javier has also recently created a blog of short stories, called 'Digital Pulp' (La Pulpa Digital).

Claire Fuller has written many short stories which always start out with good intentions, but often turn to the bad. Several of these have been published online, as well as in literary fiction journals. More examples of her writing can be found at worksbyclaire.wordpress.com. She is about to complete an MA in Creative and Critical Writing at the University of Winchester. She is represented by Jane Finigan from Lutyens & Rubinstein and her debut novel, *Our Endless Numbered Days*, will be published by Fig Tree / Penguin in 2015.

Toby Lloyd is currently studying an MFA in Fiction Writing at New York University. He has previously published stories and poems in The Mays Anthology. He is in the process of writing his first novel.

Andrew Saxsma is a small town author, surrounded by cornfields on all sides in a quaint little mid-western bore. His style is eclectic and to the point, with some polished flowery imagery for flavouring. His ideas are sharp and grisly and mostly deal with the fringes of reality, the things you hear on dark stormy nights, the things with no names. If the world of Literature was a full-bodied woman, his writing would be the hosiery, tight and fitting.

Adicus Ryan Garton lives and works in Finland. Santa Claus once asked if he was Hungarian. He is not.

Ilana Masad is an Israeli-American finishing up her degree at Sarah Lawrence College. She has been published in The Oxford Student newspaper, has won two fiction contests on Tin House's blog, and has had a story featured on the front page of Wordpress.com. Most recently, she has won the Rex Warner Literary Prize at Oxford University.

Robert Legg is a 21 year old student born and bred in Bristol. He is currently a fourth year student at Cardiff University studying physics and is a member of the Creative Writing Society there. He enjoys writing short stories in his spare time, usually based in a fantasy or science fiction setting, and is currently working on a larger novel.

Rebecca Jane Garner was born in 1982 in Aylesbury, Buckinghamshire. She was an avid poet and fiction writer from an early age, spurred on to pursue creative fantasies on an electric typewriter she was given for her ninth birthday. Rebecca received her undergraduate and Master's degree in English Literature at Cardiff University. She went on to study a part-time PhD in Gender and Madness in Victorian Gothic short fiction, whilst working at an animal rescue centre. Pursuing a second interest, she put the PhD on hold and recently moved to a career as a web content editor. Despite some years of neglect, she has taken up the pen for the purpose of fiction again and is easing herself back into writing.

Andrea Mullaney is a writer, journalist and tutor based in Glasgow, who has had a number of short stories published in various literary magazines and journals. As the Europe & Canada region winner of the 2012 Commonwealth Short Story Prize, Granta's New Voices section included her as among 'the most exciting emerging talents in the world' (no, really, they did!). She is now working on a historical novel set in 19th Century China. More info at www.andreamullaney.com

Emma Lyskava graduated from Manchester Metropolitan University with a degree in English and Creative Writing. Originally from Keighley, West Yorkshire, she now lives in Manchester. When she's not scribbling down ideas for short stories, she's training with her roller derby league the Rainy City Roller Girls.

Born and raised in Boston, Massachusetts, **Errick A. Nunnally** served one tour in the Marine Corps before deciding art school would be a safer—and more natural—pursuit. He remains distracted by art, comics, and genre novels. A designer by trade, he studies Krav Maga and Muay Thai kickboxing. Errick's first novel, *Blood For The Sun*, is available from Spence City. His work has appeared in eFiction's inaugural SciFi issue and in the anthologies *Doorways to Extra Time*, *Wicked Seasons*, *Inner Demons Out*, *A Dark World of Spirits and The Fey*, *After the Fall*, and *In Vein*.

Vince Liberato is the author of *The Unzoetic Zombies of Oz*, which can be found in the anthology *So Long and Thanks for All the Brains*, *Worlds Collide (And Then Separate)* to be published in Demonic Visions *50 Tales of Horror*, as well as *Wishing for Eternity* which will be featured in a future mystery project from Horrified Press. He lives in Texas.

Thomas Brown is a postgraduate student at the University of Southampton, where he is studying for an MA in Creative Writing. Literary influences include Angela Carter, Andrei Makine, Friedrich

Nietzsche and Thomas Ligotti. He writes dark, surreal fiction. His debut novel, *LYNNWOOD*, was released in June.